SMALL SHEN

KYLIE CHAN

With illustrations by

&

Adapted into comics-prose format by

QUEENIE CHAN

ISBN: 978-0-9945-8867-8 (pbk)
ISBN: 978-1-7430-9647-5 (ebook)

Published by Kylie Chan
First published in Australia
in 2015 by Harper Collins
Electronic book edition published 2012

Typeset in 10pt Sabon Lt Standard by Queenie Chan
Cover designed by Queenie Chan
Printed and Distributed by Lightning Source Pty Ltd (IngramSpark)

Gentle Reader,
Small Shen is a standalone story, and you don't need to have read any of my other books to enjoy it. If you'd like to see more, the end of *Small Shen* leads straight into the beginning of the first book of the *Dark Heavens* trilogy, *White Tiger*.

Also by Kylie Chan

WHITE TIGER
RED PHOENIX
BLUE DRAGON

EARTH TO HELL
HELL TO HEAVEN
HEAVEN TO WUDANG

DARK SERPENT
DEMON CHILD
BLACK JADE

Novella
THE GRAVITY ENGINE
BLACK SCALES WHITE FUR

Also by Queenie Chan

FABLED KINGDOM v1-3
THE DREAMING v1-3

SHORT GHOST STORIES: THE MAN WITH THE AXE IN HIS BACK
QUEENIE CHAN: SHORT STORIES 2000-2010

IN ODD WE TRUST
ODD IS ON OUR SIDE
HOUSE OF ODD

THE YEAR
1903

PROLOGUE

THE YEAR
1995

HONG KONG

The building at One Black Road was thoroughly sealed. Jade and Gold couldn't even materialise in the eleventh floor lift lobby — they had to enter through the gates like humans. The security guards on the ground floor called the apartment on the intercom and they rode the lift up, rigid with apprehension.

The eleventh floor lift lobby had only one door; the Dark Lord Xuan Wu had the entire top floor to himself. Gold pressed the doorbell and they waited.

A human Filipina domestic helper opened the inner door and studied them suspiciously through the large metal gate. 'Yes?'

'Let them in, Monica, I'm expecting them,' Xuan Wu said from inside.

The Filipina opened the gate for them and Jade and Gold entered. They stopped at the door and removed their shoes, then entered the large comfortable living room on the left and fell to their knees in front of the Dark Lord where he sat on the cream couch.

'Please go into the kitchen for a moment, Monica,' the Dark Lord said.

The Filipina closed the front door and gate then quickly disappeared into the kitchen across the hall.

'Wen sui, wen sui, wen wen sui.'

'Rise. Do not address me like that again in this household. Most of the staff here are human. Celestial protocols are inappropriate. A standing or kneeling salute is sufficient.' He leaned his elbows on his knees and studied them both, his noble face intent. He appeared to be in his mid-forties, wearing a pair of black cotton trousers with a small hole in one knee and a plain black T-shirt. His long hair had come out of its tie and fallen around his shoulders.

They remained standing, waiting.

'I requested that the Celestial assign you to help me in my current... predicament.'

A young European woman in her late twenties wandered into the living room from the hallway. 'Predicament, Lo Wu?' she said with the soft burr of a slightly French accent. She moved behind the couch and put her hands on Xuan Wu's shoulders, then bent and kissed the top of his head. He took one of her hands and pressed it to his lips. 'I think I am the one in the predicament.'

'I think we both are, love,' he said. 'This is my wife, Michelle. Michelle, this is Jade and Gold. They are small Shen in big trouble. The Jade Emperor has sent them to help us out.'

Michelle straightened to study Jade and Gold. She was quite tall, about five ten, with a fine-boned, intelligent, and strikingly beautiful face framed by light honey brown hair that curled under by itself and rested on her shoulders. She wore a dark blue tailored silk suit with a white silk shirt beneath. She smiled at Jade and Gold, and her warm brown eyes sparkled. 'More Shen. Just what I need.'

Jade and Gold both bowed. 'My Lady.'

Her smile widened and she waved them down. 'Please, Michelle, just Michelle.' She leaned over the back of the couch to speak to Xuan Wu, her hair falling forward over his shoulder. 'I have rehearsal in half an hour.'

'We'd better go then,' Xuan Wu said.

'Leo can take me,' she said. 'We'll be fine.'

He rose without releasing her hand. 'I will take you. I want to be absolutely positive that you are safe.'

She sighed theatrically. 'If you must.'

'Besides,' he said, gazing down at her with adoration, 'I will not pass up a single opportunity to hear you sing.'

'If you must take me, please change those awful pants, Lo Wu, find something halfway tidy.'

'For you I will.' Xuan Wu turned to Jade and Gold. 'You're stuck in human form, so you'll need to have somewhere to live. You can't stay here, I don't have room.' He held his hand out and a folder and some keys appeared in it.

'Lo Wu!' Michelle said, scolding. 'One day you'll do that in the middle of Connaught Road.'

'I did that yesterday.' He turned back to Jade and Gold. 'Here are the door codes, addresses, and keys for two apartments that I own in Happy Valley. You can each have one. Settle yourselves in, then return here this afternoon, and we will go through your duties. Do not do anything Celestial in front of my human staff — the housekeeper Monica and the guard Leo.'

Jade and Gold moved forward to accept the documents and keys.

'Where is Leo?' Michelle said, turning back to the hallway. 'He's supposed to drive me.'

Xuan Wu concentrated.

An enormous black man in his mid-thirties charged down the hallway into the living room. He was more than six feet tall, a wall of muscle, and smartly dressed in a designer polo shirt and a pair of dark slacks. 'Sorry, Mr Chen, my phone rang,' he said with a strong American accent.

Michelle patted him on the arm. 'Your phone has not stopped ringing since we arrived here in Hong Kong, Leo. I think you must be the most popular man in the Territory.'

'Ma'am,' Leo said, smiling down at her as well. 'May I drive you to the studio?'

'Leo may drive me,' Michelle said, linking her arms in Leo's and Xuan Wu's. 'And then Lo Wu may hear me sing.'

'Go,' Xuan Wu said to Jade and Gold. 'I will see you two later.'

The two Shen saluted him, and headed to the Valley.

Jade and Gold had lunch together in one of the Western restaurants in Happy Valley, close to their new apartment building.

'She calls him "Lo Wu",' Jade said. 'Old Wu!'

'She's delightful,' Gold said. 'The human retainer, the black one, he's very cute too.'

'A two-bedroom apartment each. Who would have believed it?' she said.

'He seems different.'

'I noticed,' Jade said. 'More ...' She searched for the word.

'Much more human,' Gold said. 'Kinder. Gentler.'

'You think she's done that to him?'

'If she has,' Gold said, 'then she is truly remarkable. I think I'm going to like working for them.'

What are you doing, Gold?

Jade saw Gold jump at the mental contact. 'What is it?'

Gold raised his hand. *Jade and I are sharing lunch at Happy Valley, my Lord. What time would you like us there?*

Whenever you finish. Before two.

Gold dropped his hand. 'I have a stone inside me that allows him to contact me anywhere. He wants to see us as soon as we're finished, before two.'

Jade checked her watch. 'We'd better move.'

Gold smiled as they called for the bill. It felt very strange to be living as a modern human.

The domestic helper answered the door. 'He's waiting for you in his office.' She guided them down the hallway to the third door on the right and tapped on it.

'Bring them in, Monica.'

Monica ushered them in. She glared at the desk, then turned and went out, banging the door behind her.

Gold stopped and stared. The Dark Lord had a large rosewood desk piled high with papers. A stack on one end of the desk seemed about to topple onto the floor and join the mess there. A set of ancient scrolls sat against the wall, under a filing cabinet that had one drawer hanging open.

The Dark Lord gestured for them to sit on the two chairs across the desk from him.

Jade and Gold shared a surreptitious look as they sat.

Xuan Wu closed the spreadsheet on his computer and turned to study them, leaning his elbows on the mass of paper in front of him. 'The situation is not as simple as it appears.'

Gold sagged slightly. It never was.

'Michelle is terrified of my True Form. Every time she sees it she runs from me. Eventually she said that she cannot live with the thought of me changing into something so horrifying, and she threatened to leave me unless I vowed never to take it again. So I'm stuck on the Earthly in human form, much as you are.'

'Never to take it again?' Gold said, horrified. 'Never?'

'As long as she lives, Gold, I will never take True Form. I have made the vow, and though it was on the spur of the moment, I am a Shen of my word.'

'Isn't that difficult, my Lord?' Jade said. 'For a ...' She hesitated, searching for the right word.

'Creature as large as me? Yes,' Xuan Wu said evenly. 'It is a tremendous drain. My energy levels are always low. Always. When my chi reaches a dangerously low level I make a quick trip to Celestial Wudangshan, and build the energy again.'

'If you allow your energy to fall too far, my Lord, you could lose your humanity and be stuck in True Form for quite some time,' Gold said.

Xuan Wu leaned back and studied Gold. 'I am well aware of that. The situation is very difficult.'

'I'm sure you are able to manage this, my Lord,' Jade said. 'You are a master of energy. You can control the level.'

'It's difficult because she hates going to the Celestial with me. She needs to sing. There is no audience there for her., so I go for as little time as possible.'

'Why don't you leave her here with guards?' Gold said.

'Because the demons have found out about her. Very large demons are constantly trying to kidnap her. We have had four attempts in the last two months.'

'The demons want her,' Gold said grimly. 'If they hold her they have you.'

'That is correct. So. You can help guard her. What level demon can you take in human form, Gold?'

'About level fifty, my Lord. If I was to face a low-level Snake Mother it would be a close thing.'

'Jade?'

Jade hesitated. 'I use teeth and claws, my Lord, I've never faced a demon in human form. I always change.'

'Well then, time for a test. Do either of you prefer a particular weapon?'

'I can't use a weapon in human form,' Gold said. 'There's too much of a time lag between the stone making the order and the human form carrying it out. Up to a tenth of a second. So I just use energy, chi, directly from the stone.'

'Jade?'

Jade hesitated again. 'My claws, my Lord. Always.'

'Looks like you will need some training, Jade.'

Jade lit up. 'You will teach me?'

'Of course. Let's go to the training room and see. I am already teaching Leo, two more won't make much of a difference.'

He led them down the hallway to the door at the end. It opened into a training room with soft white mats on the floor. The long wall across from the door was covered with mirrors. A fearsome array of martial arts weapons hung from hooks on the short wall. Xuan Wu led Jade and Gold into the centre of the room and turned. He lowered his head and concentrated.

The black bodyguard, Leo, appeared in the doorway, frowning. 'Sir?'

Xuan Wu gestured. 'Come in and close the door, Leo. You can help me.'

Leo glanced suspiciously at Jade and Gold, then entered the room and closed the door behind him.

'Jade,' Xuan Wu said.

'My Lord.'

'Which arts have you studied?'

Jade hesitated.

'Have you had any training in the arts at all?'

Jade dropped her head and mumbled. 'No, my Lord, none at all.'

'Very well, you are dismissed. Return to your apartment at Happy Valley. I will not need you until two in the afternoon tomorrow, from now until then the time is your own.'

Jade stood still and stared, obviously speechless.

Gold helped. 'You are giving her a whole day free from work, my Lord?'

Xuan Wu's stern expression didn't shift. 'Your working hours will be nine to six, six days a week. Sundays are your own.'

Jade and Gold shared a look, then turned back to Xuan Wu.

'We work less than sixty hours a week?' Gold said with disbelief.

'Your time outside these hours is your own. You may do as you please.' Xuan Wu smiled slightly. 'Just don't forget that you're on the Earthly plane, and you still do not have permission to take True Form. Oh.' He raised his hand. 'Obviously you've been in human form for a great deal of time, both of you look worn. You need to rebuild the energy of your human forms. You have my permission to take True Form for the next twenty-four hours, Jade, just make sure that nobody sees you.'

Jade's eyes went wide. 'May I fly and swim, my Lord?' she said, breathless.

'Of course.'

Jade grinned broadly, bowed, and saluted Xuan Wu. 'My Lord.' She glanced up at him, still grinning. 'Thank you.'

Xuan Wu waved her away. 'Go.'

She hurried out the door.

Xuan Wu turned to Gold. 'Now, let's see how good you are.'

'May I do that too when I am dismissed?' Gold said.

'Yes. Take True Form until you return here tomorrow.'

Gold couldn't control the huge grin. It had been a long time.

'Are these Shen, Mr Chen?' Leo said, watching Gold suspiciously.

'Yes. That one was a dragon, this one is a stone.'

Leo stiffened with surprise, then studied Gold carefully again. 'How about that.'

'I'm really perfectly harmless, I assure you,' Gold said, smiling his most charming smile and hoping his dimples were obvious. He raised his hands out to the side. 'Perfectly harmless.' He spoke to Xuan Wu silently. *Do we really have permission to do what we please outside these working hours?*

Yes, Xuan Wu said.

Even to the pursuit of ... liaisons?

Yes.

Gold's smile broadened. *Permission to take female human form, my Lord? And return later to visit.*

Xuan Wu's voice was full of amusement in Gold's stone lattice. *Go right ahead, Gold, I expected that from you. I have no problem with you forming a relationship with anyone. If you wish to visit Leo, and he is interested, then I have no objection.*

Gold changed to female form; slightly shorter, with long gold hair. He was still slim and elegant, and the female form had the same charming dimples. He smiled at Leo. 'Could you show me around Hong Kong? I haven't been here in over a hundred years. Let me buy you dinner to thank you.'

'Sure,' Leo said, his voice low and gruff. 'Would the other one like to come as well? I can show both of you around.'

'No, just me,' Gold said, smiling into Leo's eyes.

'There will be time for this later,' Xuan Wu said, breaking in. 'Right now, Leo, attack her. Don't be concerned about the fact that it has taken female form, these creatures are completely flexible as to gender. Treat it as if it were still male.'

'I object to being called an "it",' Gold said cheerfully, but he didn't have a chance to say more. Leo's fist shot towards his head and he sidestepped and blocked it, twisting it down and away. He used Leo's arm as a lever, stepped around him, and tipped him over so he landed heavily on his side on the mats. He bent and bound Leo's energy, effectively paralysing him, then rose and raised his hands. 'What level can this guard take? He's not very good.'

Leo struggled against the binding.

'He has only been learning from me since Michelle and I set up house together,' Xuan Wu said. ' About three months. He has a great deal of potential, but you are obviously better. Unbind him.'

Gold reached down and tapped the back of Leo's neck, releasing him. He held out his hand to help Leo up. 'No hard feelings, my friend? If you like, I'll show you that move later.'

Leo hesitated, then took Gold's hand and rose. 'That would be great, thanks. You're really good, I'm glad you're here to help guard.'

Gold didn't release Leo's hand. 'So am I.'

Leo looked down at Gold who was holding his hand, then grinned broadly. 'I look forward to seeing you later.'

'Me too.'

'Leo, go and fetch the Demon Jar from the storeroom,' Xuan Wu said.

Leo dropped Gold's hand. 'Sir.' He quickly went out.

'I have heard of this, my Lord,' Gold said, full of curiosity. 'It's true?'

'What have you heard?' Xuan Wu said.

'That you are able to turn demons into inactive fragments, and retrieve them at will.'

Leo returned carrying a massive jar at least a metre high and half that around, with a complicated metal seal on the lid. 'That's a pretty good way of describing it,' he said. 'You can't do it?'

'As far as I know the Dark Lord is the only one who can do it,' Gold said with awe. 'A gift of a jar full of demons from the Dark Lord is a high honour indeed.'

Leo grinned. 'How about that.' He placed the jar in the corner of the room. It was full of large black beads, shining like dark olives. 'I thought all of you could do it.'

'No, only him.'

'Leo, I will be pulling large demons out. You are no longer needed, but you may stay and watch if you like.'

'Please stay,' Gold said, putting on his best girlish charm. 'I'd love to show you what I can do. It's quite remarkable, I assure you.'

Leo grinned. 'Sure. I'd love to see some really big ones go down.'

Xuan Wu opened the jar and there was a hiss of escaping air. He reached in and pulled out one of the beads. 'Level twenty. Is that too high to start?'

'No, my Lord,' Gold said, readying himself. 'And I can gauge their levels myself once you've released them, no need to tell me.'

Xuan Wu tossed the bead onto the floor at the base of the mirrors. It formed into an ordinary-looking Chinese man in his mid-forties. He leapt straight for Gold.

Gold generated a ball of chi about fifty centimetres across and threw it at the demon, who exploded and dissipated into black feathery streamers.

'Generate the largest ball of chi you can,' Xuan Wu said.

'Please move back, Leo,' Gold said. 'I don't want to hurt you.'

Leo shifted so that he stood against the wall.

Gold generated a ball of chi more than a metre across.

'Is that the best you can do?' Xuan Wu said.

Gold concentrated and added another ten centimetres to the diameter of the glowing golden ball.

'Whoa,' Leo said softly.

'Can you change the colour?' Xuan Wu said.

'What colour would you like, my Lord?' Gold said.

'White.'

Gold nodded and concentrated. The gold chi turned into a shining ball of silver.

'Good. Turn it back, then re-centre it. Well done.'

Gold inhaled deeply, turned the chi back to its usual golden colour, then reabsorbed it.

'Move back, Leo, I'm going to pull out a really big one.' Xuan Wu shuffled through the contents of the jar, then held his hand above it and concentrated. A bead flew out of the jar into his outstretched hand. He tossed the bead onto the floor. It formed into a short, wizened elderly woman in a blood-red cheongsam.

Gold let his breath out in a long hiss. 'How did you catch this, my Lord?'

'It's the only one I have, Gold. Leo, watch carefully. If we're very lucky it will take True Form and you'll see what one of these looks like.'

The woman glanced from Gold to Xuan Wu. When she saw the Dark Lord her face filled with loathing. She grew. Her cheongsam turned black and tightened until it fitted her form, then disappeared completely.

Her skin disappeared as well. Her legs merged together and formed serpentine coils with black scales. She grew and twisted and lengthened until she was nearly two metres long.

Her front end appeared as a man with the skin taken off. Her back end was a black snake that writhed over the floor, spreading a deadly trail of toxic slime.

'Snake Mother,' Leo said softly.

The Mother raced towards Gold.

He held out his hands and bound it. Its tail writhed on the floor as its front end struggled to reach him.

Gold's voice was strained as he laboured to hold the demon. 'I can't kill this one with chi, my Lord, it would blow me up.'

'Leo, grab a sword and take its head off,' Xuan Wu said.

'Quickly!' Gold said.

Leo raced to the weapons rack, grabbed a dark sword, pulled it from its scabbard, and sliced the demon's head off. The head fell to the floor and dissipated quickly. The body and serpentine back end writhed on the floor for some time before they dissipated too.

Gold dropped his hands and panted. 'That was too big for me, my Lord. What level was that one?'

'Fifty-five,' Xuan Wu said. 'I thought you said you could gauge them?'

Gold was embarrassed. 'Not if they're that big.'

'If that was the best you can do then you require some work. I will spend time with you to build your skills. A stone like you should be able to produce much more than that, particularly one made of a noble metal as you are.'

Gold sagged. 'You are quite correct, my Lord. I need to be better if I am to defend your lady.'

'Good.' Xuan Wu waved to Leo and the guard returned the sword to the rack. 'Gold, Leo, dismissed. Gold, I will not need you until two tomorrow, same as Jade. The time is your own. If you wish to spend it with Leo, you have my permission, both of you. Leo, same for you. Take the afternoon off.'

Gold grinned broadly, then pointed the grin at Leo. 'Wanna take off now?

'Just let me grab a couple of things from my room and we can go,' Leo said. He bowed slightly to Xuan Wu. 'Mr Chen? My Lord?'

'Go,' Xuan Wu said, his eyes full of amusement.

Leo left the training room and Gold followed. 'Where's your room?'

'In here,' Leo said. He turned left and went to the second door along. 'There's a couple of spare bedrooms here, but Mr and Mrs Chen are planning to have a family, so —'

Gold stopped dead. 'They plan to have children?'

Leo stopped as well, his hand on the door. 'Yeah, I suppose so. Is this a big thing for you guys?'

Gold shook his head. 'The minute they have any sort of child the demons will be after it. All of them. He is Heaven's greatest defender, and the demons would give anything to have control of him.'

Leo opened the door and went in. 'Terrific.' He stopped again, just inside the room, and Gold nearly walked into him. 'What do you mean "any sort" of child?'

Gold smiled gently. 'You know what he really is, don't you?'

'Oh my God.'

'Yep. He's never had a human wife before, but he has quite a few lovely little reptilian children. His Number One Son for many years was a turtle Shen.'

Leo shook his head. 'This is so weird.'

'I'd better not show you me then.'

Leo turned to Gold. 'Show me you? That doesn't make sense.'

21

'I won't show you my stone.'

'Your stone?'

'Well, me, actually. I'm a stone. This human form,' he raised the female form's arms, 'is just a shell.'

'A shell?'

'Yep.' Gold dropped his arms and brushed one hand along Leo's bare arm. 'The real me, the stone, is inside this form. You can see it if you like.'

Leo hesitated, watching Gold, then shook his head. 'Enough weirdness for one day, I think. Maybe later. You still want me to show you around?'

'Sure.'

<hr/>

Gold leaned on the railing next to Leo and watched the tug boats pull barges through the steady stream of water-borne traffic on the harbour below them. The sky to the left faded to lilac as the sun set. The packed high-rise apartment blocks on both sides of the harbour began to light up. Across the harbour an enormous neon sign for a Japanese electronics company flared to brilliant life.

Gold sighed. 'This is wonderful.'

Leo leaned his forearms on the railing. 'I'm glad it's a clear evening so you could see.'

Gold shifted sideways to press the female form into Leo and smiled up into his eyes. 'So many wonderful things to see.'

Leo smiled back. 'You can stop coming on to me, my friend. I'm afraid you're out of luck.'

Gold turned back to the harbour and thumped the rail. 'You should have told me you're spoken for.'

'Oh, I'm not spoken for,' Leo said. He stood straighter, held the rail, and spoke softly. 'I'm HIV positive. Mr Chen somehow clears the virus from me, but I don't want to put anyone at risk.'

Gold smiled up again, cheeky. 'You won't put me at risk. I'm a stone; I can't catch any sort of virus.' He shifted closer to Leo and put the female form's arm around his waist. 'You don't need to protect me.'

Leo wrapped his arm around Gold's shoulder and squeezed him gently. 'Then it's a terrible shame, because I like you and I've enjoyed your company. But you were really much cuter as a guy.'

'This just gets better and better,' Gold said. 'Is there a place where we can go? I can't change out in the middle of the viewing platform here.'

'We can go back up to the Peak apartment if you like. I'd love to see you change again. I'd like to see the stone, too.'

Gold stiffened. 'The Dark Lord will allow it?'

Leo chuckled and his arm moved over Gold's back. 'Sure. He doesn't mind at all, he told me himself.' His voice saddened. 'Not that I can bring anyone home anyway.'

'Well, you can now,' Gold said. He laughed quietly. 'Look at us, arms around each other, perfectly normal boy and girl. Let's go up to the Peak and be a perfectly normal boy and boy.'

'None of you Shen are normal,' Leo said, his voice a low rumble. He dropped his arm from Gold's shoulder and took Gold's hand. 'Let's go.'

Gold smiled at the view before he turned to follow Leo. It had been a long time.

꒛꒛꒛꒛꒛꒛꒛꒛꒛꒛꒛꒛꒛꒛꒛꒛

'You're too big and this bed's too small,' Gold said, muffled by the covers. 'How tall are you anyway?'

'Six five.'

'Wah, that's huge. Can't you get a bigger goddamn bed?'

Leo turned over and threw his arm across Gold's chest. 'No. Deal with it.' He pulled himself up to sit. 'Hey. Can I see the stone?'

Gold sat up as well and leaned his back on Leo, relishing the soft dark skin. Leo was rock-hard muscle beneath Gold's back. 'Sure. You really want to see?'

'It's not gross or anything, is it?'

'Nope.' Gold reached into his human form's chest and pulled the stone out. He unwound the chain holding the black turtle and handed the stone to Leo.

Leo turned it over in his hands. 'And this is you.'

'Yep. Like I said, what's sitting next to you is just a shell.'

'What was that around it?' Leo said, holding the stone as if it was very fragile.

'Oh, this?' Gold raised the turtle pendant. 'The Dark Lord gave this to me about a hundred and fifty years ago so that we could communicate.'

Leo's body tensed behind Gold.

Gold laughed. 'No, no, nothing like that. I was working as an agent for him. Here in Hong Kong, actually. It was a long time ago.'

'Oh, all right.' Leo ran his hand over the surface of the stone.

23

'It's smooth and soft. I really like touching it.'

Gold shivered. 'Don't stop.'

Leo traced his finger over one of the veins of gold in the stone and Gold threw his head back into Leo's shoulder.

'Oh, now this is interesting,' Leo said. He rubbed his palm over the stone and Gold went completely rigid. When Leo stopped rubbing, Gold collapsed with a sigh.

'Very interesting.' Leo traced his fingers across the stone, turning it over in his hands. He rubbed it between both palms and Gold squeaked.

'Bad?' Leo said.

Gold panted. 'No. No. Good.' He took a deep breath. 'Very, very good.'

Leo flopped back against the bedhead and held the stone. 'You promised dinner.' He rubbed the stone and Gold moaned. 'You gonna buy us dinner?'

'After,' Gold said, and pulled himself on top.

🀫🀫🀫🀫🀫🀫🀫🀫🀫🀫🀫🀫🀫🀫🀫

'Leo.'

'Hn?'

'Thanks for dinner, I had a great time. But I have to go, and there's something I need to tell you.'

'Wha'?'

'When you see me tomorrow afternoon, I'll look at least twenty years younger.'

That woke him. Leo rolled over and screwed up his face. 'What?'

'You remember Lord Xuan said I could take True Form for a while? It's because I look so old. My normal human form is about twenty, twenty-one years old in appearance. I don't normally look this old.'

'Why not?'

Gold sighed. 'It's a long story. But when you see me tomorrow, I'll look at least fifteen years younger than you.' He dropped his voice. 'I hope that isn't a problem for you.'

Leo wrapped his arms around Gold. 'Will you still be a guy?'

Gold smiled slightly. 'For you I will.'

Leo's hands drifted lower. 'Then it's not a problem at all.' He pulled Gold closer. 'It's late, must be past midnight. Stay the night.'

'No, I have to go back to my apartment and sort stuff out.

24

And since I can take True Form for a while, it'll be much easier as a stone.'

'Your choice.' Leo brightened. 'Wanna come out on the town with me Saturday night? Meet some of my friends?'

Gold moved back slightly to grin with delight. 'You want to show me off?'

'Hell, yeah,' Leo said.

Gold moved his face closer to Leo's so that their mouths nearly touched. 'Do you always fall into bed with guys you've just met like this?'

'When they're as cute as you I do,' Leo breathed, and closed the gap.

🁢🁢🁢🁢🁢🁢🁢🁢🁢🁢🁢🁢🁢🁢🁢

Two days later Gold reported for work at the apartment at eight a.m. sharp. Leo was waiting for him. They sat at the small four-seat kitchen table together as Monica busily washed the breakfast dishes.

'The Dark Lord is practising martial arts in the training room right now,' Leo said. 'He gets up real early. Michelle, on the other hand, usually sleeps until at least ten a.m., later if she's performing. She's a real night owl.'

'So what do you do in the mornings?' Gold said.

'After the Dark Lord's done warming up, he'll give me a lesson for an hour or so; he'll probably want to teach you as well ...'

Yes. Present yourself for training with Leo in forty-five minutes, the Dark Lord said into their heads.

Leo jumped. 'I'm still trying to get used to that.'

Gold grinned wryly. 'I had a human wife once who never got used to it. In the end she just asked me to stop.'

Leo stared at him.

Gold shrugged. 'I'm not human. I'm not even really organic. I'm a stone, my friend. Gender doesn't really apply to us.'

'You gonna fool around with chicks while you're with me?' Leo growled. ''Cause if you are, we can stop now. I'm not letting you put anybody in danger.'

'I'm not going to fool around with anybody.'

Leo studied Gold for a moment, then relaxed.

'You trust me?' Gold said with delight.

'The Dark Lord trusts you. That's good enough for me,' Leo said. 'It's not the whole "be faithful to me" trash. It's the virus. I don't want to put anybody at risk.'

'You won't be.'

Leo nodded, confident. 'Good.' Monica gave him a mug of black coffee, and he nodded to her in thanks. 'After we train, we'll take Michelle to the gym. Then back here, or out to meet someone for lunch, and then after lunch down to the academy.'

'Wudang?'

'Hong Kong Academy for Performing Arts! She spends a lot of time there, they've only been running degree-level programs in music for a few years, she's been helping them to develop the programmes. She'll practise for an hour or so, then —'

'Practise what?' Gold interrupted.

'Singing, dumbass. It's what she *does*. After she's done practising, she'll spend some time there, maybe doing a master class, or mentoring some students, course development, something like that. She usually doesn't finish down there until at least five.'

'She's a busy lady.'

'When she's performing the schedule will be much more packed, she'll spend a lot of time rehearsing. She's extremely hands-on.'

'You mean she drives everybody nuts.'

Leo sighed. 'Before, she travelled the world. She toured the US. She was sought after by different opera companies. Now she's married, she's become very old-fashioned and refuses to leave her husband.'

'That is safer for her.'

'It may be, but she misses the contact with the other players.'

'So she *is* driving everybody nuts.'

About two weeks later, Gold and Leo waited for Michelle in the academy's tearoom, part of their daily routine.

'Gin,' Gold said.

'Dammit!' Leo said, 'You sure you've never played this before?'

'It works very much like mah jongg,' Gold said. 'Only simpler.'

Michelle entered the tearoom. 'Good, you are both here. I have a break for about an hour. Will you accompany me to the open space across the road? It would be good to be out of this stifling atmosphere.'

Gold and Leo rose.

'Our pleasure, ma'am,' Leo said. 'If Gold and I play any more gin, he's gonna clean me out.'

Michelle patted Gold's shoulder as they went out. 'Do not take all of Leo's money, little Shen, he needs it to buy drinks for all his friends in those bars.'

'It's okay, Michelle,' Leo said gruffly. 'Most of the drinks are for Gold anyway.'

'I'm learning a variety of alcoholic drinks that I never knew existed,' Gold said. 'Bourbon is awesome!'

'Champagne is better, especially after a successful show,' Michelle said. They crossed the busy Wan Chai street, hurrying between the slow-moving vehicles, to the park. The park was an open concreted area with benches beneath tired-looking trees in brick planter boxes. Michelle sighed and looked around. 'This is not a park.'

'The gentlemen over there playing chess would disagree with you,' Gold said.

Three elderly Chinese men sat on stools around a Chinese chessboard on a concrete table, loudly discussing their moves. The board was a piece of card marked out in a grid, some of the squares had crosses through them. The pieces were simple wooden discs with printed characters indicating the piece.

Curious, Michelle approached them. 'I have never seen a game like that before.'

As they neared the demons, Gold grabbed her arm. 'They're demons waiting for us,' he said. 'Turn around and walk away now, ma'am.'

Michelle stopped. 'Are you sure? They look so harmless.'

'Yeah, you sure?' Leo said.

Before Gold could answer, the old men all rose, studying Michelle carefully. They moved slowly towards her, crouched as if ready to spring.

'Three of them, two of us,' Gold said. 'Time to put the training to good use.'

'Move behind us, Michelle,' Leo said.

'These old men are no threat, ignore them,' Michelle said.

'These old men are after you,' Gold said.

'What level are they?' Leo said.

'Only about level twenty, slightly bigger than the ones you were practising on last week,' Gold said. 'Ready?' He moved into a long defensive stance.

'Hell, yeah,' Leo said, moving into a defensive stance as well. 'It'll be good to practise on something worthwhile.'

The three demons rushed them. Gold generated chi and blew one up, then paused before sending his fist through the head of another, making it disintegrate into black feathery streamers. He grimaced at the delay between giving the order and his human body responding. The third demon stayed out of his reach and tried to grab Michelle. Leo took it by the arm, swung it onto the ground, and ran his palm into its nose, breaking its face and destroying it.

'Ugh, what is that stuff they turn into?' Michelle said. 'It is disgusting!'

'Demon essence,' Gold said. He checked Leo, who had some essence on his hands, black and oozing. 'You'll need to wash that off, Leo. It'll burn after a while and poison you if it's left on for too long.'

'Yeah, Mr Chen told me,' Leo said. He looked around. 'No faucets here, how do they water the plants?'

'They have the water taps inside locked boxes, to stop people from stealing the water or leaving it running,' Gold said. 'Come over here to this one and wash your hands.'

'People do that?' Michelle said. 'Sometimes I dislike this place very much.'

Gold put his hand over the lock on the box and opened it, then guided Leo's hands under the running water.

'People who are accustomed to poverty will take anything that's not nailed down,' Leo said. 'Including water.' He shook his hands. 'All gone.'

Gold turned the water off and resealed the box. He turned to Michelle, who was leaning heavily on the box, her face ashen. 'Are you all right, ma'am?'

'Are you well enough to take me home?' Michelle said.

Leo took Michelle's arm. 'We'll take you home right away, ma'am.'

Michelle leaned on Leo as he guided her back across the road. He bent to carry her but she waved him away. 'No. Don't. I can walk.'

'Is this the first time you've been attacked?' Gold said.

Michelle shook her head.

'No, but it's the first time without Mr Chen along to make them explode quickly,' Leo said.

Michelle began to sob silently.

'It's all right now, Michelle, you're safe,' Leo said.

Gold moved to the other side to help guide Michelle. Her face was pale and streaked with tears as she leaned heavily on them.

'Don't pass out on us now, my Lady, we're nearly there,' Gold said gently.

Michelle glared at him. 'I am not going to faint! I am stronger than that.'

Leo caught her as she collapsed, unconscious, and carried her to the car.

Gold alerted the Dark Lord and he was waiting for them when they arrived back at the Peak apartment. Michelle had regained consciousness, but she was weak and needed assistance up to the eleventh floor. As soon as they arrived at the apartment's front door, Xuan Wu scooped her into his arms and took her into the bedroom.

'Will she be all right?' Gold asked Leo as they went into the kitchen to wait.

'Yeah, she's done this before,' Leo said. 'Very ... sensitive. She's passed out after a very big performance, too. The doctor says that she suffers from slightly low blood pressure, but really it's just 'cause things get to her.'

Gold shook his head. 'Humans. I'll never understand.'

'Women. Ditto,' Leo said.

THE YEAR
1720

BEGINNINGS

HOW DID ALL
THIS BEGIN?

HOW DID THIS STORY
COME TO BE?

HOW, IN THE
LONG-LIVED
LIVES OF THE
IMMORTAL *SHEN*,

DOES FATE
INTERVENE
AND BRING US
UNIONS

BOTH
STRANGE
AND
UNEXPECTED?

JUST AS EVERY STORY HAS ITS BEGINNING, EVERY TALE HAS AN END.

THIS TALE BEGAN 275 YEARS AGO, WITH THE MEETING OF TWO SMALL SHEN—

AN UNLIKELY PAIR IN THIS FEARSOME WORLD OF GODS AND DEMONS.

...*GOLD*, THE CHILD OF A BUILDING BLOCK OF THE WORLD.

...AND *JADE*, A DRAGON PRINCESS.

THE YEAR

1720

THE HALL OF RECORDS.

THE LIBRARY OF THE GODS. EVERY BOOK IN EXISTENCE HAS A PLACE HERE.

'What is your honoured name, Lady?' he said as he led her through the vast silent aisles of scrolls.

'Princess Jade.'

He bobbed his head. 'I am honoured, Princess.'

She waved him down. 'I am the eighty-second daughter of the Dragon King, very low in precedence. Your name?'

'I am Gold, Lady.' He smiled into her jade-green eyes, then straightened slightly as he walked beside her. 'I am a child of the Jade Building Block of the World.'

'There was a jade Building Block?'

He sagged slightly. Nobody seemed to know of his parent's existence. Gold had not spoken to his parent in nearly six hundred years.

'Yes, Lady,' he said, rallying. 'My parent was worn by the Yellow Emperor's Empress.'

'How interesting,' she said, not hearing. 'How far is it to this room that holds the Sonnets? It seems a long way.'

'We are already here.' He led her to the right through the aisles and into one of the small reading rooms.

36

PLEASE SIT, LADY.

THIS IS OUR READING ROOM.

CREAK

SURU

I WILL RETURN WITH YOUR SONNETS.

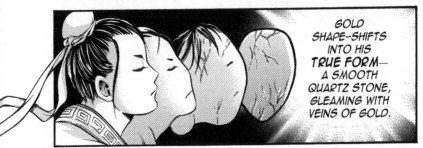

GOLD SHAPE-SHIFTS INTO HIS **TRUE FORM**— A SMOOTH QUARTZ STONE, GLEAMING WITH VEINS OF GOLD.

SHAKES-
PEARE...

SONNETS...

NOT
THERE!

Damn, he'd seen the book only a week before, but for the life of him he couldn't find it. His memory was perfect, stored in his quartz lattice, why the hell couldn't he find the damn book?

He floated over the small English section, becoming more and more frantic as the book didn't appear before him. Dragons weren't renowned for their patience. He'd better find the book soon.

Eventually he had no other choice, he had to contact the Archivist. He spoke silently without moving from the shelves.

GOLD GOLD GOLD GOLD GOLD GOLD GOLD GOLD GOLD GOLD GOLD GOLD GOLD GOLD GOLD GOLD GOLD GOLD GOLD GOLD GOLD GOLD GOLD GOLD

TELEPATHY TELEPATHY TELEPATHY TELEPATHY

Archivist, he said, *the Dragon Princess would like a copy of the Sonnets, and it is not on the shelves.*

38

She must have slipped past me when she came in, she wasn't expected until later, the Archivist said.

Number Seventeen Son of the White Tiger of the West has it. He knew she'd come looking for it and wanted to have his paws on it first. He's been courting her for nearly eight years. Send her to the Western Palace, he's waiting for her there.

Gold was astonished. *You're in on it?*

Of course I am, the Archivist said with a touch of amusement. *The White Tiger and the Dragon King contacted me, they're tired of these two dithering and want to see them safely wed. Apparently the Lady and the Tiger haven't even been intimate, they are waiting until they are married.*

Some son of the Tiger, Gold said. *Can't even bed a woman after eight years of chasing her. His father must be horrified.*

Completely. Apparently this particular son is a very powerful half-Shen, but didn't inherit his father's skills with the Ladies at all.

HMM...

Thank you, Archivist, Gold said, attempting to sound suitably respectful.

Send her off, Gold, and get back to cross indexing those scrolls, the Archivist said. *You should have finished that a long time ago.*

Gold returned to the reading room to find Jade sitting impatiently clutching the teacup.

SO, DO YOU HAVE THE BOOK?

I AM SO SORRY, PRINCESS.

I DIDN'T REALISE IT WAS YOU.

WHAT?

THE ARCHIVIST GAVE THE SONNETS TO THAT *BASTARD* WHO HAS BEEN CHASING YOU.

THAT IS HARDLY AN ACCEPTABLE WAY OF REFERRING TO HIM.

PLOP

'You didn't hear what he said, Princess'

Gold sat next to Jade, not looking at her. 'He came in here first, seeking the book as well, and the Archivist gave it to him. But I heard what he said while he was searching, and I cannot believe anybody could be so cruel. But then, he is a son of the White Tiger, and the Bai Hu is notorious for his poor treatment of women.'

Jade sat straighter, suddenly more interested. 'What did he say?'

'He said that if the sonnets didn't bring you to his bed then nothing would,' Gold said. 'And then he could settle the bet, collect his winnings, and have you thoroughly out of his fur.'

'Bet?'

'Apparently this particular son of the Tiger has a bet with a couple of the others,' Gold said, still not looking at Jade, and doing his best to appear outraged on her behalf. 'All of the Tiger's sons are aware of your...' he hesitated, searching for the right word. '*Virtue*, and there has been a bet among them as to who would be first to break through your defences.'

41

Jade studied her teacup. 'I do not believe it. He has been nothing but a perfect gentleman to me from the start.' She smiled slightly, still watching the teacup. 'In

fact, it is more me that has been trying to break down his defences.'

'That was part of the bet. The longer he could make you hold out before submitting, the more his brothers will be forced to pay.' Gold moved closer to Jade and guided the teacup out of her hand onto the table. He took her hand in his.

'You deserve much better than that furry bastard, my Lady. You have waited too long for someone to treat you with the care and respect that you deserve.'

'Much too long,' he whispered.

It had obviously been a long eight years for her, because she returned his attentions with satisfying enthusiasm. He pushed her backwards on the couch, then hesitated, concentrating, and locked the door without releasing her.

He pulled away slightly. 'I don't think your defences are so great, my Lady,' he whispered. 'I think that he has made a terrible mistake.' He gently pushed the green silk robes down over her shoulders. 'A terrible mistake.'

She smiled up and kissed him again.

Gold turned to look at Jade. 'Let's run away together,' he said. 'I have a fortune on the Earthly Plane, Princess. Nothing is holding me here. Run away with me.'

She pulled herself onto her elbow to smile down at him, and he admired her snow-white skin. 'Really?'

He nodded. 'I know a place where we can go.' He stopped smiling and mused. 'You go first, I will follow. I will fulfil my honour and my duty to the Archivist, and then join you. Do you know the Garden of Heavenly Delights?'

'Yes,' she said, breathless.

'Wait for me there in the Pavilion of Tranquil Contemplation,' he said. 'I will come in about two hours, I need to tender my resignation here. We can go to a place I know, and spend the rest of Eternity sharing our love.'

She lowered her beautiful face and kissed him. 'I will be waiting.'

'Go, my darling,' he whispered.

She and her clothes both disappeared.

He shook his head and rose, then concentrated and conjured his gold silk robes. Now for the real challenge.

Archivist, the son of the Tiger has summoned me to the Western Palace. He wishes for me to point out which of the sonnets would be most suitable for winning the heart of the lady.

Haven't you sent her on yet? the Archivist said, impatient.

I have sent her to the Western Palace, but he is waiting for some tips before he sees her.

I suppose you are the ideal person for this, Gold, the Archivist said. *But be back before dinner, I want you to finish indexing those scrolls. And no funny business.*

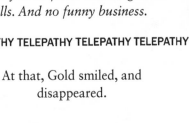

TELEPATHY TELEPATHY TELEPATHY TELEPATHY

GOLD GOLD GOLD GOLD GOLD GOLD GOLD GOLD GOLD GOLD GOLD GOLD GOLD GOLD GOLD GOLD GOLD GOLD GOLD GOLD GOLD GOLD GOLD GOLD GOLD

THE ARCHIVIST THE ARCHIVIST THE ARCHIVIST THE ARCHIVIST THE ARCHIVIST THE ARCHIVIST THE ARCHIVIST THE ARCHIVIST THE ARCHIVIST THE ARCHIVIST THE ARCHIVIST THE ARCHIVIST

At that, Gold smiled, and disappeared.

SHE'S NOT COMING, YOU KNOW.

 WHY NOT?

BECAUSE SHE WANTS TO MAKE YOU SUFFER EVEN MORE.

SLAM

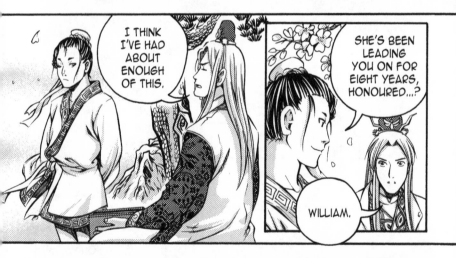

I THINK I'VE HAD ABOUT ENOUGH OF THIS.

SHE'S BEEN LEADING YOU ON FOR EIGHT YEARS, HONOURED...?

WILLIAM.

MY MOTHER IS ENGLISH,

THE TIGER'S WIFE NUMBER FORTY-FIVE.

...WILLIAM. IRONIC. I THINK IT'S ABOUT TIME YOU MOVED ON.

William sagged over his knees and sighed. 'I do love her, you know.'

'She's a dragon. Those reptiles are incapable of loving anyone but themselves.'

William stiffened slightly but didn't say anything.

Gold held out his hand. 'May I?'

'The love described in these poems is love that is true and would last the test of centuries. All that dragon would give you is suffering.'

William didn't say anything, but his face was full of misery.

AH, THE NOTORIOUS SONNET NUMBER TWENTY.

FLIP
FLIP

'A woman's face with Nature's own hand painted Hast thou, the master-mistress of my passion;'

'A woman's gentle heart, but not acquainted
With shifting change, as is false women's fashion;'

'An eye more bright than theirs, less false in rolling,
Gilding the object whereupon it gazeth;'

THAT'S TRUE...

IT'S ALL PRETENCE. ALL FALLACY. ALL LIES.

'A man in hue, all "hues" in his controlling,
Which steals men's eyes and women's souls amazeth.
And for a woman wert thou first created;
Till Nature, as she wrought thee, fell a-doting,'

'And by addition me
of thee defeated,'

Gold reached around to turn William's head towards him. He studied William's face for a long time, eyes unreadable.

This particular tiger's son was not the usual large, brawny Horseman. His skin was pale ad delicate, almost transparent, and his hair was shining platinum blonde. He was slender and young, graceful and languid. Gold smiled.

He then pulled William in and kissed him.

'Have you ever done this before?'

William didn't say anything, he just studied Gold's features, his eyes roaming over Gold's face.

'Then let's go to your quarters, and I'll show you realms of pleasure that you never knew existed.'

ᗑᗑᗑᗑᗑᗑᗑᗑᗑᗑᗑᗑᗑᗑᗑᗑ

Gold felt remarkably proud of himself as he returned to cross-indexing the scrolls. He had rescued the two fools from each other, shown young William where his true preferences lay, and had had a very enjoyable experience doing it. He quietly wondered if Jade was still searching for the non-existent pavilion. Quite possibly. Dragons weren't very good at subtlety.

He chuckled quietly as he picked up the next scroll.

PATHY TELEPATHY GET THEE TO MY OFFICE TELEPATHY TELE

THE ARCHIVIST'S OFFICE.

COME IN.

ARCHIVIST? WHO—

AH!

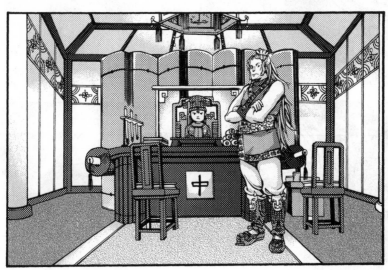

THE WHITE TIGER OF THE WEST, *BAI HU.*

LORD BAI HU.

GRR...

RISE.

ARCHIVIST ...

SIT, GOLD.

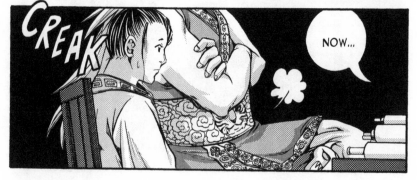

CREAK

NOW...

GOLD, PLEASE TELL US IN YOUR OWN WORDS,

EXACTLY WHAT PASSED BETWEEN YOU, PRINCESS JADE AND PRINCE WILLIAM.

'Jade came in and asked for the sonnets,' Gold said. 'I told her they weren't here, and she went away. Then William summoned me, and I went to help him find a suitable poem to win the lady.'

'Did you seduce either of them, Stone?' the Tiger said, his voice low and gruff.

Gold hesitated.

Both the Tiger and the Archivist glared at Gold.

'What will we do with it?' the Tiger said.

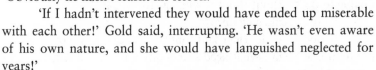

'Gold is working here as punishment for a similar transgression,' the Archivist said. 'Obviously he hasn't learnt his lesson.'

'If I hadn't intervened they would have ended up miserable with each other!' Gold said, interrupting. 'He wasn't even aware of his own nature, and she would have languished neglected for years!'

'Right now she is weeping inconsolably in the Dragon King's Palace Under the Sea,' the Archivist said. 'She attempted suicide, but changed her mind at the last minute.' Then, with emphasis, he added, 'Because she wants to *kill you first*.'

'I did both of them a favour,' Gold said.

The Archivist sighed with exasperation, banged his hand on the desk, and turned away.

'I'd like to take him to the palace and teach him some manners, but a creature like him should not be let anywhere near my harem,' the Tiger said. 'The Dragon King just wants to eat him alive—'

Gold squeaked.

'The Dragon King wants to *eat him alive*,' the Tiger said without looking at Gold. 'What do you suggest, Archivist?'

'I have a solution.' The Archivist said finally. 'Put a charm on him. Make him retain True Form, as a stone. Then set him to work lifting and carrying at the palace. Even better, put him to work in your harem. He will be close enough to touch your women, but unable to do anything about it while a stone.'

Gold squeaked again.

'Good idea,' the Tiger said, 'but I don't have power over stones, my nature is Metal. We'll need somebody with Wood alignment to do it to him.'

'I'm sure the Dragon King will be happy to oblige.' The Archivist straightened. 'Gold can finish indexing those scrolls, then I'll send him over to the Dragon King to be bound. Then you can have him until your honour is satisfied.'

'Works for me,' the Tiger said. 'How long will it take him to finish the scrolls?'

'Not more than twenty-four hours,' the Archivist said with a small smile. 'Otherwise I will ask the Dragon King to make the binding permanent.'

'This time tomorrow, you will present yourself to the Seraglio Elite Guard for assignment of duties.'

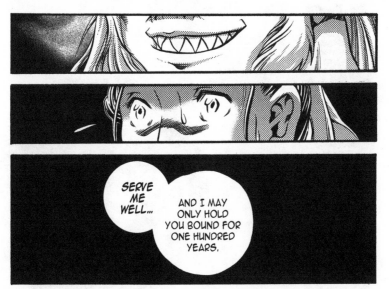

SERVE ME WELL...

AND I MAY ONLY HOLD YOU BOUND FOR ONE HUNDRED YEARS.

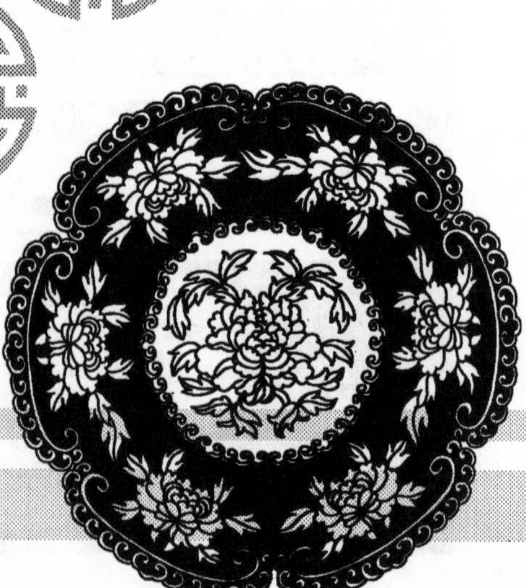

THE YEAR
1997

 # HONG KONG

Gold sighed as he entered the apartment. Michelle was having another of her tantrums; he could hear her from the front door.

Quick, Gold, come and help! Jade said into his head, desperate.

Gold hurried to the master bedroom, hesitated, then sensed that the entire household, short of Monica, was inside, and went in.

The Dark Lord was holding Michelle by her upper arms, trying to talk to her, but she wasn't listening. Tears streamed down her face and she shook her head, repeating, 'No, no, no, no!'

She's with child, Jade said. *She's worried it will be reptile.*

'It will be human child, Michelle, trust me,' the Dark Lord said. 'I give you my word, it will be nothing like that.'

'It will be a monster!' Michelle choked, her voice harsh with emotion. 'It will be a monster like you, all scales and claws! I wish I had never married you!'

'My Lady, all half-human Shen are born human,' Gold said, trying to calm her. 'Your child will be a normal baby.'

Michelle stopped and shook her arms free from the Dark Lord's grip, and he released her. She glared at Gold. 'And when it grows up? Will my son or daughter be able to change into a snake? Or a turtle? Or something even more horrible?' She glared at the Dark Lord. 'A horrible thing like you!'

The Dark Lord's face was blank for a moment, then he relaxed and crossed his arms over his chest. 'Am I really that horrible?'

Michelle jabbed her finger at him. 'You are!'

'That ugly?'

'Yes!'

'Then why did you marry me, silly human?'

Michelle opened and closed her mouth, gasping for breath. She stared at him for a while. Then she threw herself into his arms. 'It really won't be a monster?'

Time to go, Jade said.

Xuan Wu stroked her hair and nuzzled into her. 'No, my love, it will be as human, and warm, and wonderful, as you are.' He pulled her closer. 'And as exasperating as I am.'

'Then I shall love it as much as I love you,' she whispered. She pulled back to gaze up into his eyes, and they lost themselves in each other.

Out, he said, but Jade and Gold had already disappeared.

Later, Jade and Gold had dinner together at their favourite local Cantonese restaurant and compared notes.

'Never?' Jade said with disbelief.

'Never at all,' Gold said. 'He said as much to me when I helped him woo her. He's never had a relationship with a human woman.'

'Then you know she could be right. She could give birth to something black, scaly, and horrible.'

Gold shook his head. 'No half-human Shen has ever been born anything but human. Same with half-human demons. The human nature is stronger.'

'He's one of the strongest creatures there is, Gold. None of the rules apply to him. It could happen.'

'Well, if it does, I hope it doesn't break her mind,' Gold said. 'She's temperamental enough as it is.'

Jade jerked back and scowled. 'She is a wonderful woman. He is lucky to have her; she puts up with a lot from him. He is so cold-blooded.'

'Not where it comes to her,' Gold said with humour. 'Never seen a man so crazy in love.'

Jade smiled slightly and rested her chin on her hand. 'I know. The story of their love, and the sacrifices they have made for each other, will live for generations. I feel privileged to have been a part of it.' She sat straighter. 'Speaking of love stories, what is this between you and Leo?'

Gold shrugged. 'Usual guy thing. On and off. We're good pals ...'

'Pals?' Jade said with delight. 'You are around that American too much.'

'We're good pals,' Gold repeated firmly, 'and we enjoy each other's company.' He shrugged again. 'It's a guy thing, we are happy to have things the way they are. It will probably never be anything more, though. The Dark Lord said it would be okay for me and Leo to move in together here in Happy Valley, and both of us said no.'

'Why not? You two seem to have something very good here.'

Gold smiled sadly. 'Leo's heart really belongs to another. He is very fond of me, and I of him, but it cannot be the love that humans hold so dear. He is lost. He will never leave the Peak apartment, not even for me.'

Jade studied Gold quietly for a moment, then gasped. 'Oh.'

'Took you long enough.'

'The Dark Lord is famous for only liaising with females. Leo's cause is lost if he thinks that he has a chance because the Dark Lord is a Shen, like you.'

'I think Leo is aware of that. He's happy to be where he is.'

'That's very sad.'

'No it isn't, Jade. Leo's happy, I'm happy, the Dark Lord is happy, Michelle is happy — well, when she gets over this fear of giving birth to monsters — in fact, the only one who isn't getting any at the moment seems to be you.'

Jade blushed and picked up her chopsticks. 'There are many dragons here in Hong Kong, Gold, and the Dark Lord lets me take True Form occasionally.'

'So that's why you always ask if you can take True Form on your day off,' Gold said with amusement. 'What's wrong with humans?'

Jade wrinkled her nose. 'Humans smell.'

Gold nearly choked on his bean curd. 'Racist.'

Jade shrugged. 'Dragons have lovely scales. I can understand Michelle's dislike of them, being human, but a nice set of scales and a really good fin and tail ... well.' She looked down at her food. 'Michelle really doesn't know what she's missing. The Dark Lord's scales are the finest on the Celestial.'

'Even better than Qing Long?' Gold said. 'Isn't the silver and turquoise more attractive than the plain black?'

Jade was dreamy-eyed for a moment. She rested her chin on her hand, still holding her chopsticks. 'The blue and silver is pretty, but the Dark Lord's black scales are just completely bad-ass.' She snapped back. 'Hot.'

'Now who's been around Leo far too much?' Gold said.

'He tends to rub off on you,' Jade said. 'I thought about changing to male form to try him out, but he's yours, so I didn't.'

'He'd pick you a mile off and probably not be interested 'cause he sees you as a girl,' Gold said.

Jade sighed. 'Such a shame. He is shiny black, as well.'

'You have a thing for black?'

Jade smiled slightly. 'Well, the dragon I'm seeing right now is black, so ... perhaps.'

<hr>

Gold was in True Form, a tiny pebble, guarding the entrance stairs while Leo and Master Mao accompanied Michelle in the gym above. Michelle was three months along, now, and needed a new fitness regime. Master Mao had come down from the Mountain to help out.

Gold kept an eye on them with True Sight; Michelle and Master Mao on the treadmill, Leo nearby doing bench presses. Leo whispered a running commentary to Gold, who could hear every word in True Form.

'Guy just walked past and looked strangely at me, probably thinks I'm talking to myself,' Leo muttered.

You don't have to keep talking if you don't want to, Gold said.

'Relieves the monotony,' Leo said.

They were interrupted by Michelle's protestations. 'Of course I can continue to work the weights.'

'It would strain your tendons, ma'am,' Master Mao said. He had taken the form of a mid-twenties private trainer, complete with short ponytail and black tank top, to guide Michelle through her new training regime. 'As you progress further through the pregnancy, your tendons will relax to allow your pelvis to open for the birth. You can easily strain them.'

Michelle just pressed the 'faster' button on the treadmill.

Master Mao changed it back. 'Slow, ma'am. Don't push your heart rate up too high.'

Michelle raised her hands in a gesture of exasperation while still walking on the treadmill.

Enjoying the show? Gold said. *Mao took that form to tease you.*

'Oh, God, hell yeah,' Leo said. 'What's he normally look like?'

Mid-fifties, overweight, and bald, Master Mao said, grinning at Leo. He took his tank top off, revealing a smooth, muscular torso. *Glad you like it.*

Michelle burst out laughing. 'Leave Leo alone!'

Master Mao pulled his shirt back on, still grinning at Leo.

The treadmill slowed, then stopped. Master Mao nodded. 'That's it, Lady Michelle, only thirty minutes, not including warm-up and cool down.'

Michelle stepped off the treadmill and began stretching. 'It seems so little.'

'It's enough to keep you in shape while you're not performing,' Master Mao said. He bowed slightly to Michelle. 'By your leave, ma'am, I need to return to the Mountain.'

'Of course,' Michelle said, and he disappeared.

Heads up! *Sissy Wing incoming*! Gold said as the journalist passed him, heading up the stairs.

'Is her pregnancy hidden?' Leo mumbled.

I got it, Gold said.

Sissy made no attempt to pretend that she was there to work

out, she just walked up to Michelle holding a small dictaphone. 'Miss LeBlanc. May I have a moment?'

Michelle straightened and glared at her. 'Missy, if you want an interview, you make an appointment like everybody else.'

Sissy didn't seem fazed that Michelle got her name wrong. 'Miss LeBlanc, you have cancelled your concert appearances, and you haven't been seen at the Academy for Performing Arts in two weeks. Is there something we should know? Maybe you and Mr Chen have some news to share?'

Time to start the story, Gold said to everybody.

Michelle frowned. 'I have been having difficulties with my voice recently. I am seeing a doctor about it. I'm having tests.'

'What kind of difficulties?'

'We will know when the tests come back.' Michelle gestured towards Leo. 'Show her out.'

'With pleasure, ma'am,' Leo said, and moved to tower over Sissy. 'If you'll just come this way.' He moved between Sissy and Michelle, blocking the journalist's view. 'Interview's over.'

'Are you pregnant, Michelle?' Sissy said around Leo's massive form.

'If I am, you can be sure that you will *not* be the first to know,' Michelle said. She turned away and headed towards the change room.

'I'd prefer not to have to pick you up and carry you out, Sissy,' Leo said, still blocking Sissy.

Sissy looked up at Leo, studying him appraisingly. 'How much for private info?'

'Go now, Sissy, before I pick you up and carry you out,' Leo said.

'I can pay up to two hundred thousand for an inside story if she's pregnant,' Sissy said.

Leo hesitated, looking down at Sissy. Then he said, 'How much for the real story if she's not pregnant, but it's something else?'

Sissy pulled out her mobile phone, pressed a single button and put it to her ear. 'Wei? Wei? Ah Mackie ah, m'goi ... Mackie. Ngoh yao Leo Alexander la ... Kui yao story la ... M'hai pregnancy. Yao story la ... Yat man okay? Boon man? Boon man dak han la ... hola, ching deng deng ...' She looked up at Leo. 'Five thousand okay?'

'Done,' Leo said. 'Downstairs, outside, while she's in the change room.'

'Boon man hola, m'goi Mackie,' Sissy said into the phone, and hung up. As they walked down the stairs to the street, she pulled the dictaphone out of her bag again. They stood together just outside the gym's entrance, with cars and red Island taxis roaring past. Sissy held the dictaphone up to Leo. 'So what's going on?'

'She's seeing an ear, nose and throat specialist,' Leo said. 'About three weeks ago, her voice started failing for no reason, she'd be in the middle of an aria or something, and it would just stop, she'd lose it altogether.'

'What's causing it?' Sissy said.

'She's having a lot of tests, but they think it's throat polyps.'

'Is it cancer?' Sissy exclaimed with delight.

Leo snorted with derision. 'No. Throat polyps are small growths on her vocal chords, caused by overuse. They're benign. The doctors have ordered her to stop singing for a couple of weeks while they work out whether or not they need to remove them. At the moment, they're doing tests, and they're watching and waiting to see if they settle down by themselves. She can't sing while they sort it out.'

Sissy put the dictaphone away, then pulled a gold and rhinestone business-card holder out of her bag and handed Leo her card. 'Call me when they find something out. If it's cancer, I can pay as much as if it's pregnancy. More, if you tell me and nobody else.'

'Will do,' Leo said. 'But don't try to contact me, I don't want her to know.'

'Done,' Sissy said. 'Call me when you want me to hand over the cash.' She quickly walked away to one of the rare street areas not blocked with a yellow line that prevented cars from stopping, and hailed a taxi. She smiled at Leo as she was driven away.

Nice job, Gold said as Leo went back up the stairs to the gym.

'Thanks,' Leo said.

Gold's sensitive hearing heard what sounded like the hiss of scales in the change room. He hesitated, then he heard it again. He shot up off the floor, made himself invisible, and raced to the women's change room. *Leo, trouble! I hear snakes!*

Leo didn't hesitate, he ran into the change room as well.

Michelle was sitting on the tiles, cornered by two demons in female human form who were dressed in the attendants' white uniforms. All the other women in the change room lay on the floor, unconscious or dead.

'Leo, help me!' Michelle cried when she saw them. 'I've been calling for you, why didn't you come?'

Gold took human form, generated a ball of energy, and blew one of the demons up.

'I've bound the other one, Leo, kill it fast,' Gold said.

'What level is it? I can't tell,' Leo said, hesitating.

'Forty-five.'

'Glad you're here then, man,' Leo said, and ran his dark fist through the demon's head, destroying it.

The sound of scales hissed again, and a Snake Mother came around the wall separating the change room from the shower area. Leo backed up so that he was standing side by side with Gold, in front of Michelle.

The Snake Mother stopped, watching them. Then it flicked its long snake-like tongue over its face and disappeared.

'Wait,' Gold said, and checked that the demon had completely gone. He relaxed. 'We scared it off!'

Michelle buried her head in her hands in the corner of the change room and shook with silent sobs. 'You didn't come! You didn't come!'

Leo touched one of the women on the floor. 'Are they all right?'

Gold took the woman's pulse. 'They just made them unconscious.' He rose and looked around. 'I can clean this up.'

'What do you mean, "clean it up"?' Leo asked suspiciously.

'I'll sit them on the benches in front of the lockers, and bring them all around together,' Gold said. 'They'll be slightly disoriented, but they won't be aware that anything happened.'

Leo crouched next to Michelle, and held her as she wept.

Eventually she took a deep breath and looked up at Leo. 'I need to shower, I never had a chance to, I asked one of those demon things for a towel and it tried to grab me. Can you stay with me?'

'I can't, honey,' Leo said gently. 'When these women come round, they're gonna panic at the sight of a huge black man in the women's change room.'

Gold crouched next to them and took female form. 'I will take this form and stay here with you, ma'am. You have your shower, and I will sort out the other women.' He turned to Leo. 'You need to shower too, you have demon essence on you. I'll mind everything here.'

Michelle clutched Leo's arm. 'Don't leave me!'

Leo gently loosened her grasp. 'You'll be fine here with Gold, Michelle. I'll take a quick shower and be right back, standing outside just in case.'

Michelle nodded, rose, and walked into the shower area, slightly unsteady on her feet.

'Go, Leo, I'll mind things here,' Gold said.

Leo nodded and went out.

Michelle was still in the shower when Gold had revived all of the other women and had them sitting around the change room looking bewildered. He checked her; she was fine. He went to meet up with Leo at the entrance to the change room.

'The Dark Lord said that she had courage he'd never seen before,' Gold said. 'As Master of the Mountain, he's seen many courageous Disciples, so I find that hard to believe. Has she become more afraid with the demon attacks? Is it having an effect on her?'

'I think he sees what he wants to see in her,' Leo said as he leaned against the wall next to the change-room entrance. 'I wouldn't call her courageous by any stretch of the imagination.'

Gold turned back. 'She's out of the shower, I'll wait in the change room for her.'

Leo nodded. 'You do that. Stay with her, she'll be shaken for a few hours.'

'At least she didn't pass out this time.'

'She still has plenty of time to do it on the way home.'

※※※※※※※※※※※※※※※※

Later at home, Gold went into Michelle's room to make sure she was okay. He presented her with a necklace that he'd made for her; a simple polished golden cat's-eye stone in a gold setting on a twenty-four carat chain.

'This is an alarm,' Gold said. 'Hold the stone, squeeze it hard, and I'll hear you, no matter how far away you are.'

Michelle took the stone, slipped it over her neck, and studied it. 'No diamonds?'

'I can put diamonds on it if you'd like, ma'am.'

Michelle nodded. 'I'd appreciate that.'

'White, cognac, or champagne?'

'You can get champagne-coloured diamonds?'

'They're a honey brown,' Gold said. 'Same colour as the stone.'

Michelle held the pendant up and studied it. 'I think white diamonds, and if you could, change the setting to white gold as well.'

Gold waved his hand over the pendant and it changed to her specifications. Michelle looked at it again, then smiled at Gold. 'Perfect! Have you ever considered a career in jewellery making?'

'I hope one day, ma'am, when I am freed from constantly taking human form, that I can be the centrepiece of a spectacular piece of jewellery for you,' Gold said.

He saw Michelle's face, and added, 'With many diamonds!'

Michelle squeezed the stone with delight, and an alarm wailed through Gold's lattice. He quickly took her hand off the stone, making the alarm stop. 'Thank you, ma'am, I heard that very clearly.'

'How far away will you hear it?'

'Up to three li ...' Gold worked out the conversion. 'About a kilometre and a half.'

Michelle nodded. 'You will never be further from me than that anyway.' She reclined on the bed. 'Now please let me rest, it has been a difficult day.'

'Of course,' Gold said, and closed the door as he went out. Leo was waiting for him on the other side.

'That thing you did with the light,' Leo said. 'Can you teach me that?'

'Energy work? Hasn't the Dark Lord started you on that yet? You should be learning already,' Gold said.

'He's probably forgotten,' Leo said. 'How much work does it involve? Can I learn it?'

'You should be able to learn it quite easily,' Gold said. 'Come into the training room, let's see what we can do.'

They sat cross-legged on the mats across from each other. Gold had Leo do a thirty-minute deep meditation, and at then brought him out of it.

'You don't have the patience and strength of character to achieve pure detachment,' Gold said with dismay. 'You need to practise more.'

'That's what the Dark Lord says,' Leo said, 'but I just find it boring.'

'You won't be able to reap the full benefit from it until you stop finding it boring,' Gold said. 'Now hold out your hands.'

Leo held his hands out, and Gold formed them into a cup shape with his own .

'Now,' Gold said, 'focus on the chi moving through your body, your essence of life, and bring it to your hands.'

Gold was still touching Leo's hands and he felt Leo go into near-shock as he completed the exercise.

'Leo! Leo! Take the chi back out, flow it around yourself!'

Leo's face was slack; he couldn't hear Gold. Gold used his contact with Leo's hands and quickly manipulated Leo's chi so that it flowed smoothly through him again. The small concentration of chi in Leo's hands had made the virus multiply in his body, sending him into shock.

Xuan Wu rushed into the training room and crouched next to them. *Leo is not to do energy work, it could kill him.*

He didn't know?

I knew how disappointed he would be. I suppose we have to tell him now.

'Can you hear me, Leo?' Gold said.

Leo nodded slightly without answering.

'I'm going to carry you to your room, and I want you to rest for a while, and you are never, ever to try doing energy work again. The Dark Lord knows what he's doing in not teaching you.'

Leo slowly focused on Gold. 'Why?' He saw Xuan Wu. 'Why?'

'Manipulating your chi stops the check on the virus, Leo, and it multiplies like crazy in you. If you tried doing full-on energy work, the same as I do, it would probably kill you within half an hour,' Gold said.

Leo sagged.

Gold rose, slipped his arm under Leo's, and lifted him. 'Come on, my friend, you need to lie down for a day or so.'

'I have work to do,' Leo mumbled.

'You are relieved for the next day, Leo,' Xuan Wu said.

Gold took Leo back to his bedroom and stretched him out on the bed. 'Rest.'

'I feel like I've been hit by a truck,' Leo said. He put one hand on Gold's forearm. 'You need to stay here and look after Michelle until I'm rested.'

Gold shifted his hand so that it was in Leo's and squeezed. 'Don't worry, I'll stay here and make sure nothing happens.'

'Good,' Leo said, and collapsed onto the pillow.

<hr>

Six months later Xuan Wu called Jade and Gold for a meeting in the dining room. 'This is mostly a planning meeting, Jade, as the baby is due any time. Gold, an update on the deeds.'

'All taken care of, my Lord,' Gold said. 'It took me a while, but all of the properties have been registered with the relevant authorities, put in the name of your current human alias of John Chen, and your will has been updated so that Lady Michelle will inherit should anything happen. The time-consuming part of the exercise was tracking down the original deeds, because you purchased some of these properties more than a human lifetime ago, and they were still in the name of your previous human alias from a hundred years ago.'

'Wait,' Jade said, raising one hand. 'In case something should happen to the Dark Lord? Such a thing is not possible.' She looked from Gold to Xuan Wu. 'You are one of the mightiest Immortals on the plane, my Lord, you do not need a will! Why is Gold wasting his time?' She dropped her voice. 'Is there something I should know?'

'That is why I have called this meeting,' Xuan Wu said. 'The future.' He leaned back and retied his long hair, which had begun to fall out of its black tie. 'As you know, I made a vow to Michelle never to take True Form. This promise remains over me as long as Michelle lives.' He ran one hand over his face. 'It is very hard.'

'Believe us, my Lord, we are well aware of how difficult it is to remain in human form. Remember how worn our human forms were when we entered your service?' Gold said with grim humour.

'It was awful,' Jade whispered. 'We thought we were going to die.' She glanced up at Xuan Wu. 'But you die, you spend a couple of days in Hell, you return! It has already happened twice while we have been in your service! You do not need a will, my Lord, you always return from Hell, that's the Way!'

'True,' the Dark Lord said. 'But this is not a contingency plan should the human form die. It's a plan should I lose the human form altogether and slip into True Form.'

'Just change back to human form again?' Jade said, bewildered.

'Not as easy as that,' Gold said, all humour disappearing.

'I have been in human form for too long,' the Dark Lord said. 'I am so weakened that if I were to slip into True Form now, the reptile would take over.'

Jade stared at Xuan Wu for a moment, digesting this. Then she said, 'How long would you remain without intelligence, Lord? How long before the spirit could be restored and you would become more than an animal again?'

Xuan Wu studied his hands on the table for a moment, then looked up into Jade's eyes. 'I have no idea.'

'But it wouldn't be as if you had died, you would return eventually,' Jade said, trying to be positive. 'It could just be a matter of weeks, then your humanity would return, and you would come home to us. There is no need to prepare as if there is a chance you could be gone for the rest of Michelle's life.'

'All contingencies must be prepared for,' Gold said.

'I need to return to the Mountain again,' Xuan Wu said. 'I'm dangerously low on energy. I want to make a trip up there and return within a week. Michelle is into her third trimester and the baby will come soon. I must be as strong as possible to guard her and our new child.'

'Do not be concerned, my Lord, we will guard her.'

Xuan Wu sighed gently. 'I am just glad that she has agreed to stay out of the public eye during the pregnancy. I am sure that the demons do not know. You have done well.'

'The amount of mail she receives from people wishing her a swift recovery from the "throat polyps" is remarkable,' Gold said. 'There has been extensive coverage in the world press. It will not be long before she has a larger audience than before.'

'She deserves such an audience,' Jade said fiercely. 'She is richly talented, and endlessly patient with the limits we place on her because of who her husband is. She does not deserve to be locked away.'

'Guard her carefully while I am gone,' Xuan Wu said. 'I know we were just attacked and so they are likely to be quiet, but there is always the chance another demon will try us.' He nodded to Gold. 'Take my form while I am on the Celestial. Be my decoy.'

'My Lord,' Gold said.

'Your lady and child will be safe with us,' Jade said. 'We will guard them with our lives.'

'I know,' Xuan Wu said. He rubbed his eyes. 'That doesn't stop me from worrying about them.' He placed his hands on the table. 'I will leave for the Celestial Mountain first thing tomorrow morning, and return next week.'

Jade and Gold formally nodded their heads in understanding.

'Very well. Dismissed.'

<hr>

The next evening Michelle and Xuan Wu held a quiet, heartbreaking parting in the living room of the Peak apartment. They stood gazing into each others' eyes, with hands clasped, for a very long time. Finally Xuan Wu released Michelle's hands, strode through the glass of the living room window, and stepped onto the small cloud that would take him to the Celestial.

'You know you look ridiculous flying on a little cloud,' Michelle said as he turned for a last look. 'Why don't you ride something majestic, like a big black winged horse or something? Yes! Make Star fly, Lo Wu, and ride him to Heaven and then back down to me.'

'Star would panic and soil the carpet,' Xuan Wu said with a sad smile. 'We Shen have been riding clouds for thousands of years. You cannot break us from our traditions that easily.'

'It still looks ridiculous,' Michelle said. She sobered. 'Be careful, my love, and return to me —' She placed one hand on her swollen belly. 'To us — very soon.'

He held his hand out to her from the other side of the glass. 'I wish you could come.'

'Pfft.' She waved her hand at him. 'You say yourself it could endanger our little one. I will be perfectly safe with Leo, and your pet small Shen, to guard me. Now go, before I change my mind and jump onto your silly little cloud with you!'

'I love you with all my heart, Michelle, be safe for me,' Xuan Wu said, and turned away. The cloud drifted lazily upwards, then jetted off so fast it was soon invisible.

'I love you too, my silly Lo Wu,' Michelle said. 'And for once I really wish I could come with you, and be sure that our little one is safe.' She turned to the Shen and shrugged. 'Who would like ice cream? I would like some fresh air. Let's go down to the Peak Tower and walk around.'

'As long as you permit me to take the form of the Dark Lord,' Gold said.

Michelle waved one hand. 'Such precautions are so unnecessary. But if it will make you happier, go right ahead.'

Leo drove the ten-minute trip down to the Peak Tower and Galleria shopping centre, nestled between the two mountains that towered above Hong Kong Island. The Peak Tower was five storeys high, and shaped like a semi-circle balanced on two columns. The curving underside of the building was all glass, giving the shoppers and diners within a view onto the busy harbour of Hong Kong almost directly below them.

Michelle led them to the Galleria shopping centre across from the tower. It had a number of small tourist shops selling cheap local handicrafts, as well as a Western-style café and a Swedish ice-cream outlet. Leo ordered for them, then Michelle insisted that they stand near the fountain in the plaza to eat.

Jade had passed on the ice cream, and had ordered a red-bean fleecy instead — red beans and syrup in a milk drink, with a scoop of ice cream on top.

'The first time I saw a red-bean ice cream,' Michelle said, 'I thought it was chocolate. I was so surprised at the taste!'

'Did you throw it away?' Jade said, amused.

Michelle nodded, her lips pursing at the memory of the flavour. 'I have never tasted anything quite so awful. Why is it that all the Chinese desserts are so horrible?'

'Chinese desserts aren't horrible!' Gold said.

'They are all mashed beans or seeds in a soup — or even, heaven forbid, fungus, or yam, or corn, in syrup,' Michelle said. 'Who puts corn in a dessert?'

'But corn is sweet,' Gold protested.

'It's probably because this is a culture without milk,' Leo said.

'They have milk here!' Michelle said.

'Not traditionally,' Leo said. 'Your average Chinese peasant wouldn't own a cow, it would be too expensive. I think that's why they eat so much pork and chicken here — poor man's meat.'

'We are not poor!' Gold exclaimed.

Leo shrugged. 'Tell that to the old ladies who collect cardboard for a living, and sell it for less than a dollar a load.'

Michelle gestured towards the Peak Tower's viewing platform on its flat roof. 'Let's go up to the top, and watch the tourists.'

'Not look at the view?' Leo said.

Michelle nudged him with her shoulder. 'The tourists are more fun to watch.'

Leo chuckled and elbowed her back. 'Particularly the French-Canadian ones, they're so loud.'

'I know!' Michelle said, giggling, as they walked to the base of the tower.

There were expensive souvenir shops just inside, and a perfume outlet. They went up the escalators, past a freak show and the entrance to a Western restaurant, to the viewing platform above.

Gold reached to touch Leo's hand and smiled at him. *Remember when we came here as boy and girl, that first time?*

Leo smiled back without replying, his face full of longing. Gold's smile faded as he remembered — he was in the Dark Lord's form. He raised his hands and turned away.

Leo came up behind him and touched his shoulder. 'Sorry, Gold. Yeah, I remember. I'm glad I met you.'

Gold turned. 'I hope you find true happiness with someone some day, my friend. You deserve it.'

'I have true happiness right here,' Leo said, his smile returning. He looked around and sighed with bliss. 'I have everything a man could possibly want. And when the little one comes, I will have even more.'

'That's good,' Gold said. He looked around as well. 'Where's Michelle?'

The viewing platform was eighty metres to a side, and there were at least a hundred tourists on the platform, all crowded around the edge enjoying the view of Hong Kong Harbour below.

Gold stopped and concentrated, looking for Jade. She was in the ladies' room below them and felt his contact.

You're with Michelle, aren't you? she said.

'Oh, shit, Jade went to the bathroom,' Gold said. He looked

around desperately. 'Leo, we've lost her!'

Leo and Gold immediately split up and covered the viewing platform, meeting back in the middle. Neither of them had found Michelle.

I'm checking downstairs, Jade said.

Gold strode to the wall of the elevator machinery room and placed his hand on the concrete. 'Give me a minute, I'll have a look at the security videos.'

'Be quick, man!' Leo said.

Gold's awareness found the cables inside the building. Water, sewerage, no, no ... he found the power lines, and mentally slapped the young stone Shen that was surfing the consciousness-raising power in the high-voltage electricity. The young Shen, a fluorite of less than two hundred years, grinned ruefully at him and assisted him in locating the CCTV wires.

Together they latched onto the security camera input.

Gold's internal vision switched to a view from all the cameras at once — much like what an insect would see through its faceted eyes. The fluorite Shen pinpointed the display that was needed, and Gold moved to the recording device in the security room and wound it back about ten minutes.

The fluorite Shen mentally saluted Gold with an evil grin and disappeared.

Gold watched the security footage and saw a bewildered Michelle surrounded by a group of loud mainland tourists. They huddled around her, jostled her, and then one of them touched her, making her go limp. They guided her towards the escalator down.

Gold switched cameras, rewound the tape, and watched them take her outside the Peak Tower to the road in front where they bundled her onto a large coach.

Gold disconnected from the cameras, grabbed Leo's hand, made them invisible, and teleported them down to the street below.

Street below, Jade.

Got it.

The tourist bus was just pulling away from the front of the Peak Tower as they arrived. The windows were heavily tinted so they couldn't see what was happening inside. Gold seized the engine and melted it into a useless mass of metal. He raised one hand in front of the bus door and it slid open with a hiss of escaping air.

Jade stood guard on the pavement while Gold and Leo entered the bus.

Michelle was sitting in the driver's seat, staring dully at them.

Gold took her hand, checking that she was okay. 'It's all right now, ma'am, we're here to get you.'

Leo tapped Gold's shoulder. 'Uh, Gold ...'

Gold looked up, to see Leo staring at the other occupants of the bus.

All of them were Michelle, sitting and staring dully at them. Gold turned back to the driver, and checked her through his hand; as far as he could see, it was Michelle — but when he realised that she wasn't pregnant, he knew it must have been a shape-shifting demon.

'This has to be a demon, but I can't tell ...' Gold started, and the demon leapt out of its seat to attack him. He still had a grip on its hand, so he shot a blast of chi into it, destroying it.

He heard the other demons leap out of their seats before he saw them. He spun and put his hands out, ready to battle with energy.

'What level are these?' Leo said as he grabbed the first that came at them by the arm, spun it, flung it into the one behind it, and ran his fist through both of them.

'No idea, Leo, I can't even sense that they are demons!' Gold said, blowing up a couple more with chi.

There were about twenty of them on the bus, limited in their attack by the narrowness of the aisle between the seats. They could only come at Gold and Leo two at a time.

The one at the front grabbed Leo by the throat, and pushed him into the seatback of the first row of seats. Leo scrabbled at the demon, choking. Gold couldn't destroy any more with energy; the large amount of energy he'd received from the backlash in killing them was making him dangerously full, and he wasn't in contact with the ground to send it there.

Jade stormed up the stairs into the bus, pushing Gold out of the way. She grabbed the demon who was choking Leo by the neck, ripped it off him, spun it into the front-row seat on the left, and snapped its head off with both hands.

Gold checked Leo; he was fine. Leo raised his hand, and Gold summoned a sword for him. Leo and Jade stood side by side at the front of the bus to face down the remaining demons.

Gold realised with shock that all of the Michelles on the bus were glaring maliciously at them, and he couldn't pick the real one. The alarm he'd given her went off within his lattice and he concentrated to locate it — it was beneath them. 'She's in the luggage compartment!'

Jade changed to dragon form. She grabbed an incoming demon in her claws and tore its head off with her mouth. The other demons hesitated, staring at her, then rushed to the back of the bus. She swished her green tail with its gold fin, and sauntered slowly towards them, grinning with a dragon mouth full of golden teeth. *Go get her, I have this*, she said.

Gold and Leo rushed back down the stairs and to the side of the bus. Leo unlatched the luggage compartment and slid the door up. The luggage compartment was the full length and width of the bus beneath the seats. Michelle lay bound and gagged inside, her hands in front of her clutching Gold's alarm which was still shrilling inside him. When Michelle saw Gold and Leo she visibly relaxed, and lay prone inside the bus.

Leo crawled inside and carefully manoeuvred Michelle so that he could pass her to Gold, who set her on the ground. Together they untied her gag and released her hands and feet. Leo rubbed them to bring the circulation back.

Jade walked down out of the bus in human form, her green silk suit as crisp as ever and not a hair out of place in her bun. 'All fixed. That was fun.' She saw Michelle. 'Are you all right, ma'am?'

Leo studied Michelle, holding her hands. 'Michelle?' Michelle appeared semi-conscious, her head lolling and her eyes half-closed. 'Michelle, speak to me.' He turned to Gold. 'We need to take her home. Can you teleport her, or whatever it is that you do, without anybody seeing?'

'I can't teleport her, it would hurt the baby,' Gold said.

'Is my baby all right?' Michelle said weakly.

Gold surreptitiously used his inner eye to check the child. 'The baby is fine, ma'am, she hasn't been affected by this at all. All you need is some rest, and you'll be fine too, you just had a bit of a scare, that's all.'

Michelle stared at Gold. Then she threw herself into Leo's arms and held him. 'Take me home, Leo.' She waved one hand at Gold, still clutching Leo. 'And leave these creatures behind. I don't wish to see them ever again.'

Leo hoisted Michelle and held her like a child. 'I'll take you home.'

Michelle glared at Gold from Leo's arms. 'Go away, and never come back. I never want to see you again!' She looked up at Leo. 'Put me down, Leo, I can walk. Let's go home.' She leaned on Leo as he guided her back to the car park.

Jade and Gold moved to follow and she turned and glared at them. 'Go away!'

'It might be a good idea to come home a little later, guys,' Leo said. 'Just stay away for an hour or so, and come up then.'

'Never!' Michelle shouted, waving at Gold and Jade without

turning. 'Never come back!'

Leo shrugged. 'Come up in about an hour.' He guided Michelle into the car-park lift.

Jade glared at Gold. 'Excellent work, Big Mouth Stone.'

'I know,' Gold said with misery.

'She's going to hate you for a long time, Gold. We've probably lost our jobs over this.'

Gold shrugged wryly. 'Well, at least she knows for sure now that it's not a reptile. And that it's a girl.'

'After all the fuss she made about not knowing whether it was a boy or a girl.'

They hung around the Peak, Gold regularly checking with Leo by mobile phone to make sure Michelle was okay.

About forty-five minutes later, Gold received a text message from Leo's phone through his stone lattice: Come home, M in labour.

When they returned to the Peak, they heard Leo and Michelle loudly arguing in the master bedroom. 'It's not time yet, Leo,' Michelle said, exasperated.

'That's beside the point, Michelle,' Leo said, as if he'd been explaining this for a long time. 'Your contractions are ten minutes apart. We have to go now.'

'But it's not due for two weeks!'

'Two weeks either side is normal!'

Michelle shrieked, and Gold and Jade raced into the room.

Leo leaned over her, stroking her shoulders. 'Breathe, Michelle, remember your lessons.'

Michelle nodded, her face strained. She saw Gold and Jade. 'Get Lo Wu!'

'I'll take her downstairs, you get the Dark Lord,' Jade said. She went to Michelle.

'Wait until the contraction is done ...' Leo studied Michelle carefully. 'There. Walk her slowly down, take the elevator.'

Jade turned to Leo and Gold. 'Go, both of you, I'll bring her down.'

Leo raced out the door to get the car. Gold followed him. 'Leo, wait, I'll transport you down.'

Leo hesitated, then nodded. Gold took his hand, and transported him directly to the car park. Leo swayed slightly, disoriented from the travel, then shook himself and ran to the car. He turned to Gold. 'Well, go get Mr Chen. If he misses this he'll kill us.'

Gold dropped his head and disappeared.

THE YEAR
1804

THE TIGER'S HAREM

PALACE OF
BAI HU
THE TIGER,

LORD OF
THE WEST.

But Gold didn't grumble too much as he continued with the towels he had been carrying between the laundry and the Seraglio. The Tiger's wives seemed to use every towel taken almost immediately. They spent most of their time bathing, hoping that the Tiger would wander past, see them, and invite one or two of them for a small dalliance.

Unfortunately Gold saw the women all the time and, due to the particular way he'd been bound, he couldn't even tell them about their obvious charms. He wasn't just frustrated; he was way through frustration and out the other side.

But he had decided to work hard and serve his sentence with good humour. Perhaps when he was released he would be able to return and tell the Tiger's wives exactly what he'd been thinking as he'd carried the towels through the harem.

Gold placed the towels on a side table, and quickly floated in stone form to the gardens and the side of the pool, where Bai Hu the Tiger awaited in his True Form.

Gold cast around and saw a couple of Horsemen guarding the gates that led through the three-metre high wall separating the pool deck from the desert plain. One of them carried a large sword, a suitable weapon. He approached the Horsemen, floating at eye level.

'May I borrow your blade?' he asked the Horseman with the sword.

'Certainly,' the Horseman said. He pulled the blade from its scabbard at his side, and held it out.

'Thank you,' Gold said. 'I need to kill a snake with it, then I'll give it right back.'

'You do that,' the Horseman said with obvious amusement. The Horseman at the other side of the gate made a strange hissing sound, and Gold glanced at him, but his face was rigid.

Gold couldn't shrug in stone form. He turned and moved towards the edge of the pool, the sword floating behind him.

The Tiger had been wise to choose Gold to kill the snake; Gold could move silently in stone form, floating, and still wield the blade with reasonable accuracy.

The snake was a monster, more than two metres long, stretched out on the gold-coloured pavers that edged the pool. It appeared to be a cobra, but was a shiny black from its blunt nose to its pointed tail.

It seemed to be sleeping in the sunshine.

Gold approached the snake from behind, moved to the side next to its head, and raised the blade.

It had a deep, masculine hiss.

'The Tiger ordered me to kill you,' Gold said. He had been bound, and was unable to move. 'I didn't know you were a Shen, I thought you were a natural snake. My apologies. Would you mind leaving the poolside? The Tiger would like to bring some of his wives in, and he is concerned that you would frighten them.'

Something black and enormous that Gold hadn't noticed before stirred at the bottom of the pool beside the snake. 'The Tiger ordered you to kill me, eh?' the snake said.

'Yes, sir,' Gold said, distracted by the water surging in the pool. The large dark thing in the pool approached the surface; it was oval, and nearly five metres long. Gold made another attempt to move but was still bound.

As Xuan Wu and Gold approached, the Tiger obviously couldn't contain his mirth any more and roared with laughter over the top of the antelope. He laughed so hard he rolled onto his back, his paws in the air, the snow-white fur of his belly rippling as his sides heaved.

Xuan Wu flopped onto one of the deck chairs and gestured towards Gold without looking at him. 'Go to the kitchen and bring me something cold to drink. Non-alcoholic.'

'Sir,' Gold said.

'You've failed me, Gold,' the Tiger wheezed with delight, still on his back with his paws in the air. 'I ordered you to kill that goddamn snake, and instead you're going to serve it drinks.'

'And vegetarian ho fan,' Xuan Wu said.

'Sir,' Gold said.

'Go,' Xuan Wu said.

'Sir,' Gold squeaked, and floated away to the kitchen as quickly as his stone form could carry him.

'Cut the laughing and make some vegetarian ho fan for the Dark Lord,' Gold snapped loudly. 'And he wants something cold and non-alcoholic to drink.'

The demons didn't stop laughing as they hurried to prepare the noodles.

One of the demons, in the form of a teenage girl, approached Gold. 'How close did you come to cutting off the Serpent's head?' she said with a huge grin.

'I wish I'd seen that,' one of the other demons shouted from the other side of the kitchen.

'He knew I was coming from a mile off,' Gold said. 'He was just waiting to see what I'd do.'

'It wasn't your fault, Gold,' she said, still smiling. 'It was Lord Bai Hu's idea.'

'I didn't even see the Turtle at the bottom of the pool,' Gold said, miserable.

The demons all laughed again.

'Better be careful what you say near Lord Xuan Wu,' an older demon said as he approached. 'You've already managed to insult him by not recognising him. No turtle words, Gold. I know what you're like, and if you insult the Dark Lord then the trouble you're in now will be nothing compared to what he could do to you.'

'I've never seen him,' the young female demon said. 'What does he look like?'

'His human form is a tall man with long hair,' Gold said. 'Black eyes.'

'Did you see his True Form?' she said.

'You saw the Serpent? Did you see the Xuan Wu, the whole thing?'

Gold floated slightly higher, enjoying her rapt attention. 'The Serpent was lying on the poolside, then the Turtle came out of the water and I saw them join together. I saw the whole majestic Xuan Wu.'

'How powerful is he?' she said. She turned to the older male demon. 'I've heard he's very powerful. He's the Spirit of the North. How powerful is he?'

'He is second in power and majesty only to the Celestial One, the Jade Emperor Himself,' the male demon said with deference. 'He is First Celestial General. He commands the Armies of the Thirty-Six. He wields the Blade of Seven Stars. He is the mightiest demon destroyer in existence ...'

The young female demon's eyes were huge.

'He is Sovereign of the Four Winds,' Gold said, grabbing back her attention. 'He commands the other three spirits; the White Tiger of the West, the Red Phoenix of the South, and the Azure Dragon of the East.'

'He's the Tiger's lord,' the older male demon said.

'You don't get much bigger than him without entering the Celestial Palace itself,' Gold said. 'And he spends most of his time there, anyway. He is Right Hand to the Jade Emperor.'

'He spends a lot of time here, too,' the older male demon said.

'He and the Lord Bai Hu are very good friends.'

'I didn't know that,' Gold said. 'And the Tiger took advantage of my ignorance.'

'Well, from what I've heard, Gold, that would be poetic justice for you.'

Gold stopped at that. 'I suppose you're right,' he said softly.

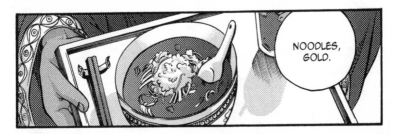

'Learn some humility or you'll join your dad,' the Tiger growled. 'Wait here, you can bring me some wives later.'

'My Lord.' Gold moved to one side and settled on the ground, resting in the afternoon sun. The sun warmed his golden veins and he nearly sighed with bliss.

'A group of missionaries from the West invaded one of my establishments in Sichuan,' the Tiger said. 'They have some interesting ideas about the nature of the universe. I'm always making plans to spend more time on the Earthly plane and gather information about this, but then find something better to do here on the Celestial.'

'Don't harm any Westerners if you can avoid it,' Xuan Wu said.

'The increasing conflict between the Qing and the traders from the West is causing us a great deal of concern.'

The Tiger stretched on the paving and curled his tail around his hind legs. 'China has no need for them. We are large and mighty. They are small and divided. They have nothing that we need.'

'They are well aware of that. But they love our tea.'

The Tiger chuckled. 'Good luck to them. So do we.'

'Chinese tea is selling for a small fortune in the West, Ah Bai,' Xuan Wu said, stirring the noodles with his chop-sticks. 'The traders see the possibility of great profits and are looking for all possible avenues to tap into this market.'

'They can buy as much tea as they want, provided they pay for it in silver or gold.'

'They are. They pay for the tea with silver.'

The Tiger pulled himself slightly more upright. 'And where are they mining this silver from?'

'Southern China,' Xuan Wu said. 'Guangdong. Fukien. Chaozhou provinces.'

'There's no silver to be had there, Ah Wu,' the Tiger said. 'What are you talking about?'

'They grow opium in India. They sell the opium in Southern China, they sell it for silver. Then they use the silver to buy tea. The streets of Guangdong province are lined with opium houses.'

The Tiger flicked one ear. 'This is very bad news, Ah Wu.'

'The Qing Emperor is planning to outlaw the sale of opium. The Western traders are willing to go to war for the right to sell it.'

'This is extremely bad. Because of the reign of the previous emperor and his corrupt little boyfriend, China's army is almost useless.'

'I am seriously considering intervening,' Xuan Wu said to the noodles.

'You're not the only one,' the Tiger growled. 'I will not see our Middle Kingdom invaded by them.'

'The Jade Emperor will shortly issue an edict.' Xuan Wu leaned back and studied the Tiger intensely. 'No Celestial may intervene in Earthly affairs. We will watch and wait. But we do not like where this is heading.'

'If we sit back and wait then it may be too late,' the Tiger said. 'The Qing Empire is becoming more corrupt all the time. The Empire is failing, Ah Wu, it is time for Divine Mandate to be removed from this dynasty. If the Empire is weak then the Westerners may see their chance to move in.'

'We will only intervene as a last resort. Only if it appears that the entire Empire will fall,' Xuan Wu said. 'Even then, we will hesitate. It is not our place.'

The Tiger sighed, shook his shaggy head, and flopped back down to lie on the paving.

Xuan Wu placed the chopsticks back onto the table. 'I've been summoned by the Jade Emperor. The Celestial wants to see me. Duty calls.'

'My Lord,' the Tiger said, bobbing his head.

Xuan Wu disappeared.

'Gold,' the Tiger said.

'My Lord?' Gold said.

'Seventy-six. Fifty-eight. Sixty. Seventy-three. Oh, and what the hell, the new one. Eighty-one. She'll have to learn to share eventually, might as well start teaching her now.'

'My Lord,' Gold said, and drifted away to collect the Tiger's five selected wives.

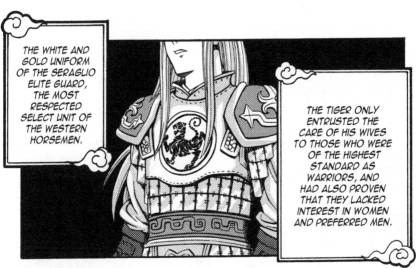

THE WHITE AND GOLD UNIFORM OF THE SERAGLIO ELITE GUARD, THE MOST RESPECTED SELECT UNIT OF THE WESTERN HORSEMEN.

THE TIGER ONLY ENTRUSTED THE CARE OF HIS WIVES TO THOSE WHO WERE OF THE HIGHEST STANDARD AS WARRIORS, AND HAD ALSO PROVEN THAT THEY LACKED INTEREST IN WOMEN AND PREFERRED MEN.

GO AWAY!

WAIT!

YOU WERE PROMOTED?

YOU MAY THINK YOU HAVE DONE ME A FAVOUR...

...WITHOUT ME YOU WOULDN'T BE HERE.

William continued, his eyes blazing. 'Nothing will undo the fact that we were made a laughing stock by you.' He turned away to hide the pain in his face. 'Everybody on the Celestial plane knows what you did, and knows what we did. Everybody knows. They still laugh when they see me coming.' He glared at Gold. 'Even the wives joke about me, they call me the "little stone's toy".'

Gold dropped slightly in the air. 'I didn't realise it was so bad for you.'

'I've been in constant contact with Jade, trying to talk her out of killing herself,' William said. 'She wants to make a trip through Hell, she wants to suffer. She says that anything she would be subjected to at the hands of Hell's demons would be nothing compared to the treatment she receives from the other dragons. Dragons are not renowned for their mercy, and in this case, they ...' His voice trailed off and he glanced away. 'In this case they have been having a great deal of fun.'

Gold dropped even further. 'I never thought of it like that.'

'Frankly, Gold, I'm not surprised.'

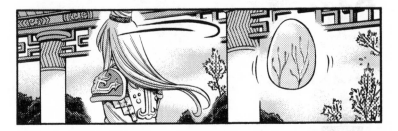

'Thinking is obviously not something
you're very good at.'

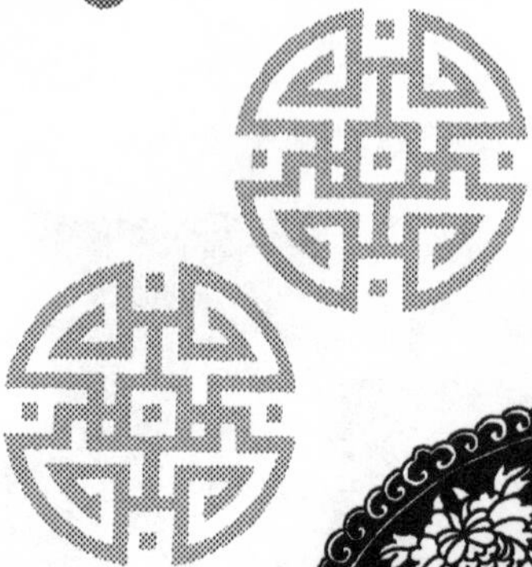

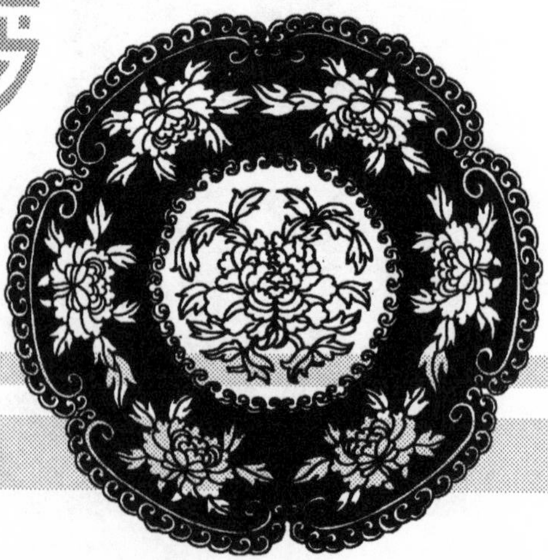

THE YEAR
1997

HONG KONG

Xuan Wu stormed into the hospital delivery room, his face fierce. He stopped dead when he saw Michelle holding the tiny baby girl. He raced to her bedside and fell to one knee, then clutched Michelle's hand.

'I'm sorry I didn't make it,' he said softly.

'Isn't she beautiful?' Michelle said with bliss. She turned, and held the baby out for Xuan Wu to hold. 'She's so perfect.'

Xuan Wu took the child as if she could shatter any moment, and stared at her with wonder as he cradled her. 'I always found human babies ugly. But this one is the most beautiful thing I have ever seen.'

'That's because she's *yours*, silly Lo Wu,' Michelle said.

The baby started to squall and Xuan Wu jumped with horror.

'It's all right, hand her back, she wants to suckle,' Michelle said. She shook her head. 'They say it will be a day or so before I have milk for her, but in the meantime it's good for her to suck, it will make the milk come sooner.'

That is so disgusting, Jade said. *Mammals! The Dark Lord must be horrified.*

Isn't the baby being bottle-fed? Gold said. *Isn't that better, to make sure that it will grow up strong and healthy?*

Leo says that it's healthier for the baby to get its mother's milk, something about fighting disease, Jade said. *It's still disgusting — like she's a farm animal!*

Xuan Wu watched as Michelle placed the child on her breast. The child nuzzled into her, then gripped tightly, making Michelle jump. It began to suck noisily and Michelle gasped.

'Are you all right?' Xuan Wu said, studying Michelle.

'I'm sore, and I'm tired, and every time she does this my stomach hurts. But they say I will be just fine.'

Xuan Wu stroked her hair. 'You have given me a greater gift than anyone ever has. I love you so much, Michelle.'

'Our gift needs a name,' Michelle said.

Xuan Wu shook his head. 'English name, I have no idea. Chinese name, we must consult an astrologer and choose a name that will offset any bad luck traits she has because of her birth date.'

'That is ridiculous, Lo Wu.'

'How about I choose a Chinese name, and you choose an

English one?'

Michelle gazed down at the content baby, who was thumping her tiny fist on Michelle's breast as she suckled. 'I would like to call her Simone, after my grandmother. She cared for me when my mother could not.' She glanced up at Xuan Wu. 'My family must come and see her!'

Xuan Wu stiffened.

'They must!'

Xuan Wu obviously relented. 'Of course. They are family, they must see their newest addition.' He touched the baby's hand and the child stopped hitting her mother and clutched her father's finger.

🉑🉑🉑🉑🉑🉑🉑🉑🉑🉑🉑🉑🉑🉑🉑

Xuan Wu sat behind his desk, grim. Jade and Gold nervously sat across from him in the visitor's chairs.

'I must return,' Xuan Wu said. 'I hardly had time to enter a trance state to begin rebuilding my energy. If I do not return soon, I may lose the form, when they need me the most.'

Gold dropped his head with misery. 'I am needed on the Mountain too. The Masters are currently working full-time assessing the students and setting their study focuses, they need me to process the latest batch of students.'

Jade shook her head. 'I do not trust myself and Leo to guard both Michelle and Simone. They are so vulnerable right now!'

'I know. The Generals are occupied administering the Northern Heavens. I have asked the other Winds, they are also unavailable. Any suggestions?'

'Er Lang?' Gold said.

Xuan Wu grimaced. 'He's filling a great deal of my role as First Heavenly General, I could not ask him to take this on as well. He feels the same way that the Celestial does about my marriage to Michelle.'

'Sun Wu Kwong?' Jade said.

'You have to be joking,' Gold said.

'I would trust the Monkey King to guard my child about as much as I trust the Demon King himself,' Xuan Wu said. He sighed. 'I will wait until Simone is old enough, then I will take both of them.'

'How old must a human child be to travel to the Celestial plane, sir?' Gold said.

'About six weeks.'

'Oh!' Jade said. 'The one-month party! You will need to start sending out invitations, and arrange a banquet hall here on the

105

Earthly for it. This will be one of the biggest things to happen on the Celestial Plane in a very long time, just about every Celestial will want to attend.'

Xuan Wu smiled grimly. 'Thank you for reminding me, Jade. The job is yours.'

Jade moaned quietly, and Gold made some barely suppressed sounds of amusement.

'You, Gold, are in charge of arranging her family's visit,' Xuan Wu said.

Gold sagged.

⊞⊞⊞⊞⊞⊞⊞⊞⊞⊞⊞⊞⊞⊞⊞⊞

'But Maman,' Michelle said, exasperated, 'why not just you? You *must* see your new little granddaughter, she is ...' she hesitated, searching for the words. 'She is so beautiful! And she does not have Chinese hair at all, it is nearly blonde, like mine, and her skin is so perfect ...' She sighed. 'Very well.' She brightened. 'Daniel? Daniel is coming?' She clapped her hands, still holding the telephone receiver, then returned it to her ear. 'That is good news. Yes, yes! Of course I will have him take photos of her! And of my house here, and my silly husband, I will have him take them all back for you! And tell Papa ...' She hesitated again. 'Tell Papa that I love him very much, Maman, and that I hope he will be here soon.'

Michelle held the telephone at arm's length and glared at it, then pushed the button to disconnect. 'Gold.' She turned and saw that Gold was already in the living room. 'Gold, my father cannot come, he has something wrong with his ears and cannot fly. They will operate soon, and they tell me he will be fine.' She brightened. 'But my brother, Daniel, is coming. He will arrive next Thursday. Lo Wu says you are to arrange this?'

Gold bowed slightly. 'Yes, ma'am. Would you prefer he stays here in the end bedroom, or would you like to put him in a hotel?'

Michelle hesitated for a moment, then said, 'In the end bedroom, next to Lo Wu's training room. He need not know about Lo Wu's ridiculous nature; it is not *that* unusual for him to be a koofoo master, and Daniel should not suspect.'

Gold smiled at Michelle's deliberate mispronunciation of 'kung fu', which she often used to annoy Xuan Wu.

'You do not plan to tell your brother about the Dark Lord's true nature?' Gold said.

'No!' Michelle vehemently shook her head. 'I do not want my

106

family to be concerned. While my brother is here, I wish you all to be as normal as possible.' Simone began to cry in the master bedroom, and Michelle lit up. 'She is awake. How can her little tears bring me so much joy?'

꧁꧁꧁꧁꧁꧁꧁꧁꧁꧁꧁꧁꧁꧁꧁꧁꧁

Jade and Gold sat quietly during the divination. The geomancer who was preparing the chart for little Simone had spent a great deal of time calculating the correct star confluences and Simone's future path.

The geomancer looked up from his charts, grim. 'There is much anguish in her future, my Lord. She will suffer greatly because of who she is.'

'I wish to minimise that suffering,' Xuan Wu said.

'You are the cause of it.'

Xuan Wu rubbed his hands over his face. 'I know.'

'How much of her future can you see, my Lord?'

Xuan Wu shook his head. 'With her, I have a blind spot. With the women I love, I cannot see. The paths are murky, the future twists. A number of futures are visible, all equally likely. Some are full of joy, some are full of grief. And all of them become imperceptible, when they approach these two.'

The geomancer nodded slightly. 'This is a good thing. Heaven protects you.' He glanced at Jade and Gold. 'You two are too small to see anything?'

Jade and Gold nodded.

'Very well.' The geomancer rose and rolled up the charts. 'Her name is to be "Si Min".' He drew the characters in the air, leaving a golden trail with his finger. 'Si, for remembrance, thought, meditation. Min, for speed. She must never forget who she is, even in the heat of battle. She will be immensely powerful, and must always remember to control this power. She must think quickly when in conflict, and have the intelligence to decide the right path, or those around her will suffer.'

Xuan Wu gazed up at the geomancer. 'Nothing to protect her from her future of pain?'

The geomancer flipped the hem of his robe. 'It is more important that those around her be protected. For her, there will be suffering, and that will temper her spirit and give her wisdom. It is for the best.'

'Will she lose me?'

The geomancer looked down. 'You are Immortal, my Lord. She

can never lose you, because you cannot die.'

'That is not what I asked.'

'I will register her name with the Hall of Records,' the geomancer said. 'Make sure the fung shui in her room leans towards the Yang; because you are her father, she is more likely to be Yin and therefore cold-blooded.'

'Will she lose me?' Xuan Wu said.

The geomancer disappeared, but his voice remained. 'She will lose one, then gain one, then lose three, then gain five.'

'Which one will she lose?' Jade whispered.

'I hope it is either you or me,' Gold replied.

'Do you love her, like family?' Xuan Wu said.

Jade and Gold shared a look.

'Then it will probably be me. Heaven knows who the two are. In the end, however, she will have more who love her than she loses. Is Michelle awake?'

Gold concentrated. 'Yes, sir.'

'You cannot see her?' Jade said.

'I need to travel to the Mountain. As soon as Simone is six weeks old, I will take both of them, and spend ten days there. How are the preparations for the banquet?'

'The Tiger has offered the use of the ballroom in his hotel in Sha Tin. His staff are demons; your guests will be able to take True Form,' Jade said with obvious satisfaction.

'And Michelle will have a heart attack,' Gold said. 'You know how she hates it when they take True Form.'

Jade opened her mouth and closed it again. 'I forgot.'

'Michelle's family?' Xuan Wu said.

'Her father has a tumour in his inner ear that does not allow him to change pressure; he cannot fly at the moment,' Gold said. 'Her mother will stay with her father while he has surgery to remove the tumour, and they check whether it is cancer.'

'If it is cancer, your Serpent can cure it,' Jade said, pleased. 'They would certainly appreciate that!'

'If I had my Serpent,' Xuan Wu said.

Jade, Gold said, *Wherever you left your brain today, could you please go fetch it?*

I know! Jade wailed.

After a few moments of uncomfortable silence, Gold spoke. 'Lady Michelle's brother, Daniel, will arrive next week and take some photos to give to her parents. He will stay in the room closest to the training room.'

'She wants him to stay *here*?'

'He's family, my Lord.'

Xuan Wu made a soft sound of exasperation. 'I'm just glad her parents are not coming as well.'

'They will, eventually, my Lord.'

Xuan Wu waved one hand over his desk. 'Dismissed. Go tell Michelle the baby's name. That should please her, to have such a clever name for her child.'

༺༻༺༻༺༻༺༻༺༻༺༻༺༻༺༻

'Si Min?' Michelle cried, horrified.

'Si Mun in Cantonese,' Jade said.

'It's a good name,' Gold said. '"Smart Girl", your daughter will be very clever with a name like that.'

'And it sounds like Simone!' Jade finished for him triumphantly.

'It sounds like *semen*!' Michelle wailed. 'Where is Lo Wu, we must change this immediately!'

Jade gasped. 'Oh, no!'

'Um ...' Gold hesitated. 'Ma'am, the name has already been registered on the Celestial Record. It cannot be changed. And it was chosen by the Jade Emperor's own magician, it is the name that she should have.'

'Ugh.' Michelle turned away from them. 'Get out of my sight.'

Jade and Gold teleported out as quickly as they could. They did not want to see the fireworks when Michelle nailed Xuan Wu down.

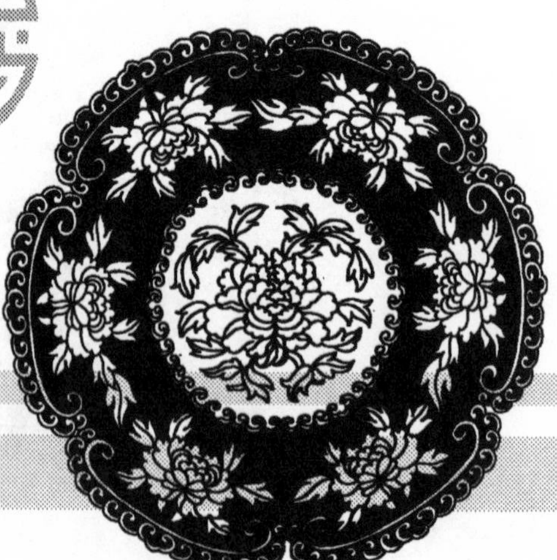

THE YEAR
1820

FREEDOM AND THEFT (1)

IT WAS THE YEAR

1820

113

Gold floated closer to the table, then dropped six inches in the air. 'This humble stone is present. My Lords. My Ladies.'

'How long have you served me, Golden Boy?' the Tiger said, his voice low and gruff.

Gold counted, then felt a wild rush of hope. 'Exactly one hundred years, my Lord.'

'Do you wish to be released?'

Gold tried to keep the enthusiasm from his voice. 'I do, my Lord.'

'What have you learnt from your hundred years of serving me?' the Tiger said, his golden eyes blazing.

Gold nearly said, 'how to carry towels', but swallowed it. 'I have learnt to think twice before meddling in the affairs of others, my Lord,' he said. 'In pursuing my selfish interests I harmed both William,' he bobbed in the air, 'and the Princess Jade.'

'My honour is satisfied,' the Tiger said. 'He has served me well. I have no objection to his release. Princess?' He nodded to Jade.

Jade glared at Gold, her green eyes flashing. 'I agree to his release on one condition.'

'Anything you wish, my Lady,' Gold said.

'Stay well away from me and mine,' Jade said.

Gold swallowed a retort and made his voice suitably even. 'If you do not request my company then I swear I will not approach.'

Jade placed a pale slender hand on the table, still glaring at Gold. 'I agree.'

'William?' the Tiger said.

'Same for me,' William said. 'Don't come anywhere near me, stone, or I swear I will have your human head.'

Gold flew backwards then moved forward again. 'I thought of you as a friend, William,' he said softly. 'Often when I was alone in my niche during these long hundred years I have thought of you. I was looking forward to seeking you out once I had my freedom and regained my human form. I thought I was your first.'

William leaned forward over the table and glared at Gold. 'Stay well away from me!' he spat. 'You come near me, I will tear you to pieces! My tiger form has never tasted human flesh.' He grinned with menace. 'I would be happy to make you my first.'

'I've seen enough,' Jade said. 'Don't come near me, Gold, or I'll have your head in my teeth.' She disappeared.

'I have things to do,' William said, and also vanished.

'Honour is satisfied,' the Archivist said. 'You have been warned, stone.' He nodded to the Number One Son of the Dragon King.

'Yi Long, you may proceed.'

The charm fell away from Gold, but he waited until the dragon's hair had completely fallen back before attempting the human form.

Even after a hundred years the form was simple to take. He fell to one knee and saluted the Tiger, the Archivist, and the dragon. 'My Lords, I thank you.' He pulled himself back to his feet. 'You have scrolls for me to index, Archivist?'

'I have no further need for your services, Gold,' the Archivist said with a small smile. 'You'll have to find gainful employment if you want to live as a human.'

Gold glanced at the Tiger.

'Don't even think I'm giving you a job near my women while you're in that form,' the Tiger said with amusement. 'I still don't trust you. You have ten minutes to get your carcass out of the palace, and if you ever return I will take off your head.'

'I hear there is plenty of work in Guangdong,' the Archivist said.

'Why not go there? Business is booming, there is much need for Shen with mathematical ability, and you stones are famous for your aptitude with an abacus.'

Gold didn't salute them or say a word. He just disappeared. He had no intention of ever seeing any of them again.

116

CITY OF HONG KONG,

SOUTHERN CHINA

AND SO HERE I AM.

FINALLY RELEASED AFTER A HUNDRED YEARS, AND LOOKING FOR SOMETHING TO DO.

THE EARTHLY PLANE HAS COME A LONG WAY.

HONG KONG SEEMS A LOT OF FUN.

I LOVE THIS IDEA. WHO THOUGHT OF IT?

A HUMAN.

IT'S DEVELOPED FROM THE SNACKS SERVED AT TEA HOUSES IN SOUTHERN CHINA, THAT'S WHY IT'S CALLED YUM CHA,

'DRINK TEA' IN CANTONESE.

BUT WHY DO YOU NEED A JOB? WHAT FOR? YOU'RE A STONE.

UNLIKE US DEMONS, YOU DON'T EVEN HAVE TO EAT.

'Ah,' the demon said, understanding. 'You need a soft bed.' The demon had taken human form to meet with Gold; he appeared to be a middle-aged Chinese businessman, one of many found in this part of Southern China who dealt with the opium traders from the West.

Gold smiled through a mouthful of dim sum. 'Precisely.'

'I have no need for a book-keeper right now,' the demon said, pouring the tea and then placing the lid sideways on the pot to indicate that it needed filling. 'You're out of luck if you want work from me.'

Gold chuckled. 'Who says I want to work?' He inspected the steamer carefully. 'What would you pay for one of the Tiger's wives? To hold for ransom?'

The demon took several wheezing breaths before he calmed himself down, and sipped the tea again.

'I can enter the seraglio,' Gold said. 'I served there for a hundred years. Many of the wives know and trust me. What would you give for one of them?'

'It wouldn't be worth it,' the demon said. He took another sip of tea. 'The White Tiger is nearly as formidable a demon destroyer as the Xuan Wu. It would come after me and destroy me.'

Gold thought quickly. 'How about this, then? I take the wife, you hold her. I rescue her, and pretend to destroy you. I return her to the Tiger, and we split the reward.'

The demon studied Gold over the tea for a long time. Then he placed his teacup on the table and put his hands, palms down, on either side of his bowl. 'I like it. But the harem is like a fortress. The guards are the Tiger's finest sons. There's no way you could get in.'

'I can get in anywhere,' Gold said. 'I could steal the Great Seal of the Jade Emperor if I wanted.'

'Oh, now *that's* an interesting claim,' the demon said. 'The Hall of Celestial Treasures is damn near impenetrable. You couldn't possibly do it.'

'If I can't get you a wife then I'll get you the Great Seal,' Gold said.

'I have a tea plantation in Fujian province,' the demon said. 'It produces the finest silver-tipped tea in China. Nearly five qing, the largest tea plantation on Drum Mountain. If you can get me one of the White Tiger's wives, you can have the plantation and half the reward.'

'Does the plantation have a manor?' Gold said.

'Of course,' the demon said. 'Fifty rooms, human servants thrown in. Plenty of lovely soft beds for you to take your pleasure in.'

'If I can't get you a wife then I'll get you the Great Seal,' Gold said.

'A young wife,' the demon said. 'A pretty one.'

'They're all pretty, you know that,' Gold said. 'The Tiger only wants beautiful women.'

The demon raised his teacup. 'It's a bet.'

Gold raised his own tea. 'Good.'

'To the Tiger's beautiful wives,' the demon said.

'To my own personal tea plantation and manor,' Gold said.

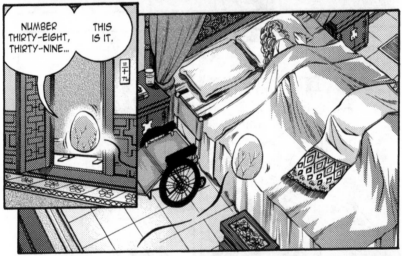

PERDITA.

MMM.... FLORIZEL?

MARY,

I HAVE COME TO RETURN YOU TO THE KING. HE HAS SENT ME TO BRING YOU.

...HUH?! GOLD?

YES, MARY.

YOUR FLORIZEL WANTS TO SEE YOU.

Mary pulled herself as upright as she could, her useless legs dragging under the covers. 'I am happy here, Gold. The Tiger is more man than Florizel — than George ever was.'

'The King would like to see you, one more time, my Lady,' Gold whispered. 'He discovered that you are not dead after all; he learnt that you are here. He wants to apologise to you, and beg your forgiveness.'

She was silent, her eyes wide.

'He is dying, Mary. If you were to do this for him, he would die with a clear conscience.'

She turned away. 'I am old and ugly now, Gold. I do not wish my Florizel to see me like this.'

'He has seen your portrait and says you are as beautiful as ever, and I agree with him,' Gold said. 'Come with me, and I will take you to see him. I will return you here as soon as you wish.' Gold took human form, sat beside her on the bed, and reached to her. 'Take my hand, and I will take you to see your Florizel.'

She turned to him, smiled gently, and took his hand. Gold carefully lifted her in his arms, and then dropped his head and concentrated.

William grinned menacingly at Gold. 'Congratulations, Gold. You have truly outdone yourself this time. Permission to return and watch the sentencing, my Lord.'

'Oh, shit,' Gold whispered.

'Granted,' the Tiger growled.

'I just wanted to forgive Florizel,' Mary said from the floor, desperate. 'I would have returned straight away.'

'I know that, my darling,' the Tiger said. 'I know you have a good heart. But this little piece of shit stone was going to take you to a demon, not to your old love. That one has completely forgotten about you, and if he saw you today he would not love you nearly as much as I do.'

'You are my heart, Tiger,' Mary whispered without looking up.

'And you are mine, Mary,' the Tiger said. 'Now return with Seventeen to the seraglio. I am not displeased with you, and to prove it you will grace my bed tomorrow night.' Mary dropped her head. 'You alone.'

Mary burst into tears, and William gently lifted her from the floor and carried her out.

HEH...

The Tiger linked his hands behind his back in front of Gold. 'Now. What to do with you.'

Gold couldn't control his trembling.

'Kneel,' the Tiger said.

Gold flopped to his knees without being aware of the movement.

BLADE.

SHA

'The demons in Hell are going to have a great deal of fun with you, little stone,' the Tiger said, hefting the blade.

'Mercy, my Lord,' Gold whispered. 'You may even run into the demon that you were taking Mary to,' the Tiger said. 'I'm sure he has a few words he would like to say to you.'

'Mercy,' Gold choked. 'Lady Kwan Yin, hear my cries.'

'Oh, the Goddess is a long way away right now,' the Tiger said.

'I believe she's in retreat. Feel free to call on her. From. Hell.' He hefted the sword again.

Gold couldn't control his quivering

DO IT.

The Tiger strode forward, sword raised high...

...and sliced Gold's head from his neck

with a single

swift stroke.

Gold finally emerged after three months of torture in the Hell of Trees Full of Swords and the Hell of Red-hot Grates.

Normally Shen such as he were escorted directly to the Tenth Level of Hell and then released back to the Earthly plane. But this time the judges had seen fit to punish him for his misdemeanours.

Gold quickly headed for the hills of western Guilin province, where the mountains were thick and vertical, clustered around the Li River. He found a cave in a mountainside overlooking the Li and hid.

He was too slow.

He heard the rush of wind and tried to run, but the demon blocked his exit from the cave and sauntered closer. The demon had taken True Form; ten feet tall, black and scaly, with squinting eyes, tusks, and tufts of red hair on its head.

'No idea what you're talking about,' Gold said. 'Are you sure you have the right stone?'

'Oh, definitely the right stone,' the demon said. 'The Golden Boy, child of the Jade Building Block of the World, yes?' The demon gestured and a ceramic table with two stools, suitable for outdoor use, materialised on the damp floor of the cave. 'Sit, Gold, I believe we have things to talk about.'

'I didn't see you in Hell,' Gold said, sitting on one of the stools as far from the enormous demon as possible. 'I wondered what happened to you.'

'Business is very good,' the demon said. 'We buy their opium with our silver. We sell our tea for even more of their silver. We sell the opium for a great deal of gold. Business is very, very good.'

'Oh, I'm glad for you,' Gold said, relieved. 'So you need someone to keep the accounts, do the sums for you. Well, you've found the right stone. I'll be happy to work for you in return for a soft bed and a bowl of rice every day.'

'Oh, I already have someone to do that for me,' the demon said, leaning back and placing one scaly clawed hand on the table. 'What I don't have, though, is the Great Seal of the Jade Emperor.'

Gold squeaked.

YOU HAVE TWO FULL MOONS TO BRING ME THE SEAL.

IF YOU DO NOT PROVIDE ME WITH THE SEAL, THEN YOU ARE UNABLE TO PAY YOUR DEBT TO ME.

AND YOU ARE MINE.

The Great Seal of the Jade Emperor was hewn from the finest green Celestial Jade. It was also exceedingly heavy, but nothing that Gold couldn't handle.

Gold carried the Seal behind him as he floated in stone form out of the Hall of Celestial Treasures. It was midnight; the palace was quiet. It looked like he was going to make it.

The hall was sealed; Shen could only travel in and out through the main door. Gold floated along the final silent corridor to the door.

The lower half of the walls were wood panels; elaborate paintings of birds and flowers adorned the walls above. The wooden floor had been polished to a high silken sheen by centuries of passing feet.

Gold silently floated closer to the door, full of desperate hope.

If he could get the Seal through the door, then he could travel directly out, disappear, and take the Seal to the demon in Hong Kong. Just a few more centimetres ...

Gold stopped at the door and listened. Not a sound. He pulled the Seal slightly closer to him and concentrated. The door wasn't locked.

It swung silently open.

It was Xuan Wu, in full majestic Celestial Form, at least twelve feet tall. He was garbed as Celestial General in his black lacquer armour, worn over his black silk robes.

'Come with me.' He turned, and walked away without looking back, the floorboards creaking under his massive weight.

Gold checked behind him; the Seal was gone, leaving a dent in the floor where it had landed. He turned back and followed Xuan Wu.

Xuan Wu led him through countless corridors in the Celestial Palace. The lamps brightened as they approached, then darkened behind them, a pool of light following them through the silent halls.

'My Lord ...'

'We are going to my audience room, where you will tell me the whole story,' Xuan Wu said softly without looking at Gold, his deep voice rumbling. 'Until then, remain silent.'

Gold did as he was told, and followed Xuan Wu through the corridors. If he was lucky, he would just be executed. If he was unlucky, he would be executed and the demon would be waiting for him again when he emerged from more suffering at the hands of the residents of Hell.

Xuan Wu stopped at a pair of dark wooden doors and they slid silently aside. He led Gold into his audience room.

The room was very plain; a cold stone floor, bare wood walls, a slightly raised dais at the end with a large rosewood desk set upon it. A large brass plaque with calligraphy of 'Xuan Tian Shang Di' in the Jade Emperor's own hand hung on the wall above the desk — 'Supreme Emperor of the Dark Northern Heavens' — Xuan Wu's full Celestial Title. The infamous Seven Stars sword hung beneath the calligraphy on the wall — nearly two metres long, and as dark and menacing as its owner.

Xuan Wu moved around the desk and sat. Gold settled on the cold stone floor in front of the desk, took human form, and fell to his knees, touching his head to the floor.

'*Wen sui, wen sui, wen wen sui,*' Gold said. Ten thousand years, ten thousand years, ten thousand ten thousand years.

'Rise,' Xuan Wu said. 'Retain human form, I want to see your eyes. Tell me why you have done this.'

Gold carefully didn't look into the Dark Lord's eyes. 'After I was released from the Tiger's service, I needed to make a living. I did a foolish thing; I made a pact with a demon. We arranged to hold one of the White Tiger's wives for ransom.'

'I am aware of your attempted kidnapping of Wife Number Thirty-Nine,' Xuan Wu said. 'At the time I found it difficult to believe that even you could be so stupid.'

'I thought it would work,' Gold said. 'It didn't. I was caught. The Tiger sent me to Hell.'

Xuan Wu shifted in his seat and placed a hand on his desk. 'And you obviously still have not learned your lesson, even after what happened to you in Hell.'

'I made a bet with the demon, Celestial Highness,' Gold said. 'I foolishly boasted that I could steal the Seal. We made a bet that if I could not give a wife to the demon, then I had to give him the Seal.'

'Ah.' Xuan Wu leaned back. 'If you cannot provide the Seal to the demon, then you belong to the demon.'

'Celestial Highness,' Gold said, dropping his head with misery.

'If you had not made the bet with the demon, stone, what would you have done with yourself when you were released from Hell?'

Gold decided to tell the truth. 'I don't know, my Lord, truly. I only know that if I had a choice, it would be something legitimate. I would search for somebody who would be in need of my particular skills. Someone who needs my mathematical abilities.'

'Look into my eyes,' Xuan Wu said.

Gold froze, looking into the eyes that held the Yin force of the universe. Xuan Wu was Yin personified: dark, cold, water, winter, death. All of those things were in his eyes.

Gold shivered, and the ice-cold power that held him snapped off.

Xuan Wu rose with the grace of a true Master of the Arts of War. He walked around the desk, and stepped down off the dais.

Gold still felt cold, and shivered on the floor as the Dark Lord approached him. It was all he could do not to run.

Xuan Wu stopped in front of Gold. Gold carefully gazed at the elaborate silver embroidery of snakes and turtles on the Dark Lord's black robes without looking up.

'Rise,' Xuan Wu said.

Gold pulled himself to his feet and resisted the urge to hug himself against the cold.

'Come with me,' Xuan Wu said, and disappeared.

Gold followed. He had no choice.

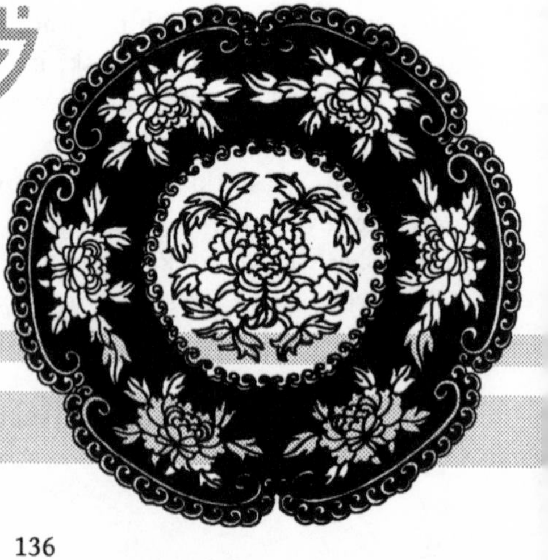

THE YEAR
1997

HONG KONG

Next Thursday came quickly, and Daniel's arrival was breathlessly anticipated.

'But of course, I must go collect him!' Michelle said, 'Monica can mind Simone for an hour or so.'

'Ma'am, it's only just over a week since you gave birth, you can't go out yet!' Jade said.

'Of course I can go out. What, you will keep me a prisoner? I am fine, I have healed nicely, the doctor said so just yesterday. If I could go to see the doctor, why can't I got to the airport?'

'It's just not done,' Jade said.

'The lady who has just given birth must not leave the house for six weeks. That's the way it's done,' Gold said.

'And you must not bathe,' Jade said. 'You could catch your death of cold, you are weak!'

Michelle rose from the piano stool and pushed both of them aside. 'This is ridiculous. You wish to continue to keep me prisoner now that I have had the child? This is stupid. I am coming to the airport to greet my brother, and that is final.' She glared at Jade. 'Not bathe. Really. How ridiculous.' She waved one hand at them. 'Do your Shen thing and disappear. Tomorrow, we will go to the airport, and collect Daniel.'

The next day, Leo hovered over Michelle, concerned. 'Are you sure you're all right? You're not still sore? It's a long drive,' he said.

'I am fine.' She nodded to Monica, who was tucking Simone into a wicker cradle decorated with pink teddies and tiny elephants. 'If she becomes hungry, I have left milk in the fridge.'

'I know what to do, ma'am,' Monica said. She smiled down at Simone. 'I have cared for about twenty of my nieces and nephews, and I love caring for babies. Particularly babies as beautiful as this one.'

Michelle patted Monica's arm. 'I know, and I trust you, dear Monica.' She turned to Leo. 'Are the silly Shen coming?'

'Gold will be in the car with us, Jade will meet us there,' Leo said. 'Where is Lo Wu?'

'He is in a meeting with his Generals in the dining room,' Leo said. 'He's staying here with Simone.'

138

Michelle waved one hand. 'The Generals are annoying, they take up far too much of his time.' She brightened. 'Well, let us find Gold and be on our way.'

蹈蹈蹈蹈蹈蹈蹈蹈蹈蹈蹈蹈蹈蹈蹈蹈蹈

They waited in the arrivals hall amidst the huge crush of people.

'I will be glad when the new airport opens,' Michelle said. 'This one is so old and cramped! And dirty!'

'I won't be glad to see Kai Tak go,' Gold said, 'It's grown and changed so much over its many years. I remember when this was a long way from anywhere.'

'Well it's in the centre of the city now,' Michelle said, 'and the landings are terrifying. I will not miss that checkerboard.'

'The pilots like bragging about the landings they've done here,' Jade said. 'They love sharing stories about it.'

Michelle glanced at her. 'And how many have shared their stories with you?'

Jade blushed and didn't reply.

'Dating pilots?' Gold asked, without turning away from the arrivals doors.

'Dragonair is not called that for no reason,' Jade huffed. 'Many of us are pilots. It is in our nature to fly.'

'There he is!' Michelle cried, and jumped up and down, waving one arm. 'Daniel! Daniel! Here!'

Michelle's brother was tall and slim, with short black hair and matching dark eyes and olive skin, a contrast to his sister's fair complexion. His face lit up into a huge smile when he saw them, and he waved casually back. He pushed his luggage trolley through the throng of shouting locals and as soon as he was close, he threw his arms around Michelle.

She jiggled in his arms with delight. 'It has been too long!'

Daniel released Michelle and held his hand out to Leo, who shook it. 'Leo! Good to see you still taking care of my silly little sister.' He grinned at Jade and Gold. 'Who is this?'

Michelle waved one hand dismissively at the Shen. 'Don't mind them, my husband makes them come with me everywhere to make sure I behave.'

Gold held his hand out to Daniel. Daniel surprised him by pulling the handshake into a hug and whispering in his ear. 'You are adorable.' Daniel pulled back, still grinning at the breathless Gold. 'I'm sure you have a very difficult job.' He turned to Jade, took her hand, bowed over it and kissed it, making her blush furiously. 'Michelle, you did not warn me that you had such stunning friends.' He straightened, then pulled Jade into a hug as well, and whispered into her ear, making her eyes go wide.

'He's still at it,' Leo said under his breath so that only Gold could hear.

Gold didn't reply.

㊉㊉㊉㊉㊉㊉㊉㊉㊉㊉㊉㊉㊉㊉㊉

'So who are these delightful Chinese people anyway?' Daniel said from the back seat in the car, next to Michelle.

'I am ...' Gold nearly said 'the Dark Lord's' but stopped himself in time. 'I am Mr Chen's lawyer, and the lady, Jade, is his accountant. We are more like personal assistants, though.'

'And the little one, Simone? How is she?' Daniel asked Michelle.

Michelle clutched Daniel's hand. 'Ah, Daniel, she is so very beautiful! I just wish Maman and Papa were here.'

Daniel sobered. 'Michelle, did they tell you that Papa's ear is very bad?'

Michelle was confused. 'It is a benign tumour, yes?'

Daniel looked grim. 'It may be cancer, Mimi.'

Michelle blanched. 'No!' She turned to the front of the car to speak to Gold and Leo. 'I must go to Quebec and see them!'

'No,' Daniel said. 'Maman says it's better that you do not go until they are sure what it is. Besides, you have just had the little one. Taking a tiny baby for such a long flight is not a good idea.'

Michelle dropped her head. 'I suppose you are right. But the minute both Papa and I have recovered, I will have them here to visit. Now ...' She squeezed Daniel's hand. 'What is this I hear of you going to Europe?'

'Paris,' Daniel said. 'I have been poached by a newspaper. They loved my piece on the city, and they have asked me to be a staff photographer.'

'You will need to learn their version of French,' Michelle said with amusement.

'I think I shall be all right.' Daniel looked out the window of the car. 'This road is very steep! How far up are we going?'

'All the way to the top, Lo Wu has an apartment up very high,' Michelle said. 'Hong Kong is small and steep. All high rises — no gardens, no parks, no ... no *space*.'

'Wonderful view,' Daniel said as the harbour came into view below them.

'We will have dinner when we get home; but Lo Wu is vegetarian, and only eats Chinese food,' Michelle said.

'I love Chinese food,' Daniel said to the back of Gold's head.

'Not every day,' Michelle said. 'Don't worry, Monica, my housekeeper, cooks very well, my chef from Florida came out and taught her.' She gestured as Leo eased the car up the long, overgrown drive off Black Road. 'Here we are, Lo Wu's apartments. He owns the whole building.'

'Does he, now?' Daniel said appraisingly.

Leo grimaced in the corner of Gold's eye.

'What did you call him?' Daniel said as they got out of the car.

Michelle grinned. 'Lo Wu. It means "Old Wu". "Wu" is his Chinese name. Lo Wu is also the name of the extremely nasty crowded train station that you pass through when you cross into China.'

'He is nasty and crowded?'

Michelle gestured for Daniel to follow her into the lift. 'When he wants to be, yes!'

꒰꒱꒰꒱꒰꒱꒰꒱꒰꒱꒰꒱꒰꒱꒰꒱

After dinner, while Michelle and Daniel were in the master bedroom cuddling Simone and catching up, Gold tapped on Leo's door.

'Who is it?'

'Me,' Gold said.

'Come on in, pal, you know you don't need to knock.'

Leo was lounging on the couch in the living area of his suite, watching an American action film. Gold sat next to him. 'This Daniel — has he always been like this?'

Leo nodded. 'He led me down a merry garden path before I realised — he does that to everybody.'

'Do you think he'll even try the Dark Lord?'

'He'll have a go at *Monica*, man. He plays the "dashing man about town" to the hilt.'

'He is very dashing,' Gold said ruefully.

'Look.' Leo ran one hand over his face. 'Michelle doesn't know. I think it would be better that she doesn't. Can you talk to Mr Chen for me?'

Gold nodded. 'Done. First thing tomorrow, when he is finished with the morning's briefing.'

Leo grinned. 'Got anything planned for the rest of the evening?'

141

Gold smiled, coy. 'Why, did you have something in mind?'

Leo shifted closer. 'Maybe. Maybe I'd like to have a feel of your stone.'

Gold reclined so his head was in Leo's lap. 'You've never called me dashing.'

'I've never called you a love rat, either,' Leo said, his voice rumbling through his body.

'Love rat, eh? That's a good name for it.'

'Complete lack of integrity.' Leo traced Gold's collarbone through his shirt. 'Glad you're not like that. You showed me the stone the first day, and didn't hide anything.'

'I'm glad I'm not like that too.'

Gold went in to see the Dark Lord the next morning. The Dark Lord's hair was greying at the roots and his face was lined with worry; he was losing energy quickly and needed to return to the Mountain.

'Are you sure you will last five more weeks, my Lord?' Gold said, concerned.

'I must.'

'Leave a couple of days before we take Lady Michelle and the baby up, sir.'

'No.'

Gold rubbed his hands over his face. 'We have a slight problem.'

Xuan Wu turned away from the database of the latest intake of Mountain students. 'Wonderful. What now?'

'Lady Michelle's brother, Daniel.'

Xuan Wu's face became grim.

'Has he tried you as well, my Lord?'

'I did not understand what he was suggesting for a very long time, as I could not believe that anyone could be so without integrity. He would betray his own sister! If he was a subject of mine, he would have been executed for such gross indecency. I take it that Michelle does not know.'

Gold shook his head.

'How much longer is he here for?'

'Thirteen days. We need to protect the household, my Lord.'

'He wouldn't try Monica out, she is middle-aged and plain of feature, even though her heart is made of solid gold.' He smiled slightly. 'Her golden heart is purer than yours, stone.'

'Her age and plain appearance wouldn't stop him, my Lord. He would perceive Monica as belonging to both you and Lady Michelle, and therefore will try to take her from you.'

'Then try to keep him away from her. There is not much else we can do.'

Gold hesitated; but the Dark Lord was right. They couldn't lock Daniel away, all they could do was try to protect Monica and hope he didn't harass her.

'We just have to keep him busy, I suppose,' Gold said.

'Take him out, show him around,' Xuan Wu said. 'Wear him out.'

Gold smiled without humour. 'Good idea.'

Michelle announced her singing comeback over lunch a week later, two weeks after giving birth to Simone.

'It's not right for you to go out yet. New mothers are supposed to stay indoors at home for the first six weeks,' Xuan Wu said.

'I want to go out. I want to make an announcement that my "throat polyps" have healed.'

'Even if you do, the baby can't go out,' Xuan Wu said. 'The demons don't know that she exists, and she must stay a secret, especially while she is so tiny and vulnerable.'

'A journalist is coming over tomorrow so I can announce that I am returning to the stage,' Michelle said. 'Simone need not go out, she can go on the bottle, and Monica can care for her at home.'

'It's better for her to be breastfed, Michelle. It's healthier,' Leo said.

'She will be perfectly fine on the bottle, most Chinese babies are bottle-fed by their amahs while the mothers return to work.'

'You don't need to return to work, though!' Leo protested.

'You have no idea, dear Leo, how much I *do*. Now, where is Monica? We must start arranging for Simone to be weaned off me so I can have my freedom back! Monica! Monica?'

Xuan Wu concentrated, and Monica came into the dining room from the kitchen. 'Ma'am?'

'Monica, after lunch, Leo will take you to the department store down in Central, and buy all the bottle-feeding equipment you will need.'

Monica lit up. 'You're putting her on the bottle? It's for the best, ma'am.'

'It's not for the best,' Leo growled.

'Can I take the baby into my room as well, ma'am? At night?' Monica said.

143

'Only if I am performing, but I will probably have a comeback concert soon,' Michelle said.

Monica nodded. 'I understand, ma'am.'

'Where is Daniel? I haven't seen him all day.'

'Master Daniel and Miss Jade have spent the day together,' Monica said. 'They have been spending quite a lot of time together.'

Michelle frowned. 'Ugh. I hope there is no chance of them forming a relationship, because Shen are very hard to deal with.' She grinned mischievously. 'Right, Leo?'

'Absolutely,' Leo said.

'Ma'am ...' Monica began, then trailed off.

'Hmm?'

'Uh ... Nothing.' Monica smiled around the table. 'Is that all?'

'Yes, Monica, thank you,' Michelle said.

Later that evening, Jade tapped on Leo's door. 'Enter,' Leo said.

Jade hesitated outside the door. *I'm not interrupting anything am I?*

Come on in.

Jade opened the door and poked her nose around, then smiled and entered when she saw that Leo and Gold were playing on Leo's Playstation. She sat on the couch.

'What, Jade?' Gold said, then, 'Dammit! That's three to zero, you're cheating!'

'Not cheating, you're just slow, noobie,' Leo said. He turned to Jade. 'What's up?'

Jade looked down at her hands and smiled shyly. 'I think I am beginning to understand the human concept of "love" now.'

'That's wonderful, honey,' Leo said. 'Is it one of the pilots?'

'Oh, no, no, no,' Gold moaned. 'Not Mrs Chen's brother. Please say you haven't fallen for him.'

'Oh no way,' Leo said.

'He is so charming.' Jade's smile widened. 'And so gallant. He says that he has never met anybody like me before.' She sighed with bliss. 'He is so caring! Will you help me to explain our true nature to him? I don't want to scare him, but I think that he should know.'

There was a tap on the door: Monica.

'Come on in, Monica,' Gold said. 'You might as well.'

Voices down in there, Xuan Wu said to all of them. *Michelle is exhausted, and you'll wake Simone.*

Sorry, my Lord, Gold said.

Monica came in, and Leo rose from his desk chair so that she could sit on it. She fidgeted in the chair, obviously miserable.

'You too?' Gold said, disappointed.

'It's Mrs Chen's brother, Master Gold,' Monica said. 'I am flattered, really, but ...' She looked up, desperate. 'It's not what I want! It feels wrong!'

'You are mistaken,' Jade huffed. 'Master Daniel has asked me to be his girlfriend.'

'And he's asked me and Leo to be his boyfriends, Jade,' Gold said. 'He's a ...' He hesitated, trying to remember the term that Leo used.

'Love rat,' Leo finished for him. 'He will seduce anything nearby. Once he's gotten what he wants, though, he'll ditch you faster than you know what's happened.'

'Can you ask Miss Michelle to tell him to stop annoying me?' Monica said. 'This is so strange, she is so noble and elegant — and all he wants is one thing!'

'You are all mistaken!' Jade said.

'Jade, watch.' Gold replayed an episode between himself and Daniel, shortly after they'd arrived at the Peak apartment. Daniel had asked Gold if he was interested, and then offered to take him out to dinner.

'You led him on!' Jade said, then lowered her voice. 'That is just like you!'

'He is just like I was,' Gold said. 'I recognise what I used to be in him.' He grimaced. 'And it is not pretty. He didn't come home with you, Jade, where is he right now?'

'He is shopping in Wan Chai,' Jade said.

'It's eleven p.m., all the shops are closed,' Gold said. 'I have a pretty good idea where he is. Follow me.'

They found him in the second nightclub that they visited. He was surrounded by Filipinas, all of whom were on the hunt for wealthy expatriates to hook up with, and escape from their lives as maids.

He didn't see Jade and Gold as they approached, and he stole a kiss from one of the maids, who giggled and blushed. He then turned and did the same thing to a second, groping her breast at the same time. 'Would a couple of you like to go to a hotel with me? We could have some fun together.' He glanced around at the women. 'I hear you can rent hotel rooms by the hour in Hong Kong. Who's interested? Let's have a party!'

'Seen enough?' Gold said.

Jade disappeared.

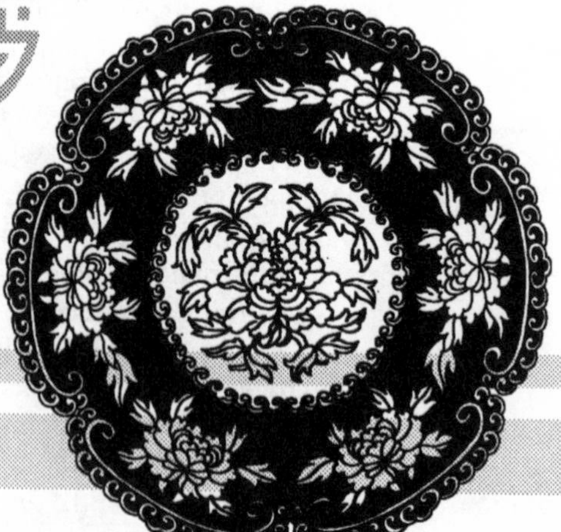

THE YEAR
1820

FREEDOM
AND THEFT (2)

148

Xuan Wu had taken human form as a wrinkly old man as they materialised in Spring Garden Lane in Hong Kong. The lane was bordered on both sides by brothels with large numbers outside; the infamous 'Big Number Brothels'.

Of those, Number Eighty-eight was the largest and most well-kept on the street, with elaborate white Corinthian columns on either side of the door.

Xuan Wu stopped and studied the building.

Xuan Wu glanced at Gold, his dark eyes emotionless. 'The demon is there. Many demons are there. You will have many to serve.'

Gold sighed and dropped his shoulders. 'I don't want to belong to this demon, my Lord, I beg you. Do not give me to it.'

'You should have considered that when you made that foolish bet, and then tried to steal the Jade Emperor's Great Seal. Come.' Xuan Wu slid effortlessly through the crowds of people that lined the street, despite his stooped posture.

When they reached Eighty-eight they stopped.

'Don't take your grandpa in there, boy,' a coolie shouted from the other side of the road. The coolie was well over sixty, wearing nothing but a loincloth and a filthy straw hat. A basket of protesting ducks hung suspended from each end of a bamboo pole over his bony shoulder. 'Don't take the old man in there, sonny, he'll use up all his ching and die on you.'

'Not grandpa using his ching,' a rickshaw driver called as he hurried past. 'Grandpa showing little Number Three Grandson where to put it!'

'Anywhere he likes, in Number Eighty Eight,' the coolie said. He hefted the pole holding the ducks and hurried away into the crowd with the peculiar sliding gait used to avoid upsetting the load. His voice faded. 'They even got foreign devil women in there.'

The doorman was a huge Indian; a Sikh, with a white silk turban and a red embroidered jacket. He eyed the two Shen suspiciously through his fierce, bearded face.

Xuan Wu didn't hesitate. He walked up to the door and nodded to the doorman. The doorman opened the door with one hand and collected a one-dollar note from Xuan Wu with the other.

You are to remain silent, Xuan Wu said to Gold. *You are only to speak if asked a question. That is an order. Disobey and things will go very bad for you.*

Gold nodded. His only thought was to where the demon was. He cast his eyes around suspiciously as they entered the brothel.

OOOH! CHEN SING SAN!

IT'S SO WONDERFUL TO SEE YOU HERE!

I ONLY CAME HERE TO PROVIDE A BIRTHDAY PRESENT FOR MY NUMBER ONE GRANDSON HERE,

BUT I THINK I MAY BUY A PRESENT FOR MYSELF!

YOU KNOW YOU CAN HAVE ANYTHING YOU LIKE HERE,

CHEN SING SAN.

Xuan Wu reached into his robe and pulled out two small jade ornaments, tiny carved rabbits embellished with gold on solid gold chains. 'For you, because you are so very beautiful.'

The girls took the rabbits. One of them squealed like a schoolgirl and jiggled with delight. 'This is real!'

'Of course it's real,' Xuan Wu said, sounding like a jolly grandfather at New Year with a pocket full of lai see. 'Now where's that Mr Wong? I want to give him a present as well.'

The two girls giggled as they led Xuan Wu through the parlour, one on each arm. Gold followed silently.

HOW LONG HAS THIS ONE BEEN HERE?

ABOUT TWO WEEKS. DOESN'T SPEAK CHINESE. BUT SOME OF THE GWEILO MEN LIKE THEIR WOMEN BLACK.

CAN'T SEE THE ATTRACTION. DIRTY, SMELLY, BLACK DEMON WOMEN. *HUMPH.*

<I AM GOING TO GET OUT OF THIS HELLHOLE IF IT'S THE LAST THING I DO!>

<YOU ARE AMERICAN?>

<YOU SPEAK ENGLISH, SIR?>

<PLEASE HELP ME AND CALL THE POLICE! I'M HERE AGAINST MY WILL!>

154

Eyes blank, the black woman fell back to sit on the couch, mesmerised.

A burly young Chinese rushed through the back door, racing straight up to Xuan Wu and the black girl. She slowly turned to look at him, her eyes empty.

'She said she's happy to be working here,' Xuan Wu said to the guard in Chinese. 'She wants to give me special attention.'

'I'd like to visit with this lovely old man,' the black girl said in English. 'I hope he chooses me.'

The young Chinese guard relaxed. 'You want to see Mr Wong?' he asked Xuan Wu.

'I haven't seen my old friend in years,' Xuan Wu said. 'I thought I'd pay him a visit before my grandson enjoys his birthday present. But after seeing this little black rose, I may give myself a present as well."

155

The Chinese girls on his arms pouted.

'Now, girls, don't worry, one is enough for this old man. I'll give you two to my grandson, and if you entertain him well, I'll have special little gift for both of you.' The two girls giggled again and nodded, sneaking delighted glances at Gold.

Play along, Xuan Wu said.

Gold forced a flush to his face and looked away, making the girls giggle even more.

'He's too old for his first time,' one of them said. 'He looks more than eighteen already.'

'He's been sheltered by his mother. I finally got him out of her clutches, the evil old dragon,' Xuan Wu said with good humour.

The guard bobbed his head, turned, and gestured towards the back of the house. 'We will prepare the girls for you while you visit with Mr Wong. Please pass me any weapons that you are holding.'

Both Xuan Wu and Gold raised their arms. 'No weapons,' Xuan Wu said.

The guard didn't attempt to search them. 'Come this way, then, sir.'

The guard showed them into a bright and airy office containing an enormous rosewood desk. Small high windows allowed rays of afternoon sun to light up the hardwood parquet floor.

The guard bobbed his head, 'the Master will be here shortly,' and went out.

'I think you will enjoy working here, Gold.' Xuan Wu studied the ink paintings on the wall across from them. 'I thought it was this particular demon that made the bet with you. I was right.'

Gold remained silent. He couldn't speak unless a question was asked of him, and Xuan Wu knew it.

'We have some time before we meet Mr Wong,' Xuan Wu said to Gold, voice casual. 'He'll make us wait so that he will gain face. Do you think you will like working here?'

'My Lord, this poor American girl is held here against her will!' Gold cried softly. 'We have to get her out of here!'

'Don't you want to know my connections with the owner of this establishment?'

'No,' Gold said. 'All I want to do is make sure that none of these women are here against their will. And to get that poor black girl out of here.'

'If you worked here, you could do that,' Xuan Wu said, studying the painting.

Gold silently considered his options, then nodded once sharply. 'I can use my skills as a Shen to help them if I'm working here.'

'You are a very small Shen, Gold. I doubt if you could carry them very far. How will you get that girl all the way back to America?' Xuan Wu turned to study Gold. 'The owner probably wouldn't care if you took your pleasure with the girls when they're not working. You have the finest young women in Hong Kong here for the taking.'

'This isn't like you at all, Gold.'

'I know.' He raised his head. 'I suppose after being held in the palace, and then Hell against my will, I know what it is like to be a prisoner.'

'Silence,' Xuan Wu said softly. The demon approached.

WELCOME, HONOURED GUESTS—

CLOP CLOP

The demon stopped dead and went completely white when he saw Xuan Wu and Gold. He spun to escape, but Xuan Wu quickly bound him and held him motionless.

Xuan Wu pulled himself to his feet and transformed from an old man into his usual human form; long hair and sculpted face. He strolled to the demon and held his hand in front of its face.

The demon's face went from horror to blank.

Xuan Wu moved his hand, and the demon followed, its eyes never moving from Xuan Wu's palm. Xuan Wu turned the demon and then walked towards the desk, his hand still in front of the demon's face. The demon followed like an automaton.

'This is the Number Twelve Son of the Demon King,' Xuan Wu said conversationally as he led the demon to the desk. 'How many girls are you holding here against their will, Twelve?'

'Thirteen, here,' the demon said.

'Other places?'

'I don't know.'

'Twenty? Forty? Fifty?'

'Probably about fifty.'

Xuan Wu glanced at Gold. 'Fifty like that American girl.' He strode around the desk and fell into the large office chair, then placed both hands, palms down, on the desk. Not a single scrap of paper sat on the desk; its only residents were a large brush and ink set and a priceless jade ruyi, a sceptre that granted its owner fulfilment of his will.

'Number Twelve here,' Xuan Wu said, gesturing dismissively towards the hypnotised demon, 'has been planning for years to make an attempt against his father, the King of the Demons. He has amassed an army in the hills above Guangdong province. Human and demon.'

'Normally I let the demons sort this type of thing out among themselves,' Xuan Wu said. 'The current demon king has been around for a long time, though, and his behaviour has been reasonably honourable. His word is good and he doesn't create half-human demon hybrids to use as weapons against us.' Xuan Wu rose, walked back around the desk, and stood next to the demon still standing motionless in front of the desk. 'This one, however, is not particularly trustworthy and treats humans with contempt. If it were to gain the position of king, many humans would suffer.'

'You cannot interfere directly, my Lord,' Gold said. 'Celestial interference in demonic dominions is forbidden unless they attack us first.'

'I am well aware of that,' Xuan Wu said, studying the demon. Gold blanched as he understood. 'No.'

'You may do your best to free the captive women while you work for the demon. I can help you if you require it. These women must be freed. But, apart from that, all I want is for you to provide information. On the opium trade, on the tea trade, on the prostitution and organised crime, and particularly on the planned bid against the king. You are cunning, Gold, and your intelligence has been going to waste. I think now is a good time to begin using it.'

Gold hesitated, thinking. Then he nodded once. 'If you can help me, I think I can get some of them out.'

'Good.' Xuan Wu held out his hand, and a small black jade turtle appeared in it, hanging from a light gold chain. 'Take this. Connect with this jade, stone to stone. It will allow you to communicate with me. Be aware that if I am on duty to the Jade Emperor, the Celestial takes precedence. Even if the demon is about to take your head.'

'I understand, my Lord.' Gold took the turtle and slipped it around his neck. He had an inspiration; a black turtle around his neck was an obvious giveaway of his connection with the Dark Lord. He absorbed the turtle and chain into his human form and wrapped them around the stone, deep inside his body, where not even a demon could see.

'Good thinking, Gold, I think you will do well at this.' Xuan Wu held his hand in front of the demon's face. 'I am going to walk it back to where it entered the room. Then I am going to give you to it. You know how to behave. Ready?'

Gold returned to his seat. 'Ready.'

Xuan Wu walked the demon back to the door, and concentrated. Then he went back to the rosewood chairs next to Gold.

The demon froze.

'I am not here to interfere in your dealings,' Xuan Wu said. He gestured dismissively towards Gold. 'This Shen has an honour debt to you, I believe. I caught him trying to steal the Great Seal of the Jade Emperor.'

The demon slowly turned back, its horrified expression changing to one of cunning. 'You are here to ensure the debt is paid?'

Xuan Wu rose. 'I am. That is all I am here for.' He waved one hand at Gold. 'This worthless stone is yours.'

The demon bent to study Gold, grinning with avarice. 'I will put it to good use, my Lord.'

'You are bound to this demon's servitude until the Celestial judges your debt discharged, stone,' Xuan Wu said. He disappeared.

Gold fell to his knees in front of the demon. 'I am yours. I can only trust that you will treat me well.'

'Can you take female form?' the demon said with barely controlled greed. '*Attractive* female form?'

'If I must. But, my Lord ...'

He gazed up at the demon. 'I am sure I would be more useful managing your administrative dealings. As I am bound by the Celestial, I am completely trustworthy, and you can pass me the management of your accounts without concern.'

The demon straightened and studied Gold. 'You have a point. Managing the Little Brothers is a pain.' He gestured dismissively towards the desk. 'Behind the desk is a cabinet full of documents that need to be sorted, and in the basement there are outstanding reports that need to be brought up to date. Can you do that?'

Gold rose and bowed slightly. 'I am more than capable. I can manage the whole operation with minimal supervision, my Lord. And you can trust me.'

'Sounds good, I ate the previous manager of this particular house last week, he was skimming takings into a private account. You won't do that, will you?'

'I cannot,' Gold said. 'I am bound.'

The demon grinned, jolly. 'I think the Xuan Wu has given me a very useful

little toy. You can handle all of this while I deal with more important matters. I haven't tallied the earnings in a while, it's too much trouble. You can tell me when you've worked it out.'

Gold bowed slightly again. 'I will be delighted to.'

The demon slapped Gold on the back. 'Let me show you where the documents are.'

JUST RELAX.

I-I'M TRYING TO... IT'S JUST... ALL RIGHT.

DO IT.

THANK YOU SO MUCH, GOLD.

FOR EVERYTHING. I'LL NEVER FORGET YOU.

GIVE YOUR LITTLE GIRL AN EXTRA HUG FOR ME.

164

Gold went back downstairs, and sat at the desk in the demon's office. He pulled out the records of the days' takings, and began to add the figures when noises erupted outside the door.

One of the junior demon guards rapped on the door and charged in. 'We lost another one.'

'Damn,' Gold said, rising. 'Was it bad opium again?'

The demon gestured towards the door. 'No, I think she just took too much. Deliberate overdose.'

'Call the Master,' Gold said. He led the way up the stairs. 'Which one is it?'

'Anne,' the demon said, then disappeared into the back of the house to call the Master.

The demon Master appeared next to Gold. 'Is she dead?'

'Yes, my Lord,' Gold said. 'Don't worry about it, I will take care of the body.'

'Dump it in the harbour or something,' the demon said. 'Damn! This black one was expensive. And popular. Where the hell are we going to get another one?'

Gold rose and turned. 'My Lord, we are losing too many to this. I think it would be better if we only used girls who choose to be here. The ones we hold against their will always end up killing themselves.'

'Deny the opium,' the demon said.

'If you deny the opium then they are too distraught to serve the customers,' Gold said. 'Either way, we lose. I think the best option is just to use girls who want to do it. There's plenty over the border who will give anything to come and work in Hong Kong.'

'Very well,' the demon said with resignation.

'Permission to release the rest of the girls as we find replacements for them,' Gold said. 'At the rate we're losing them, the growing pile of corpses will attract the attention of the authorities.'

'I pay the police very well to leave us alone,' the demon said.

'I am not talking about the police.'

The demon was silent as he understood. 'The Celestials won't intervene. It's none of their business.'

'If enough humans are suffering, a Celestial may take it upon himself to do something,' Gold said. 'I recommend that you release the rest of the girls, my Lord.'

'Very well. Take care of it, Gold. I have other, more important things to attend to.'

'My Lord.' Gold bowed slightly. 'Don't worry, it will all be taken care of.' He ventured a question. 'How soon will you make your bid, my Lord?'

'Another two, three weeks, that's all,' the demon said slowly. 'Then I may promote you to oversee all of my Earthly establishments.'

Gold bowed. 'I would be profoundly honoured, my Lord.'

The demon chuckled. 'A Demon King with a pet Shen. Who would believe it?'

'You will be the most powerful and ruthless king that Hell has ever seen,' Gold said.

The demon laughed and slapped Gold on the back. 'You are worth more to me as a slave than any wife of the Tiger would have been.'

Gold bowed again. 'I thank you, my Lord.'

'Now sort this mess out,' the demon said, gesturing towards Anne. 'Get rid of it and the rest of the slaves. You're right, they're more trouble than they're worth.' He hesitated. 'But if you could find another black one that wants to do the job, I'll give you a special bonus.'

Gold grinned. 'I'll see what I can do.'

The demon disappeared. Gold quickly closed the bedroom door. He stood in the centre of the room, lowered his head, and concentrated.

Yes? Xuan Wu said.

I have another one, my Lord, Gold said.

I'm sending somebody right now.

A tall European woman appeared next to Gold. Without saying a word, she moved to Anne and took her hand.

'Well done,' the European woman said. She glanced up at Gold. 'My name's Meredith, I'm one of the Dark Lord's lieutenants.'

Gold couldn't hide his amusement.

'Westerners can gain Immortality as well, Gold,' Meredith said, turning back to Anne. She put her hand over Anne's face. 'Good job.'

She concentrated, and Anne jerked as if shocked, then took a deep gasping breath. Her eyes snapped open and she cast around.

'It's all right, dear,' Meredith said. 'I'm taking you home.'

Meredith and Anne both disappeared.

Gold lifted the opium pipe and returned it to the cupboard, then headed back downstairs. He had a lot of recruiting to do.

MY LORD XUAN WU.

TELEPATHY TELEPATHY TELEPATHY

I KNOW. KEEP YOUR HEAD DOWN.

HEY, I'M THE CHIEF OF POLICE!

I'LL SEE YOU SHUT DOWN FOR THIS!

GET THE GIRLS INTO THE BASEMENT AND GUARD THEM!

EEEK!!

ARRGH!!

THE DEMON APPROACHING HERE...

...IS NOT THE MASTER OF THE HOUSE!

THE EXISTING KING...

...MUST HAVE SUCCESSFULLY FOUGHT OFF THE COUP!

CLICK

Gold was sitting quietly in his office when a demon appeared. Gold rose, walked around the desk, and bowed. 'Good day, sir.'

The demon was in human form, appearing as a Chinese in his mid-thirties, slim and good-looking. 'You are Gold?'

'I am, your honour,' Gold said.

The demon grinned. 'Number Twelve's pet Shen.'

'No more, I believe, my Lord,' Gold said.

'You're free now, stone,' the demon said. 'What are you doing here?'

'Waiting to see the new proprietor of this establishment,' Gold said. 'I have enjoyed working with the women, and if you are as understanding as the previous owner, I may choose to stay. What is your honoured name, sir?'

'I'm the One Hundred and Twenty-Second Son of the King,' the demon said. 'You can call me Mr Wong. I provided my father with a great deal of assistance in the recent altercation, and I have been granted all of Twelve's property as reward.'

'I will show you the deeds, sir,' Gold said.

The demon gestured dismissively. 'Let's see.'

Gold opened a cabinet behind the desk and pulled out the books. 'These are all of the establishments possessed by the late Number Twelve. There are thirteen brothels similar to this one. There are three export traders in Hong Kong, and six in Guangdong.' Gold flipped through the papers. 'A few other minor holdings, real estate, restaurants, businesses.' He pulled out a set of books tied with a red ribbon. 'These contain details of underworld activity; the names of the gangsters, their ranks, and the amount of protection money they are collecting from businesses.'

'How much is it all worth?' the demon said.

'Seventy-five million Hong Kong dollars,' Gold said.

The demon whistled through his teeth. 'Yes.'

'The girls are hiding in the basement, sir,' Gold said. 'They are delightful ladies, all working here of their own free will, not even held by debt. Would you like me to call them up so you can inspect them, try some of them out? They'd probably like to meet you.'

'Go right ahead,' the demon said, moving to the desk to inspect the books. He spoke without turning away from the deeds. 'Seventy-five million. Excellent.' He glanced up at Gold. 'How many women?'

'Fifteen here, my Lord. All human.' Gold said.

'Oh, yes,' the demon said with relish. 'Humans. Any spare?'

'My Lord?'

The demon focused on Gold. 'Are any of the women excess to our needs? Not satisfactory in performance? Do any of them need to be ...'

'*Punished?*'

'Every single woman here is a good worker and well behaved, my Lord,' Gold said. 'None of them are excess.'

The demon shuffled through the books. 'I think I shall go and inspect my other properties. My other women.' He glanced up at Gold. 'Have the women here ready for me when I return. I will inspect them last.'

'My Lord,' Gold said.

Gold watched the demon depart, and waited until it was a good distance away. He turned and quickly scrabbled through the cabinet behind him. For a horrible moment he couldn't find what he was looking for; then pulled it with triumph from the back. He unrolled the document; the deed to the tea plantation in Fujian, the one that the previous demon owner had used in their bet. Gold rolled the parchment up and shoved it into his human body.

He slipped down the stairs to the basement, and opened the door.

'Girls, listen,' Gold said. 'There is a new Master and he's a bad one. He will hurt you. Come with me, I can help you.' Gold felt a rush of remorse; he couldn't do anything for the girls in the other houses. He straightened. He would do what he could for these ones. 'Come with me, I'll take you to Guangdong train station, and you can go home.'

The girls silently followed him up the stairs. They grabbed what they could and ran.

THE YEAR
1997

 HONG KONG

A few days before Daniel was due to leave, Michelle tapped on Leo's door. 'Leo, are you in there?'

Leo opened the door. 'Can I help you, ma'am?'

Michelle saw that Gold was in Leo's room on the couch. 'Good, both of you are here, I need your help.'

Leo opened the door and Gold shifted on the couch so that Michelle could sit. She rubbed her hands over her face and sighed.

'What's the matter, honey?' Leo said.

'Daniel has said that he doesn't want to return to Canada, or take the job in Paris. He says that he wants to stay here in Hong Kong. He says he'll live here for a few weeks, if that's all right with John, and then find an apartment of his own.'

Leo and Gold were silent for a moment, then Gold said, 'That's great, ma'am.'

'No, it isn't!' Michelle exclaimed. She lowered her voice. 'He will run rampant here and destroy everything! He will spend all his time chasing the Filipinas and eventually find his way back into the drugs. He was coming along so well, until he came here!' She slapped the arm of the couch. 'We must make him go to Paris, and take his job there. He must stop his disgusting habits. He has broken poor Jade's heart, he has harassed Monica, he has probably annoyed both of you. From the look on Lo Wu's face, I'd say he's even tried to seduce *him*.' She looked away. 'He is so shameful!'

'We didn't know you knew, ma'am,' Gold said.

'Of course I know,' Michelle said. 'He promised me he had given it up. He promised me he would settle down with someone, and stop chasing everyone he meets, man or woman.' She dropped her head, her voice thick. 'He promised me!'

'Short of drugging him and dragging him onto the airplane, ma'am, I don't think there's much we can do,' Gold said.

'Do that then,' Michelle said.

Both Gold and Leo snorted with amusement.

'I don't think that's an option,' Gold said.

'Can you do something with his mind, Gold?' Michelle said.

'That's really not allowed, ma'am.'

'In this case, it would be doing him a favour,' Michelle said.

'It would be doing us a favour as well,' Leo growled.

'Exactly!' Michelle said.

'The Dark Lord is in his office, let's go talk to him,' Gold said. 'He might have a suggestion for us.'

The three of them went into Xuan Wu's office together. Leo and Michelle sat on the visitor's chairs, and Gold stood behind them.

'This looks serious,' Xuan Wu said.

'To cut a long story short, sir,' Leo said. 'The Lady Michelle is well aware of her brothers ... habits ... and is unhappy because he has decided to stay in Hong Kong.'

'He had a job lined up in Paris, correct?' Xuan Wu said.

The three of them nodded.

'Would he be better off in Paris than he is here?'

'There are no desperate Filipinas in Paris,' Michelle said. 'The women there will not accept his advances so easily. He will also be kept extremely busy in his new job. If he stays here he will probably just live on our generosity without even seeking work!'

'True,' Xuan Wu said. 'And you want to discourage him from staying here, without resorting to anything ...'

'Unnecessary,' Gold finished for him.

'Easily fixed,' Xuan Wu said. 'Take him out to look for rental accommodation. Show him what is available on the budget of a freelance photographer — one that is not being financially helped by me, because I am so offended by him.'

Leo's face filled with understanding. 'He won't be able to afford anything bigger than about two hundred square feet!'

'In Western District,' Xuan Wu said with grim humour. 'Next to both the crematorium and the abattoir.'

Michelle clapped her hands with glee. 'Oh that is perfect, Lo Wu! You have such a streak of cruelty in you sometimes!' She raced around the desk and kissed him.

Xuan Wu bobbed his head, his smile wide. 'I thank you, my Lady.'

'Come on, gentlemen, let's find him a truly awful place to live,' Michelle said to Gold and Leo.

'The major real estate agents have websites with full information on all the flats available, with floor plans and prices,' Gold said as they walked back to Leo's room. 'Give me a couple of hours, and I can sift through them all, check the buildings, and choose the very worst.'

'Then we can call an agent, and take Daniel to see some tomorrow,' Michelle said with delight. 'Oh, this will be fun.'

'Does that mean you're gonna be offline for a couple of hours?' Leo said as he opened the door for them.

Gold nodded. 'Yes, I'll have to thoroughly phase out for a search like that.'

'What do you mean?' Michelle said, curious.

'He sits like a zombie on my couch, eyes wide open, processing data,' Leo said. 'It's freaky.'

'Can you display the search results somehow?' Michelle said.

Gold nodded. 'I can show you on the TV or computer monitor.'

'Fascinating,' Michelle said. 'And all of this because you are stone?'

'Yes,' Gold said. He sat on the couch and wriggled to make himself comfortable. 'Once I shut down, you won't be able to rouse me unless you call me or email me; I'll be in full data mode. Is that all right?'

'Go right ahead,' Michelle said. 'I would like to see this.'

'There goes our evening of gaming,' Gold said to Leo ruefully. 'Sorry.'

'Oh!' Michelle said. 'No! Do not work after hours!'

'It's fine, if it helps us to shift Daniel,' Gold said. His eyes went blank. 'Shutting down, if you need me, email me or call me.'

'You were planning to play games with him?' Michelle asked Leo.

Leo gestured towards his Playstation. 'Yeah, he's complaining that I always beat him on the racing game.'

'Racing game, eh?' Michelle said. 'Want to show me?'

Leo grinned. 'Sure!'

幽幽幽幽幽幽幽幽幽幽幽幽幽幽幽幽

'I've already told Cynic that your budget is a maximum of about two hundred and fifty Canadian a week, which adds up to roughly six thousand Hong Kong dollars a month,' Gold said to Daniel as Leo drove them in the Mercedes to meet the real estate agent at the first property. 'Her name's Cynic, but she pronounces it "Kainick".'

Cynic was waiting for them at the base of the building. She was about twenty, with a broad face pock-marked with acne that was concealed by a heavy layer of extremely pale make-up, making her look as if she was wearing a white mask. She wore a poorly fitting pink polyester suit and carried a folder and keys for the properties they were visiting. She greeted them without smiling, handed Gold a business card with both hands and a small bow, then marched into the building with them trailing behind.

The building was a nondescript grey-tiled high rise tower, ten metres across, with two small shopfronts on either side of the residential entrance. Above the single glass door the name of the building was inscribed in brass in both Chinese characters and English: 'Wealthy Mansion'.

'The building is a wealthy mansion, perhaps it can lend me some money,' Daniel joked as they went in.

Cynic turned to Gold, obviously confused.

'Just a little joke about the name of the building,' Gold said in Cantonese.

Cynic nodded without smiling and led them past the rusting letterboxes in the lobby. At the end of the dirty, green-tiled corridor there was an ancient wooden desk with a half-asleep elderly bodyguard.

'Yar A,' Cynic said to the guard, and scribbled her name on the guest book, then turned and pressed the button for the lift.

The lift had green laminated doors. Inside, the buttons were worn down with use and the walls were black with dirt. Gold, Leo, Michelle, Daniel and the agent altogether barely fitted.

At the twentieth floor Cynic walked through the grimy lobby to a dirt-encrusted door on one side. A single bare fluorescent tube buzzed and flickered in the middle of the whitewashed ceiling's peeling paint. More green tiles, the grout black with dirt, covered the floor and halfway up the walls of the lobby.

Cynic opened the door with an "A" on it. 'A flat, studio, six thousand, good location but no facilities. New decoration.'

They went in. The flat was a roughly whitewashed concrete box two metres by three metres with a hardwood parquet floor and a set of three metal-framed windows at one end. At the left of the entrance, a tiny bathroom had been separated from the rest of the area by a painted wooden partition; inside the bathroom was a cheap toilet, small sink, and a flow-through water heater with a showerhead. The bathroom was too small to have a separate shower cubicle; bathing had to be done over the toilet.

The rest of the studio was taken up by a double bed jammed under the window, filling the space from one side to the other. A bookshelf had been placed against the wall between the bed and the front door, and that was all there was space for. There was no kitchen.

Daniel looked around. 'How much did you say this was again?'

'Six thousand,' Cynic said.

Daniel did the math in his head. 'That's nearly a thousand

Canadian a month. How many square feet is it? I've been in bigger hotel rooms!'

Cynic checked her folder. 'Two hundred square feet gross. Most apartment six thousand dollar, two hundred, three hundred max. You want bigger?'

'Gross?' Daniel said.

'They include all the lift lobby space and the fire stairs in the calculation of the unit sizes,' Gold said. 'And divide it up among the units, so the real size — the "net" size — is about seventy to eighty per cent of what they say. With older buildings like these, with no clubhouse, it's about eighty-five per cent, but with newer ones it can be as low as sixty-five. So a thousand square foot flat is really only six hundred and fifty square feet.'

'Why do they measure all their real estate in square feet?' Daniel said. 'Wouldn't square metres be easier?'

'They take it down to the last square foot,' Gold said. 'Give us a break, some of us are still struggling to convert from li and catty to feet and pounds, let alone kilometres and grams.'

'I can't do that kilometre and gram stuff either,' Leo said. 'Too complicated for me.'

'So you want to rent this one or not?' Cynic said impatiently.

'Do you have anything with at least a kitchen?' Daniel said.

Cynic checked her folder. 'I have one, further west. Slightly more expensive, but much better decoration, and has a Western kitchen. You will like.'

Daniel grinned broadly. 'Sounds perfect.'

To get to the next building, they picked their way through the wet market, the ground between the tiny stalls slippery with blood and vegetables.

'Convenient location next to market,' Cynic said to Daniel, who had his hand over his nose at the overpowering odour of rotting fruit and stale meat.

The wet market was an old-fashioned street market, a rarity as they were being replaced by government-owned multi-storey market buildings that still had floors awash with blood and rotting vegetables. Daniel stopped when he saw a butcher stall, its metal racks holding a variety of cuts of pork and beef hanging in the heat, as well as the hearts, lungs, and livers. He recoiled with horror when he saw that the large bushel bamboo basket of trash next to him held a cow's head on top of a pile of glistening intestines, the head's blank eyes staring dully.

'Good for fresh meat,' Cynic said. 'This is a good market, plenty of fresh vegetable and meat.' She pointed to a nearby stall where the stall holder grabbed a live chicken out of a cage, took it to a large bin, slit its throat, then tossed it into the bin to die. 'Very fresh, fresher than America, eh?'

Another stall holder had a large flat tabletop of polystyrene foam with pieces of carp and eel laid out, the hearts still beating in the middle of the display of blood, water, and scales. 'Very fresh!' Cynic said.

'I don't think I want quite that fresh,' Daniel said, eyes wide.

The next apartment building was slightly newer, with shiny grey tiles in the lobby rather than faded green ones. It was in a very old part of town, the gutters filled with trash and ancient stores selling a variety of pungent dried seafood across the road, the shopkeepers yelling to passers-by in Cantonese. They went through the sign-in procedure with another elderly guard, and went up to the flat.

This one was about the same size, but it had a tiny separate kitchen and bathroom with a miniscule shower cubicle. The kitchen had a clothes washer installed into the cabinets under the single-burner electric stove. The front door opened on the long side, and across from it was a small leather sofa, with a small TV on the wall next to the door. The end of the unit was once again taken up by a double bed, but this one had a cupboard that hung over the end of the bed, providing some closet space over the bed itself.

'Is this the same size? Two hundred square feet?' Daniel said.

Cynic checked her folder. 'Yes, two hundred, only seven thousand a month, very good value.'

Daniel let out a long breath. 'Are there any around this price that have actual bedrooms?'

Cynic flicked through her folder. 'One is two bedroom, again further west, bigger again, very good value.' She glanced up. 'But not new decoration.'

'I don't care too much about decoration, provided it's clean,' Daniel said. 'I don't need fancy wallpaper and curtains, if it's bigger that'll make it much better.'

'Okay.' Cynic led them along the waterfront of Western District, the barges in the water unloading bundles from the freight ships moored in the harbour. A few people stared curiously at the group as they passed.

'Not many foreigner seen around here,' Cynic explained.

The stores in this area were mostly open shops selling plastic ware or groceries, with elderly Chinese shopkeepers staring suspiciously at them. They stopped outside a large, gleaming fast food restaurant with cafeteria-style chairs and tables inside, one of Hong Kong's chain restaurants.

'You can get all three meals a day and snacks here,' Cynic said. 'Very clean, very cheap, you really don't need kitchen.'

'But they don't speak any English,' Gold said, waving one hand at the Chinese menu board.

'Do they have any English restaurants here? Or American style?' Daniel said, beginning to sound desperate.

Cynic stared blankly at Daniel. 'This one serves Western food too.'

'But I can't go in there, I don't speak Chinese!' Daniel said.

Cynic's face cleared. 'You need to learn language if you live here. I can find you language teaching service. Only English restaurant are in mid-levels, where most foreigners live.'

'Well, show me an apartment there, then,' Daniel said.

'I can, I have a good one, two bedroom, nice view, clubhouse, gym, above three good Western restaurant and bars, Hollywood Road, new building,' Cynic said. 'Big apartment, you like very much, new decoration, six hundred and twenty square feet gross.'

'How much?' Gold said with amusement.

'Thirty thousand only,' Cynic said. 'Very good value.'

Daniel hesitated.

'That's four thousand, seven hundred and thirty dollars, and forty-three cents a month Canadian,' Gold said. He quickly remembered to conjure a calculator behind his back, and held it up. 'I just worked it out for you. That's ...' He pretended to use the calculator. 'Ah, a thousand and ninety-one dollars and sixty-four cents a week.'

'A thousand dollars a week for six hundred square feet? About sixty square metres?' Daniel said, incredulous.

'What is net on that?' Gold asked Cynic.

'Sixty-five,' Cynic said. 'New building, nice clubhouse.'

'Actually it's more like four hundred and three square feet,' Gold said.

'Two bedrooms in an area twenty by twenty feet?' Daniel said, horrified. 'For a thousand Canadian a *week*?'

Cynic shrugged. 'Mid-levels, Expat area, more expensive.'

'Show me the cheaper one, the two bedroom one, near here,' Daniel said, beginning to sound discouraged.

Michelle, who had remained silent throughout the entire process so far, patted Gold on the shoulder as they turned to go.

They walked through the dingy streets of Western District, one of the oldest parts of Hong Kong. This area wasn't frequented by tourists, and many of the residents were elderly people who'd come from China during the turmoil of the Cultural Revolution. It was a small piece of Old Hong Kong in an otherwise extremely modern city.

As they arrived at the building, the breeze from the ocean about a hundred metres away carried a bad stench that seemed to be a combination of burning tyres and dusty faecal matter. Daniel stopped, horrified. 'What is that?'

Cynic gestured dismissively towards the harbour. 'Not often breeze blows that way, but is "meat killing place". Not close, you won't get smell often, no worry.'

Daniel stared at Cynic, obviously not believing her, then shook his head. 'Let's see the flat.'

'The smoke from the crematorium shouldn't be much of a bother either,' Gold said. 'They have advanced air filters.'

'Where's that?' Daniel said.

'Next to the abattoir and refuse transfer station,' Gold said cheerfully.

'Refuse transfer?'

'All the garbage trucks take the rubbish there, and they put it on barges to take it to the dump, which is an island offshore somewhere.'

Daniel said something under his breath and followed Cynic into the apartment building.

The building was sixties vintage, not even tiled, just plain whitewashed concrete walls, the whitewash so cheap that it formed a powdery white coat over the pockmarked peeling paint layers beneath. The narrow, grimy corridor had a linoleum floor, the red colour in the centre of the hallway worn through to white by years of passing feet. At the end of the corridor, in the narrow lift lobby, three elderly Chinese sat loudly gossiping. They were sitting on tiny stools only fifteen centimetres tall, open newspapers around them providing a makeshift floor cover. The two women, both wearing black polyester pants and jackets, stopped and stared suspiciously at the group; but the man, who wore pyjama pants and an undershirt pulled up over his rotund belly, ignored them and continued to lecture loudly in Cantonese. One of the women picked up her stool and turned her back on them as they walked past, making a loud 'tch' noise. The elderly man laughed raucously and said something in Cantonese that made her shake her head.

The lift had a metal gate that slid closed before the external double doors.

'This lift is ancient!' Daniel said.

'Don't worry, all the lifts are checked yearly. In fact, this lift was probably checked by that professional gentleman sitting outside with those lovely ladies,' Gold said, enjoying himself.

Daniel silently shook his head.

The floor of the fifth floor lift lobby was green bathroom tiles without grout between them. The walls had been green a long time ago, but now they were a grimy shade of tan, with a thick layer of dust on the door frames and window ledges. Outside the doors of the five apartments on this floor were red plastic buckets with lids, the rubbish collection for the day, and small altars with jars of sand holding pungent incense burning for the door gods.

Cynic took them to the end of the lobby and slid a filthy metal door gate aside, then attacked the lock in the gloss painted metal door with her key. After much fiddling and grunting she finally managed to heavily shove the door open, slamming it against the wall.

The room they entered was a metre and a half by two metres, with two doors side by side on the far short end, and another two doors on the long side. A faded laminated television unit stood between the two doors on the long side, with a torn black leather couch against the wall across from it, allowing only twenty centimetres room to walk between them.

'Oh, yes, is part furnish,' Cynic said.

The walls were the same colour as the lift lobby walls; originally a green that had turned brown from the polluted air. Rough areas on the concrete walls were coated with a thick layer of dark brown dust.

Cynic took them to the two doors at the end of the room. 'Kitchen on right, bathroom on left.'

The kitchen was a metre square, with a tiny window thirty by sixty centimetres, covered in self-adhesive plastic. A single bathroom-style sink was on a bench forty centimetres long on the left, and a lower platform went from one side of the room to the other on the right. All of the tiles were beige, with a thick layer of slimy black mould in the grout. The floor tiles were cracked beige tiles as well, with another thick layer of mould around the bottom corners of the floor.

'Where is the stove?' Daniel said.

Cynic pointed at the tiled platform. 'Put stove there.'

'Hong Kong people cook with a double-burner gas stove, you put the gas bottle under the bench,' Gold said.

Daniel looked around. 'Where does the fridge go?'

Cynic shrugged. 'Can go in living room, plenty of room.'

Daniel went and looked at the bathroom, which was the same size as the kitchen. Once again the tiles were covered with a thick layer of slimy mould. The bathroom sink had a large black crack running through it, and a single cold water tap. A filthy flow-through water heater hung on the wall above the small toilet, a hand-held pink plastic showerhead hanging between the cold and hot water taps. A rusty steel towel rail was attached to the wall, and some transparent plastic shelves, grown opaque with age, next to the tiny window.

Daniel went out and into one of the bedrooms. A double bed sized mattress, ten centimetres thick, was leaning against the wall. The hardwood parquet floor had a thick layer of dust in the gaps between the slats. The room was a metre and a half to a side, only just enough room to fit the double mattress with twenty centimetres to spare to clamber past it when it was placed on the floor.

'Where do you hang your clothes?' Daniel said.

'You can put nails in the wall and hang your clothes on them,' Gold said. 'You can fit four or five items of clothing on each nail that way. And you can put them in boxes under the bed, if you decide to go with a bed frame.'

Cynic touched the mattress as they went back out. 'Good mattress. New. Thick.'

'Ten centimetres is thick?' Daniel said.

'Most mattresses are only three or four centimetres thick,' Gold said. 'We like our beds hard, good for the back.'

The other bedroom had a single bed mattress, two centimetres thick, leaning against the wall as well. When the mattress was placed on the floor, it would go from one end of the room to the other, and leave ten centimetres of space on one side to walk around it.

Cynic walked them back out to the living room. 'This one has furniture, but not new decoration, so not as good as last one.' She glanced down at her folder, then up at Daniel. 'You sure you don't want to look at stuff in mid-levels? I have apartments that are more than a thousand square feet, very luxurious, clubhouse, room for maid, only fifty-sixty thousand dollars a month.'

'Seven thousand ...' Gold trailed off, then rallied. 'That's about seven thousand nine hundred to nine thousand five hundred a month Canadian, which works out to about eighteen hundred to twenty-two hundred a week.'

'I think I need to think about this,' Daniel said wanly.

'No problem,' Leo said. 'Go downstairs, and I'll bring the Merc around.'

'So how much does an apartment in our building cost to rent?' Daniel asked as they returned to the Peak.

'Our building?' Leo said.

'He means Lo Wu's building,' Michelle said.

'The apartment three floors down, half the floor, is three hundred and eighty thousand a month,' Gold said. 'About sixty thousand Canadian a month. A villa up on the Peak, one of the top-end ones with a pool and clubhouse, at least five thousand square feet, will go for about half a million dollars a month — that's about eighty thousand Canadian a month, or twenty thousand a week.'

'People can afford that?' Daniel said.

Gold shrugged. 'Obviously. Top-end residences in other cities, like Paris, can cost similar amounts.'

'I didn't know,' Daniel said. 'they were going to provide me with an apartment, so I never checked prices in Paris.'

'Free accommodation included in the job? Sounds like a sweet deal to me,' Leo said. 'I save a fortune by being a live-in bodyguard.'

'What if I stayed with you?' Daniel said.

'My husband does not want you around,' Michelle said stiffly. 'For some reason he has taken an extreme dislike to you.' She turned in the seat of the car to glare at him. 'He did not want to tell me exactly what it was that you did to annoy him so much.'

'Oh,' Daniel said, and remained silent the rest of the way to the Peak apartment.

Later that evening, Michelle tapped on Leo's door.

'Come on in,' Leo said.

Michelle looked around the door and smiled when she saw that Leo and Gold were playing on the Playstation again. She sat on the couch, still smiling. 'He is going to Paris after all. He's out having one last fling now, and he'll be leaving tomorrow. We did it.'

Leo put down his controller, reached over, and gave Michelle a quick hug. 'That's great.'

Michelle patted Leo on the arm and released him. She sat on the couch, hesitating.

Gold held his controller out to Michelle. 'Play if you want, ma'am.'

Michelle didn't take it. 'I don't want to impose on your private time, gentlemen. I have bought one for myself, and I need you to attach it to the large screen TV in the television room for me, if you would.'

Gold and Leo shared a look, then turned to Michelle.

'Three way knockout on Speed Drift 2?' Leo said.

'I can beat you!' Michelle said.

Gold whooped with delight, and Simone started crying in Michelle's room. 'Whoops, sorry, ma'am.'

Michelle opened the door and called out. 'Monica, please take Simone, I am going to be busy for the next hour or so beating these neebies.'

'Noobies,' Leo said, correcting her.

'Neebies, noobies, prepare to be beaten!' Michelle exclaimed, excited.

Monica came down the hallway, her smile wide. 'Yes, ma'am. Mind if me and the little one watch?'

'Of course, I love an audience when I am outstanding,' Michelle said, cheeky.

'You still can't beat me,' Leo said.

'That's only a matter of time, neeb.'

THE YEAR
1851

FORTUNE KNOCKS

189

SIP...

1851

GOLD'S TEA PLANTATION IN FUJIAN.

MY LORD GOLD!

CLACK CLACK

YES, FIFTEEN?

WE HAVE VISITORS.

VISITORS —?!

DO NOT BE CONCERNED, MY LORD.

CLATTER

IT IS A HUMAN. A EUROPEAN. HE IS ACCOMPANIED BY A FEMALE DRAGON ...

...WHO HAS GIVEN ME A MESSAGE TO PASS TO YOU.

Gold sat back down, and scanned the piece of paper. Strangely, it was written in English, but that proved little problem for Gold as he took in the words with surprise.

This European knows nothing of Shen, but he has a noble heart and his cause is worthy. Please help us to free our nation from the slavery of the opium trade.

Jade

Jade.

Gold snorted with amusement. After all this time, she was looking for him. He glanced up at the demon servant. 'Show them up to the house, and tell the maids to prepare guest rooms. How big is their entourage?'

'The Dragon Princess, the European, and three servants,' the demon said.

'The Princess is acting as interpreter?' Gold said, surprised.

'This European does not require an interpreter,' the demon said.

'He speaks High Beijing dialect like a native.'

'Interesting.'

A flash of light erupted from the hillside below them; the sun reflecting off steel. Gold scanned the paths leading to his manor, and saw them. Two sedan chairs, and three walking servants.

'I wonder what she really wants,' Gold said. He smiled slightly. 'Maybe her memory of me is one of the best she has.'

'I believe it is something to do with the tea,' the servant said. He bowed slightly. 'By your leave.'

'Go.'

SO THAT IS ALL WE WANT. TEA SEEDS.

ROBERT FORTUNE

Robert Fortune leaned forward over the table to speak earnestly to Gold.

'Tea is the root of all the problems in China. The opium to tea trade is killing your people. If we can take the tea trade out, then the British won't bring the opium into China.'

'If I let you have the tea seeds, I am giving you the seeds to my own downfall,' Gold said. 'You won't need to buy my tea any more.'

'We've been planting the tea in India,' Fortune said, 'and the results are unsatisfactory. The plantations in Ceylon are performing slightly better, but we will never have the same quality as you, the climate just isn't suitable.'

'So?' Gold said.

'So, your tea will always be superior,' Fortune said. 'You can provide the finest China tea to the gourmet market, at a higher price. Our tea will be the low grade drink for the poor of England.'

'The China tea trade will continue,' Gold said. 'They will still bring the opium in.'

'Not if they are dealing in smaller quantities,' Fortune said. 'They will be able to find enough silver to pay for the tea if they deal in premium quantities.'

Gold considered the proposition. Fortune was offering him a great deal of money for the tea seeds. He already had seeds from a number of different plantations; he was offering Gold even more money for Drum Mountain's famed silver-tipped tea, only produced in this part of northern Fujian province. Gold glanced up at Fortune's earnest face. The European really did have the best interests of China at heart; a refreshing change after so much of what had happened during the wars. The Europeans had bludgeoned the Dowager Empress into granting more and more concessions; half of Shanghai was now European concessions. The entire island of Hong Kong had been ceded to Britain; and Macau to Portugal.

The Empress was weak and the foreigners were strong. If they wished, they could take over China as easily as they had gained control of India. But if they could grow their own tea, then it would not be worth the effort. China had nothing else the Westerners wanted.

I'M DOING THE RIGHT THING HERE.

'I'll do it,' Gold said. 'I'll provide you with all the seeds and seedlings you need.'

'I also need trained staff to tend the plants,' Fortune said. 'You know that what I am doing is highly illegal, and any workers found leaving the country to assist me would be sentenced to death if discovered.'

Please provide him with some demons, Gold, Jade said.

'Very well,' Gold said. 'For the lady.' He smiled at Jade, but her expression was remote. 'I will provide you with three of my staff to help tend the plants.'

Fortune jumped up and grabbed Gold's hand, shaking it vigorously.

Fortune continued to shake Gold's hand until Gold felt he would shake it off. 'Thank you. You have saved your country. You will be a national hero.'

I'm a hero, Gold said to Jade.

She gazed directly into his eyes, her pale serene face expressionless. *Don't even think about it.*

Fortune turned to Jade and took both her hands in his, then kissed her on the cheek. 'Thank you so much, Lady Jade.'

Jade was obviously embarrassed and blushed furiously.

'Oh, sorry,' Fortune said. He released Jade and returned to his chair. 'I forgot.'

'That's quite all right, Robert,' Jade said, still blushing. 'I know that Europeans do things differently.'

'I cannot thank you enough,' Fortune said to Jade.

Oh, I see, Gold said, making no attempt to hide his amusement.

Nothing happening, Jade said, her lie obvious to Gold. *Europeans are just more ... demonstrative.*

195

Fortune raised his teacup. 'Here's to a prosperous future for the people of China.'

Jade and Gold raised their cups as well.

AND FREEDOM FROM THE TYRANNY OF OPIUM!

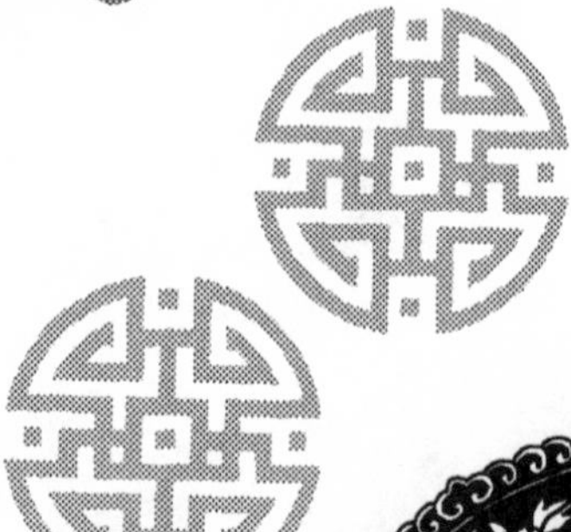

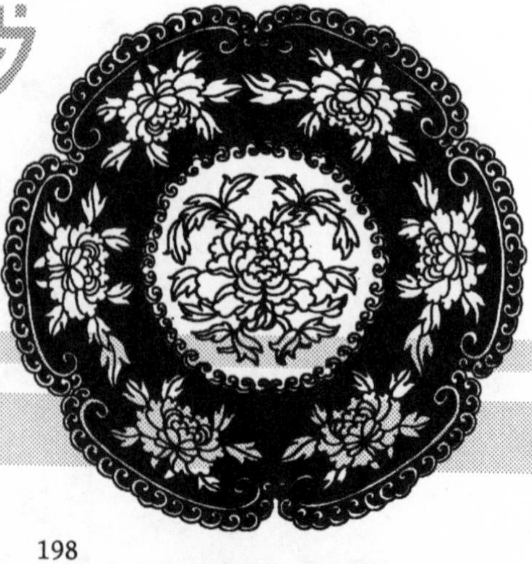

THE YEAR
1997

HONG KONG

Gold and Jade stood at the entrance to the hotel ballroom greeting guests as they arrived. Every Celestial who could get their hands on an invitation to Simone's one-month party was there; some had even tried to bribe members of the household to be permitted to attend. The hall was full.

The guests sat around large round tables, each set for twelve people with silver plates beneath their bone-china rice bowls. Waiters ran between the tables holding trays carrying cans of soft drink, filling everybody's glass. Michelle and some of the more modern Shen drank red wine from enormous balloon glasses; Xuan Wu and the more old-fashioned guests drank black tea out of tumblers.

Gold and Jade showed the guests to their tables. Jade seemed full of satisfaction as the hall filled; she had done well organising the party. A raised platform held the table of honour, its red tablecloth making it stand out from the rest. At this table sat Xuan Wu, Michelle, Leo, the other three Winds, Er Lang representing the Celestial, two of the Dark Lord's most senior Generals, and two of the most senior Celestial Masters from the Mountain.

When all of the guests had arrived, Gold and Jade closed the hall doors and took their seats at the head table between Michelle and Leo.

Gold tried to keep his head down and not attract any attention, and Jade seemed to be doing the same. Lowly retainers such as them should not have been sitting at the head table, but Michelle had insisted upon it. Er Lang sat, scowling, in his chair, occasionally shooting disgruntled looks at them. Qing Long, the Blue Dragon, had noted their existence and acknowledged their salutes with the slightest of nods, then pointedly ignored them. The White Tiger was too busy leering at all the female Shen in the hall and working to quickly empty his bottle of rice wine; the Red Phoenix, Zhu Que, seemed oblivious to all but baby Simone, who she cradled and cooed at. The Generals and Celestial Masters were deep in a quiet discussion with Xuan Wu and thankfully seemed unaware of their existence.

The wait staff had finished serving the drinks, and began to serve the large platters of the first course. Each platter contained a whole roast suckling pig with large maraschino cherries stuck into its eye sockets with toothpicks. The pigs were cut into bite-size pieces, the skin of the animal mouth-meltingly crispy over a fine layer of tender meat. Next to each platter of suckling pig was a platter of vegetarian entrees, small pieces of mushroom and shredded fungus, with bean curd sheet wrapped around bamboo shoot and lotus root.

The wait staff placed the platters on the tables, then proceeded to use serving spoons and forks as tongs to lift a small amount of each dish into a serving bowl for the dinner guests.

'How many courses?' Gold asked Jade softly.

'Twelve, standard banquet, whole coral trout for fifth, "Buddha Jumps Over the Wall" for seventh, vegetarian options all the way through,' Jade replied.

'Good job.'

The hall doors flew open, and the Dark Lord and his lieutenants shot to their feet. A few guests shrieked with surprise and ran from their tables to hide behind the dais.

'Guard Michelle and Simone,' Xuan Wu said, and moved to the front of the dais, his lieutenants flanking him. All except the Dark Lord changed to Celestial Form. The White Tiger became seven feet tall wearing white and gold scaled armour, with a long flurry of white hair down to his waist. The Red Phoenix grew into a tall, willowy woman in a red Tang robe, holding a pair of red swords. Er Lang changed so that he was taller, wearing green scaled armour and a war helmet. They moved into position at the front of the dais, a protective shield in front of Michelle and Simone.

The Demon King strolled into the hall in human form. He appeared to be a Chinese in his mid-twenties, wearing a blood-coloured polo shirt and a pair of black designer slacks. His long hair was also the colour of dried blood, and swept unbound down his back.

He was attended by four Snake Mothers, all of them in human form — appearing as tall, gorgeous young Chinese woman wearing blood-red cheongsams. They moved with graceful menace through the hall towards Xuan Wu.

The Demon King stopped at the base of the dais, then elegantly fell to one knee and saluted Xuan Wu. 'Xuan Tian Shang Di, Demon-conquering Celestial Worthy, Celestial Minister of Jade Emptiness, Master of the Glorious Teachings of the Primeval Chaos and the Nine Heavens.'

Xuan Wu nodded to the Demon King. 'Loathsome Majesty Wong Mo, King of all the Demons and the Humanity-crushing Horde of Hell, Drinker of the Blood of Innocents, Slaughterer of the Unworthy, Torturer of the Unbeliever.'

The Demon King rose and grinned at the White Tiger. 'Your

seals fail, my friend.'

'Whoever raised them will feel my claws,' the Tiger growled.

'Pass the failure over when you're done, the ladies haven't eaten Shen in a while,' the Demon King said, and the Snake Mothers grinned with malice. He beamed around at everybody. 'So what's the occasion? I heard there was a party, is it someone's birthday?'

He doesn't know, don't tell him! Xuan Wu warned everyone. *Keep the child out of sight!*

Michelle pushed her way through the Shen and stood glaring at the Demon King. 'Why have you interrupted my comeback celebration? All of these people were here to hear me sing, and now they cannot because you have ruined it!' She waved one hand at him. 'Go away, you horrible little man!'

The Demon King bowed slightly to Michelle. 'I would love to hear you sing, Lady. The Dark Lord has given up his duty and dominion for you, it had better be worth it.' His grin grew vicious. 'With him on the Earthly here all the time, Heaven is like an orchard full of Celestial peaches, ripe for us to pluck.'

Er Lang stepped forward slightly. 'The Thirty-Six and the Celestial Vanguard protect our subjects, Wong Mo. You are no more able to threaten us than you ever have.' He summoned his halberd, and tapped the end on the floor. 'Return to Hell.'

'Tell you what,' the Demon King said casually. 'Michelle can sing a song for us, and then we'll go.' He shrugged. 'No trouble, no conflict, one song and we're gone.'

'One second,' Michelle said, before anyone could reply. She returned to the table, sipped a glass of water, and glanced at Leo, who was holding tiny Simone, silent and wide-eyed, in his arms.

She is bound, Lady, Jade said to Michelle. Do not be concerned, she cannot make a sound. The Shen are all blocking his view of her. He will not be able to see past them.

Michelle nodded to Jade, and returned to the front of the dais. She coughed slightly, then visibly relaxed and sang for the Demon King.

Her voice was loud enough to make Gold's ears protest at her proximity; some of the higher notes sounded muffled as his ears could not handle the volume. Her voice was piercingly sweet, filling the hall to all corners. She sang a medieval French love song, warm and lilting. She did not hesitate as she struck the difficult scales in the middle of the song, and faultlessly skipped over them, even though she hadn't warmed up. She concluded with a slower passage, full of longing and love, and the final note faded through the hall.

There was complete silence, all attention focused on the Demon King. He stood, staring at her, for a moment, then smiled gently.

'Lady, the Dark Lord was right to leave his dominion for that, your voice is exquisite,' he said. He glanced at his glowering Snake Mothers. 'I can understand now why there is such a large attendance to welcome you back to the concert circuit. Watch for us in the audience.' He saluted Xuan Wu. 'Xuan Tian. See ya.' He and the Snake Mothers disappeared.

'Wait,' Xuan Wu said, and nobody moved. All of the Shen concentrated for a few uncomfortable minutes, then they relaxed and retook human form.

The White Tiger, Bai Hu, fell to one knee before Xuan Wu. 'This stupid Shen has failed you most miserably, my Lord.'

Xuan Wu stared emotionlessly at Bai Hu. Then he said, 'What's done is done, he still does not know of the existence of the child. Find what has caused this! It is of great concern if they are capable of breaking Celestial seals!'

Bai Hu rose and nodded. 'I don't know what caused it. But I will find out immediately.'

Er Lang glanced around the standing guests, then pointed at some of the other Shen present. 'Li Fu Long. Zhang Lei Gong. Zhou Guang Ze, Guan Yu. Take up positions to guard the doors, we cannot have a repeat of this, and the seals must be completely down now.'

The four named Generals rose, took Celestial form, and took up guard positions, one on either side of the two double doors to the hall.

Jade released the binding on Simone, and the baby started to squall. Michelle rushed to take her, patting her back and talking softly to her. Simone soon settled in her mother's arms.

Gold studied Michelle. She was shaking, but all her concentration was on her child. Michelle looked up and called to Xuan Wu. 'Come, let us finish our dinner. We must not let horrible little people like that spoil it for us!'

'You are quite right, my love,' Xuan Wu said. He glanced around the hall, then he and the other Shen retook their positions at the table. Jade concentrated, and the waiters began to bring out the next course, deep-fried scallops with dipping mayonnaise, and a deep-fried mushroom vegetarian alternative. Each table was also served with whole pigeon soup, with bean curd and winter melon soup as the vegetarian option. Michelle nodded to Jade, Gold, and Leo as the plates were placed in front of her. 'You all did a fine job of protecting my little one. I thank you.'

'You were so brave, ma'am!' Jade said, her voice full of approval. 'To stand up there and sing so courageously, when your child was threatened!'

'Pfft.' Michelle waved them down, her hand still shaking. She emptied her wineglass in a single swallow, gesturing for a waiter to fill it again. 'I will not let anyone threaten my child. Any mother would do the same.'

The White Tiger filled his wine cup from his old-fashioned teapot-shaped silver wine jug. 'Whoever set those seals will feel my claws,' he grumbled quietly. 'Five of them came in with no difficulty at all.'

A demon servant slipped into the back of the hall, approached the Tiger, and whispered urgently into his ear. The Tiger grimaced and rose.

'The Demon King couldn't leave without having a little fun first,' the Tiger said. He saluted Xuan Wu. 'By your leave, my Lord, I need to replace some of the wait staff; the king's entourage realised that they were tame demons, and killed a few of them before my White Horsemen could intervene.'

Xuan Wu nodded. 'Go.'

酉酉酉酉酉酉酉酉酉酉酉酉酉酉酉酉

'Michelle, we are only going for two weeks, and anything you need can be brought up for you,' Xuan Wu said when he saw the four suitcases on the living room floor.

'Only three are mine, one is Simone's,' Michelle said.

'Who will take the ladies?' Gold said.

'Jade,' Xuan Wu said. 'She is faster, she can travel to the plane more quickly than any of us.'

Jade nodded and stepped forward. 'Hold on tight to the Princess, ma'am, and close your eyes.'

Gold grumbled under his breath about taking so much luggage, changed to True Form, and lifted all the suitcases with his stone to carry them to the Mountain.

Leo stood in the living room, forlorn. 'Take care, everybody.'

'Look after Monica, Leo,' Michelle said, but Jade had already taken her.

The journey to the Mountain on the Celestial plane was a long one. Celestial Wudang, Xuan Wu's Mountain of Martial Arts, was at least an hour from any Earth-based location, even at dragon-speed; and as far from the hordes of Hell as any place on the Celestial. This did not stop the Demon King and his multitudinous children from occasionally attacking the Mountain, hoping to break the back of the Celestial army that held them at bay.

Jade writhed quickly away as a dragon, her wingless form sliding sinuously through the air. They travelled high and fast, covering the distance between Hong Kong and Hubei province quickly, the clouds far below them. Jade had gently sedated Michelle and Simone as she carried them on her massive green front legs, and they rode cradled in her arms, oblivious to the height and travel.

When they arrived at the Earthly Wudangshan, Jade and Gold travelled almost to the edge of the atmosphere and through the gate that led to Heaven. The gate, one of many, was at least a hundred metres wide, with three red pillars topped with golden tiles. Live guardian dragons writhed up and down the pillars on either side. Jade whisked through with her human and half-Shen passengers, and Gold toiled solidly behind, lugging the increasingly heavy luggage. Xuan Wu, riding his Celestial Cloud, glided past Gold without a glance in the stone's direction.

'Did you get a tip, busboy?' one of the guardian dragons sniped at Gold as he passed through the gate, but passage through the veil between Earth and Heaven did not permit him to reply.

Once through the gate, they travelled for another forty-five minutes on the Celestial plane. The Northern Celestial landscape was a mountain range, with high, sharp peaks separated by deep valleys. Each valley had its own internal light source, glowing from the hillsides, so although they were shadowed by the mountains during the day, the valleys never lacked light. The valleys had green meadows and tree-bounded rivers, with Celestial villages nestled into the riverbanks. Most valleys had a waterfall where a river cascaded from the mountain cliffs into the valley below, and were unreachable by foot; the only way to visit a village in the Northern Heavens was to fly.

They travelled towards the craggier mountains further west, and Celestial Wudangshan towered majestically before them. The Mountain comprised seven peaks, joined by impossibly soaring bridges over deep gorges. The base of the Mountain was perpetually in cloud; and ancient, twisted pine and spruce trees clung to its craggy sides. The buildings of the Wudangshan Academy spread between towering walkways, with small open areas where the Dark Lord's Disciples could perform their martial arts sets.

When Gold arrived at the Mountain, Jade and the Dark Lord had already landed on one of the open practise areas. The Mountain's household staff, all tame demons in the traditional black and white of servants, were fussing over Simone and Michelle. Simone was wailing, and Michelle was unconscious, unable to be roused.

Gold dropped the bags and went to Jade and Xuan Wu, concerned. 'Is Lady Michelle all right?'

Xuan Wu was on one knee next to Michelle where Jade cradled her in her dragon arms. 'She lent her energy to allow one so small to make the passage to the Celestial and it has exhausted her.'

'She will be okay, my Lord?'

Xuan Wu rose and nodded. 'She will be fine. Jade, take her to our quarters.' The servants were all attentive and eager to assist, and listened carefully as he addressed them. 'Keep watch on Lady Michelle. Take the child to her room, and care for her.' He turned away. 'I must go now to my private wing and rebuild.' He glanced around. 'Do not disturb me unless lives are threatened, and only if those lives are Michelle's or Simone's.'

'What if the Celestial summons you, my Lord?' Gold said.

'Tell him to go to hell, I'm taking a nap,' the Dark Lord said with grim humour.

Twenty-four hours later, Michelle could still not be roused and Gold met with the two most senior Celestial Martial Arts Masters to see what could be done.

When he had first arrived to take up duties as the Dark Lord's Retainer at the Mountain, he had been surprised to discover that the academy's head Energy Master was the same European woman who had assisted him in rescuing the American woman, Anne, from the brothel so many years ago. Her name was Meredith, and she was married to the Shaolin Master, Liu. Both of them hurried back to the Dark Lord's quarters with Gold when he told them that Michelle had not regained consciousness.

'What about the baby?' Meredith asked as they walked quickly along one of the narrow paths that clung to the side of the Mountain, a chasm of a thousand metres on the other side of the stone balustrade.

'The demon staff are caring for her. Lady Michelle had her put on bottle-feeding a good month ago, and there are demons who are trained in the care of little ones. She is perfectly fine.'

'It's just Michelle, then,' Liu said. He shook his head. 'It must have been a tremendous drain on her to protect one so small. Normally we wait until the child is at least two or three years old before bringing it to the Celestial, it strains the mother too much protecting them from the transfer.'

'Michelle is strong,' Gold said.

'And the Dark Lord didn't have much of a choice,' Meredith said. 'I could feel how drained he was when he arrived. It was frightening how little of his energy remained. It was like a black hole had arrived on his Mountain, trying to suck all nearby energy into it.' She shook her head. 'He must not touch her when he is like this, he could suck the life right out of her.'

'He didn't,' Gold said, remembering. Then he realised with shock, 'They can't have normal marital relations while he's like this?'

'Absolutely not. He's best not to touch her at all.'

'No wonder she's been in a filthy mood lately!'

'That, and she hates being here,' Meredith said.

They arrived at the Dark Lord's private apartments. The buildings were set on the highest part of the Mountain, on a specially cleared platform that had been flattened and terraced into the slope. The buildings flawlessly complied with the rules of fung shui; a courtyard shape with a front entrance facing out towards the smaller mountains below Wudang. The building was constructed of Celestial hardwood from trees grown in Heaven, in the traditional pillar and beam construction. The black-tiled roof swept up at the corners.

The front entry had a large veranda with a carved wooden balustrade. The double doors then opened into the entry hall, where Xuan Wu would entertain his closest guests. Gold led the Masters into the entry hall which opened into the central courtyard beyond.

The courtyard was bordered on all four sides by the house, and was a hundred metres each side. A sparkling clear pond of koi carp sat in one corner, with a fountain in the shape of the Xuan Wu — turtle and snake — in onyx pouring water into the pond. Some bonsai pine trees, obviously extremely old, stood on carved stone benches on either side of the courtyard. Another veranda encircled the courtyard, allowing an open air walkway between the rooms of the house.

Gold led them up the stairs in the entrance hall to the second storey. They went through the private living room with a large widescreen television, library of DVDs, and baby grand piano to the bedroom beyond. The bedroom was decorated with carved rosewood furniture and an enormous rosewood Chinese-style four-poster bed with black and silver sheer silken canopies.

Michelle lay on the thin, hard mattress, her head on a soft Western pillow next to the traditional ceramic Chinese pillow favoured by the Dark Lord. She lay on her back, her face ashen, her breathing so slight it was almost undetectable.

Meredith went to her bedside and took Michelle's hand, her face rigid with concentration. Then she relaxed and breathed a sigh of relief. She smiled up at Gold. 'She's fine. I don't even need to feed her energy. This is a normal sleep. She'll probably sleep for another eight or nine hours, then wake up starving.'

Gold rubbed his hands over his face, sharing her relief. 'I'll let the demon servants know, and they can have something ready for her.'

'Do they know how to cook any Western food?' Master Liu said. 'She prefers that to Chinese.'

Meredith gazed down at the sleeping Michelle. 'She'll be so hungry when she wakes, that she won't care.' She glanced around. 'Where's the baby?'

Gold led them to the baby's room next to the master room, at the back of the house in the safest location with the rear wall nestled against the stone spine of the Mountain. A demon in the form of an elderly Chinese woman sat in a chair next to Simone's cradle, gently rocking Simone. Gold, Meredith and Liu went to Simone's bedside and Meredith lightly touched her hand.

'She has been distressed at being separated from her mother, and she has fallen into an exhausted sleep, Masters,' the demon said. 'I am on duty, and three others are on standby. We thought only one at a time would be best, as it is what she is accustomed to.' She glanced into the next room. 'Will the lady be all right?'

Meredith released Simone's hand and straightened. 'Both of them are well and should recover soon. I expect Lady Michelle to be up and around in the morning. Simone will stop fretting when she is in her mother's arms again. I suggest that if Simone frets, put her next to her mother. It may wake Michelle, and the familiar scent of her mother may settle Simone.'

The demon nodded. 'Yes, ma'am.'

Meredith turned to Gold. 'You've done well. Michelle should wake soon.' She shrugged. 'Then you have to deal with her being completely bored.'

'The television and movie library are for Michelle, ma'am,' Gold said, 'but she says that the Dark Lord has impossible taste in movies, and she threw many of them away.'

Meredith leaned into Gold and spoke softly. 'Michelle's right.' She patted Gold on the shoulder. 'I'll leave you to it. Don't we have a bunch of students to review tomorrow?'

Gold sagged. 'Yes. The Dark Lord should stop the student intake while he's living on the Earthly.'

'What, and stop supplying our trained people to other Celestials to act as guards and weapons masters?' Liu said.

'Yes!' Gold said.

'And the Jade Emperor's Elite Guard too?' Meredith said. 'If the Jade Emperor says that he needs a few new swords, we just tell him, "no"?'

Gold hesitated.

'And the demon students that graduate from the academy, when they're ready to take up duty in the Vanguard of the Thirty-Six, we just hold them here indefinitely?' Liu said.

Gold raised his hands in defeat. 'I concede. We need to continue bringing in new students. But the Dark Lord is always working with outdated information. I really need to find a way to network the Mountain with his home computer, so that he has the latest data. The other day, he promoted a student who had already been moved up the day before.'

Meredith winced. 'He would hate something that makes him look out of touch like that. He prides himself on knowing the status of every student in the academy.'

'Tell me about it,' Gold said wryly. 'He wondered out loud what temperature gold melts at.'

Liu snorted with amusement. 'Get a few of your stone friends to create the data link. They can just sit there, and work like a computer network, transferring information. It's what you stones do all the time anyway.'

'I've asked, nobody wants to volunteer,' Gold said.

'Why not?' Meredith said. 'It would be a simple solution.'

'It'd be too boring,' Gold said. 'Nobody I've asked has been interested.'

'Not even if we paid them very well?' Liu said.

Gold shrugged. 'For most stones, payment is irrelevant, if we need to purchase something, we just create a precious gem to sell for the money. If we agree to work, we agree because we are interested in the task.'

'Any other stones held in servitude because they did something stupid?' Meredith said.

'Just me, and I'm full-time dealing with the legal matters and assisting the Dark Lord,' Gold said. 'Don't worry, I'm working on a way to link up the computers, it's just a matter of time.'

'Make it biological, not geological time, Gold,' Meredith said.

'There's a difference?' Gold said innocently.

━━━━━━━━━━━━━━━━━━━━━

'Final item,' Gold said.

'About time,' Xuan Wu said. 'We've been here a couple of hours now.'

The office door opened slightly. Gold and Xuan Wu both looked, and saw nothing. Then a tiny set of fingers appeared at the edge of the desk. A pair of bright hazel eyes, topped by a short wispy mop of honey-coloured hair, appeared over the edge of the desk at them.

'Hello, Simone,' Xuan Wu said with warm affection. 'Are you visiting Daddy?'

'Daddy!' Simone said. 'Daddy and Gol.'

'Gol — d,' Gold corrected her.

'Gol.'

Gold sighed.

Simone toddled around the desk and pulled herself up into her father's lap.

'What is the final item, Gold?' Xuan Wu said, and Simone busily tried to poke her fingers up his nose. He turned her around on his lap and she brushed at the papers on his desk.

'We have received a missive from the Celestial one. The Jade Emperor would like to see Simone. She will be turning a year and a half old soon, and it is time for her to be presented, and to be formally invested as Princess of the Dark Northern Heavens.'

'You're a princess,' Xuan Wu whispered into Simone's ear, making her giggle. He spoke louder for Gold's benefit. 'It's a good idea. She can see her Celestial heritage, meet those she will one day serve.'

Gold grimaced. 'She is so young to be a servant.'

'It is the fate of all the rulers on any plane,' Xuan Wu said, 'to serve those who they rule. But first, I must travel to the Mountain, and rebuild my energy. It would not be acceptable for me to present myself to the Jade Emperor looking as weak as I do.'

'When, my Lord?'

'I am planning to travel up there for a week on Monday. Michelle and Simone will accompany me; Leo and Monica will stay here, as usual.'

Simone stopped moving the papers around and looked up at her father. 'Mountain?'

He smiled down at her. 'Yes, Simone, we're going to the Mountain.'

She raised both arms in the air in triumph. 'Yay!'

Monica's head appeared around the door. 'There you are, you silly girl, let Daddy and Gold do their work.'

'Gol!' Simone squealed. She pointed at Gold. 'Gol!'

Monica came into the room and nodded as Xuan Wu passed the kicking Simone to her. 'Sorry, sir.'

'She is a welcome interruption,' Xuan Wu said. 'Gol is boring.'

'Gol is boring!' Simone said as Monica lowered her to the floor. Simone scuttled to Gold and poked him on the arm, then grinned up at him. 'You're boring!'

'And you are very cute,' Gold said down to her. 'Want to see a magic trick?'

Simone's eyes went wide and she nodded.

'Is that all, sir?' Gold said.

'Dismissed,' Xuan Wu said.

Gold disappeared.

※※※※※※※※※※※※※※※※※

The next week they held a student intake and assessment while the Dark Lord was in retreat at the Mountain. Gold met Meredith and Liu at Dragon Tiger Platform outside the Dragon Tiger Palace. The platform was a large open area a hundred metres to a side, paved with slate-grey stone slabs.

The palace at the top of the flights of stairs behind them served as an imposing backdrop while they reviewed the students who had been recently recruited. Gold and Meredith sat at tables and Meredith wore her formal Tai Chi Master outfit of a plain black cotton jacket and pants with white trim on the sleeves.

Master Liu had changed out of his usual jeans and T-shirt and was wearing the full saffron-coloured robes of a Shaolin Master, carrying his preferred weapon — a simple hardwood staff. With his elderly appearance — bushy white brows, long beard, and completely bald head — he fitted the students' preconceptions of a Martial Arts Master perfectly and he enjoyed intimidating them.

The students had all been fitted with the Mountain uniform of a plain black cotton jacket and pants with traditional cloth toggles and loops. They were a mixture of all races and had come from all over the world — the Dark Lord's scouts monitored martial arts schools and hand-picked those with the talent and attitude to join the ranks of Celestial practitioners. Some of them were demons who had turned and been tamed by Celestials, and some were Celestial denizens — Shen in human form — sent by their parents for training in the martial arts. They stood quietly in three rows of six, some of them still appearing unsure as to what they'd gotten themselves into.

Liu strode up and down in front of the nervous novices, grinning with malice. 'You are here because you are possibly the best of the best. We are going to test each of you in turn, and see if you have what it takes.' He stopped, turned, and tapped the end of his staff on the ground next to him. 'Any questions?'

The novices were silent.

'Very good. Move back and stand around the edge of the arena. We will see you one at a time, humans first.'

As the disciples moved back, a young American of about twenty years hesitated.

'Yes?' Liu said.

'Uh ... Master ...' the student said, then, 'Did you say humans first?'

'That I did. Move back,' Liu said.

When all the students were standing around the edge of the platform, Liu moved to the middle and held out his hand. He swept a look around the students, then pointed at one who appeared to be only fourteen or fifteen years old; a small, slender boy. 'You. First.'

The student took three steps forward, his bony joints standing out within his Mountain uniform. He dropped to one knee and saluted Liu, then stood, confident, waiting.

'You are Lee from Goat Village, yes?' Meredith said, studying the papers in front of her and Gold.

Lee saluted Meredith. 'Yes, I am Lee from Goat Village, Master.'

Meredith shifted the papers around. 'Proceed.'

Liu raised and dropped his outstretched hand, still holding his staff with the other. 'Take this stone from my hand. Any way you wish.'

Lee grinned, then his face went slack. He blurred for a moment, then disappeared.

The other human students present gasped; even the Shen and demon students appeared shocked.

Liu stood silently, waiting. There wasn't a sound except for the breeze whispering around them.

Suddenly Liu swung his staff in a whirl of saffron, sweeping it low along the ground and striking Lee loudly. Lee appeared in front of him, on his back on the ground, gasping.

'Good try,' Liu said. He returned his staff to his side. 'Up you get, and return to the group.'

Lee picked himself up and shook his head. He returned, cowed, to the rest of the students.

Liu turned to look at all the students, then pointed at the young American. 'You next.'

The American stepped forward. He had blond hair and freckles across his nose, and had obviously been working hard at the arts; he had a very solid muscular frame. He stood in front of Liu, fidgeting with nervousness.

'Jensen from the US, correct?' Meredith said.

Jensen jumped, then quickly fell to one knee and saluted Liu and Meredith. 'Apologies. Yes, I am Jensen, Masters.'

'Up you get.' Liu held out his hand. 'Try to take the stone.'

Jensen hesitated, studying the stone in Liu's hand. Then he relaxed. 'Even invisible, Lee couldn't take the stone off you. There is no way I could take it.'

'Of course there is,' Liu said, friendly and jovial.

Jensen's face cleared. He bowed to Liu. 'May I have that stone, sir?'

'You certainly may.' Liu dropped his hand to his side. 'But I would like something in return.'

'What is that, sir?'

'Any martial arts set that you know. Anything at all. If you want to do a weapon set, there are weapons on the side in the rack. Or unarmed. It doesn't matter.'

Jensen saluted. 'I only hope I am good enough to be taught by you.'

'Of course you aren't!' Liu said, laughing. 'If you were, you'd be a third year, not a novice. Now show me what you've got.' He took three steps backward, then stopped again. He raised his hand, still holding the stone. 'Oh, one other thing.'

Jensen bowed slightly. 'Sir?'

'Don't make it too long, boy, you'll bore me to death.'

The rest of the students tittered as Jensen grinned broadly and saluted Liu again. 'Yes, sir!' Jensen moved back a couple of paces, took a few deep breaths, and shook out his shoulders. Then he began to do a Chen-style tai chi set.

'Oh, very nice,' Meredith murmured next to Gold. 'He's been taught by Richard Bociano in San Diego. Good practitioner. Lucky kid.'

'He moves his chi well,' Gold said. 'Good control.'

'Definite Energy candidate, this one is mine,' Meredith said softly with satisfaction, and scribbled on the papers in front of her. She nodded to Liu, obviously communicating silently.

'Enough,' Liu said, and Jensen stopped and saluted Liu.

'My lovely wife would like to know why you chose a Chen-style tai chi set, when from your build and the way you move, it is obvious you have been trained in harder arts by Master Bociano in San Diego,' Liu said.

Jensen shot a quick, shocked look at Meredith, then pulled himself together. 'Uh ... I know a few different styles, but this one is the oldest, and I think the most pure. Master Bociano said that Chen style's been handed down unchanged for hundreds of years.'

'Your Master is correct,' Liu said. 'I've seen enough. Move back.'

Liu pointed to the next student, and the student stepped forward, then stopped dead when a dragon landed lightly on the pavement between him and Liu.

The students backed away, intimidated. The dragon was fifteen metres long, with a green body and darker green fins and tail. It bowed slightly to Liu in dragon form and spoke in a warm human woman's voice. 'Master Liu. I apologise for this interruption. There is a demon prince on his way to the Mountain with a cohort of about fifty, many of whom are Snake Mother size. You should expect them to arrive here in the next ten minutes; they are riding fliers.' The dragon looked around. 'Where is the Dark Lord? I must inform him.'

'The Dark Lord is in retreat,' Meredith said, rising. 'We can handle this, we are fully manned and able to take a threat as small as this. What is your honoured name?'

The dragon dropped its head slightly. 'My human name is Cynic.' It winked at Gold.

'Are you on duty for the Celestial? You're not one of the academy's dragons,' Liu asked Cynic.

'No, my Lord, I was just coming up to the Mountain to visit my friend Gold when I passed the demons.'

Bells began to ring in the four bell towers situated at the corners of the Mountain complex; each five hundred metres away from the other.

'About time,' Liu said. He nodded to Cynic. 'Thank you, Madam. I suggest you stay while we fend off this attack.'

'Mind if a lend a claw?' Cynic said, her eyes glittering.

'Be my guest,' Liu said.

214

Cynic launched herself into the air, then shot upwards to hover about two hundred metres above the ground.

Liu moved forward to speak to the students. 'You will go with Gold. You will remain calm. The demons will not be able to breach the walls of Wudangshan; no demon ever has. You are safe, so what we really need is for you to stay out of the way.' He gestured with one hand. 'Gold, come and take these kids to the barracks and make sure they're not in the way.'

Gold stepped forward. 'Please come with me.'

'I want to help!' Lee shouted as the rest of the students gathered around Gold. 'I can fight, let me help!'

'I'd like to help too,' Jensen said, and a few of the other students chimed in to agree.

'Quiet!' Liu roared, and they all went silent. He dropped his voice, but could still be clearly heard. 'If you can't do as you're told, you might as well go home now. I told you to go with Gold, and you'll damn well do it or go home right now. Is that understood?'

The students nodded, intimidated. 'Good,' Liu said. 'Gold, take them to the central barracks, out of the way. This probably won't take long if there's only one cohort of demons. Can't imagine why the demon prince is wasting his time.'

'Yes, sir,' Gold said. 'Stay together, if you get lost you'll be in everybody's way. Let's go.'

He led them to the barracks, a number of long halls nestled against the mountainside in one of the safer locations towards the back of the complex.

'I wish we knew what was happening,' Lee said as they walked single-file along a path beside one of the deeper gorges. 'I've fought demons before, I know how to handle myself.'

'You've fought demons before?' Jensen asked.

'Yeah, in Goat Village we train against small ones,' Lee said.

'You have a village full of goats?'

'Nah,' Lee said. 'It's one of the twelve animal villages. Goat Village is the home of the art of invisibility.'

'In here,' Gold said, and led them in to the mess hall. Inside, the tame demons who would normally be busy preparing lunch for the students were nowhere to be seen, and all the stoves were deserted. 'Don't go to the bathroom by yourselves, and if any of you sneak off and try to join the battle, Master Liu will probably kick you out of the academy so fast and so hard that your ass will be sore for a week.' Gold searched the academy grounds for another stone to relay the events, but couldn't find one. He contacted Cynic instead.

How's it going?

They're nearly here, they're close to the southern wall. A very small band, I don't know why they're wasting their time, they're all dead.

Do you mind relaying for me? I have some green novices here who are itching to know what's going on. Probably wouldn't hurt them to see the real thing.

Oh, my pleasure, just relay back some of the reactions, please!

I never did get to thank you properly for helping out with Lady Michelle's brother, Gold said wryly as they established the link.

Why do you think I'm here? Cynic said with amusement. *I've heard about you, little Stone Toy.*

Where did you hear me called that? Gold asked with astonishment.

Oh, around. Why?

About three hundred years ago, I wronged a Celestial and he was nicknamed the 'Little Stone's Toy', Gold said ruefully. *Looks like the nickname given to him has attached itself to me in the retellings.*

If you wronged someone, then it serves you right, Cynic said.

I've made some monumental blunders in my long life, Gold said. *One day I'll have atoned for them all. Until then, I'm stuck serving the Dark Lord.*

The demons are here, I'll establish the link for you. You must tell me the whole story later.

'Everybody, gather round,' Gold said. 'I'm going to show you what's happening out on the south wall.'

The students, some holding tumblers of water, quickly gathered near Gold.

Gold snapped open the link with Cynic and passed the image on to the students, who gasped. All of them were now floating with Cynic about twenty metres above Wudangshan's south wall.

'The demons are approaching from the south,' Cynic said, enjoying her commentator role. 'There is a single demon prince, and a cohort of very large demons — some of them bigger than level fifty. You have all learned the levels and strengths of Hell's demons?'

'They have a rudimentary knowledge, I think they've attended one or two classes in basic Demon studies,' Gold said.

'Two,' Jensen said, as if from a million miles away. 'Didn't think I'd see one up close for a while.'

'Don't worry, all in due time,' Gold said.

'Ah! I see them,' Cynic said. She used her dragon vision and homed in on the approaching demons. They rode large fliers — demons with four legs, wings, and glowing red eyes. The demon soldiers were in True Form; roughly human-shaped, but their skin was black or red with scales, bulging eyes, and tusks. They all wore armour and carried swords.

'No Snake Mothers today,' Cynic said. 'But these are big enough to provide the Masters of Wudangshan with some entertainment.'

I would like to know why this demon prince is throwing these obviously powerful demons to their deaths, Liu said into everybody's heads. *So I would appreciate at least two or three of these taken alive for questioning.*

What about the prince? someone said.

One less demon prince in the world isn't something I would lose sleep over.

The south gate of Wudangshan was made of shining black stone with the image of an enormous red phoenix carved into it. The doors slid soundlessly apart, disappearing into the walls, and a group of about thirty black-clad warriors emerged with a single standard bearer in the middle of them. The standard was a black flag on a long pole arm, with the seven stars of the Big Dipper the only insignia on it.

The warriors moved forward down the steep hillside below the wall, and the south gate closed behind them.

'They appear to be young — are they students?' Cynic said, sharing her voice with the watching students.

'Yes,' Gold said. 'I recognise them, they are Master Liu's third year Weapons class. They'd normally be doing some theory revision right now, obviously he's decided to give them a bit of practical.'

'Cool,' Jensen said softly.

Cynic's dragon view swept over the wall, and a group of black-clad archers could be seen at the top.

'And on the wall?' Cynic said.

Those are mine, Meredith said into their heads. *They are fourth year Energy Work students, who have been doing some chi bow in the last three weeks.*

One of the archers on the wall grinned up at Cynic and waved, and a few of the watching novices chuckled.

'Oh, that's my fourth year mentor, Enrico Sentoza,' one of the students said.

'Hi Frannie!' Enrico called up to Cynic. 'I hear you're watching!'

'Hi Rico!' the student called back to Gold.

'Heads up!' Meredith said sharply, and the student turned back, nocking his bow. 'Incoming!'

The fifty or so demons riding the fliers landed down the hill from the waiting Wudang students, who drew their weapons. Most held swords, but a few carried different weapons of the arts, including poleaxes and staves. The demons dismounted from the fliers, who pulled themselves back into the air and swept towards the students on the wall.

The archers on the wall loosed arrows at the flying demons. Each arrow had a glowing ball of chi on the point which made the demons explode on contact.

The ground-based demons advanced swiftly on the Wudang students and they hit each other with an audible clash of weapons. Liu moved amongst the students, giving direction and occasionally assisting them as they battled the demons. The students didn't have much difficulty, outclassing the demons easily.

The fliers swooped over the wall, attempting to rake their claws over the archers, but with each swoop the archers took out about ten of them without being touched themselves. Another group of students ran into the bastion behind the wall and attacked the fliers with blasts of glowing golden chi energy.

'This is a walkover,' Cynic said. 'I wonder why they bothered.'

A student appeared in the doorway of the mess hall. 'I got lost! Is this where we're supposed to be?'

Gold turned and saw that the student was a demon, dressed as a student of the academy. The demon must have been at least level seventy, easily able to destroy Gold.

Help, Master Liu, he said. *The prince is here at the mess hall, and it's way too big for me to take.*

Gold faced the demon. 'Get back, kids, that's a big demon.' He generated a large ball of chi and prepared to do his best to hold the demon off until someone skilled enough to destroy it turned up.

'Stop right there,' Xuan Wu said from the doorway behind the demon. He was wearing the same black Mountain uniform as the students, armed with a sword in each hand, his long hair loose from its tie.

The demon hesitated, looking at the Dark Lord, then dropped his head and disappeared.

Xuan Wu disappeared as well.

'Was that him?' Jensen asked with awe.

'Oh!' Cynic said. 'Look!' She relayed the image for them.

Xuan Wu appeared on the wall among the archers, still with a sword in each hand. He leapt from the top of the wall, somersaulted, and landed lightly on the ground twenty metres below. He swept through the demons, moving so fast that he was a black blur of swords and flying hair. The students stopped, watching with bewilderment as he destroyed the demons with ease. He grabbed the last demon by the scruff of the neck before it could escape and again disappeared.

Shut the gates, battle stations, he said to everybody. *The prince is still here. Gold, connect with the structure, and find the demon. Energy workers, trace it! I want this demon found! Celestials Liu, Mak, Park, Wong, to Purple Mist. Let's see what this one will tell us.*

The bells on the towers in the corner of the academy sounded again, this time in a higher pitch: battle stations.

Master Liu strode into the mess hall. 'I will watch them. You run the trace.'

Gold checked; it really was Master Liu. He quickly took True Form and flew outside to the stone-paved square in the centre of the barracks area. He made his stone form paper-thin and spread over the paving, sending his awareness through all of Wudangshan, seeking the demon prince.

Gold did a lightning-fast inventory of all the staff and students present in Wudangshan, comparing every person present with the list he held internally. Five people were unaccounted for, and Gold quickly sent the information about them to Xuan Wu.

Good job, Gold, I am sending Masters to check these five people. Gold watched as the Masters approached each person in turn. None of them was the demon prince.

It appears to have taken off, Gold said.

Do a sweep to confirm. Check the seals, the Dark Lord said.

Gold lifted himself up off the paving and took True Form again. He quickly rose and moved his consciousness through the Wudangshan complex, meeting up with the minds of other Shen as he did. The demon prince was nowhere to be seen. Surprisingly, the academy's seals appeared to be intact; the demon must have somehow not registered on them.

Gone, my Lord.

Come to Purple Mist and assist in the interrogation of this demon.

Gold took human form and walked to the south-west corner of the complex, to the Hall of Purple Mist. The hall had been erected two thousand years previously, and was one of the oldest buildings in the complex. It was a perfect rectangular shape, with traditional nail-less pillar and beam construction, its upward-sweeping roof tiled with black tiles.

When Gold entered the hall, a number of the Celestial Masters, all in their black uniforms, were gathered around the Dark Lord and the demon. The demon was still in True Form, black and scaly with bulging eyes and tusks at the corner of its mouth; but its face was limp and slack-jawed.

'Good, you're here, Gold,' the Dark Lord said. 'Record these proceedings, we may need to review them later.'

'Has it turned?' one of the Celestial Masters said.

'No,' Xuan Wu said. 'I'm holding it bound.' He stood in front of it. 'What number are you?'

'Three nine five,' the demon said.

'Third generation this big. Disturbing,' one of the Masters said. 'The king is losing his touch, allowing creatures like this to be spawned without his direct control.'

'The king always has his reasons, even if they aren't apparent at the outset,' Xuan Wu said, still studying the demon. He focused on it. 'What is the name of your master?'

The demon opened its mouth, then its eyes went wide and it exploded in a cloud of black foul-smelling demon essence all over everybody present.

'Dammit!' Xuan Wu said.

'Very disturbing!' one of the Masters said. 'Not just large, but with a self-destruct mechanism as well!'

'Gold,' Xuan Wu said, without turning. 'I want this data link up between Heaven and the Earthly as quickly as you can make it. Five of the students on the database here weren't on the one in my office. A demon prince tried to take advantage of our ignorance and insinuate himself into the school. I need my information up to date.' He strode out of the building towards his private wing.

'Yes, sir,' Gold said, his voice small.

As Gold returned to the barracks to collect the students for the remainder of the evaluation, Michelle's singing soared over the compound, accompanied by the grand piano in Xuan Wu's quarters. Gold felt the music try to lift his spirits as he pondered how he would be able to create a data link between the Celestial and the Earthly realm. He shook his head. He was an expert at the manipulation of stone and energy to produce information, but even this could possibly be beyond him.

Cynic landed on the walkway in front of him. 'That was fun!'

'No it wasn't, the prince tried to take the form of a student and insinuate itself in. The database between Heaven and the Earthly was out of sync. It's a disaster.'

Cynic dropped her head and gazed at Gold with her jade-green eyes. 'It'll be fine. The demons didn't hurt anybody.' She raised her head and changed into human form, this time a slender beautiful young woman wearing a jade-green Tang-style robe. 'So when are you off duty? Want to meet up later?' She smiled seductively. 'Like you said, you owe me some thanks for helping with Lady Michelle's brother.'

Gold hesitated, then, 'Thanks for the offer, lovely lady, but I am in a relationship at the moment, and don't think that such a thing would be proper.'

Cynic stared at him. 'Are you sure you're the Golden Boy? The one I've heard so much about?'

Gold bowed slightly. 'People change, ma'am. I'm sure many of the stories you've heard about me have been grossly exaggerated.'

Cynic's frown deepened. 'Humph. Very well then. Guess I'll go visit with someone else.' She disappeared.

Gold continued back towards the student barracks, thinking of Leo, all alone on the Earthly. He wondered if he could warrant a brief visit home, but then quickly shook his head. He had more pressing matters to attend to; a whole computer system to update for the Dark Lord.

Leo would have to wait.

THE YEAR
1903

THE
SENTENCING

1903
GOLD'S TEA PLANTATION IN FUJIAN.

LORD GOLD!

IT'S— IT'S—

WHAT IS IT?

IT'S— IT'S—

LORD XUAN WU...

EVERYBODY OUT.

'*Wen sui, wen sui, wen wen sui,*' Gold said.

'Rise,' Xuan Wu said. He gestured towards Gold's chair. 'Sit.'

Gold flopped into the chair.

Xuan Wu didn't sit; he clasped his hands behind his back. 'How did you come by this tea plantation?'

'When Number Twelve was ousted, I lifted the deed for this property,' Gold said. 'Nobody else knew that Twelve owned it.'

'Theft,' Xuan Wu said.

Gold raised his hands, palm up. 'The new owner didn't even know that the plantation existed. I prefer to think that I inherited it.'

'Tell me about Robert Fortune,' Xuan Wu said. He sat in one of the chairs and conjured a pot of tea for himself.

'He did a great thing,' Gold said with pride. 'He worked to free our nation from the tyranny of the tea and opium trade.'

'You were aware that the Celestial has forbidden interference in human affairs?'

'If the human asks for assistance, is it interference?'

Xuan Wu poured himself some tea. 'You are very sheltered here in the hills of Fujian. Let me tell you what has been happening elsewhere.'

'Please,' Gold said. 'I would love to hear.'

'After the tea was grown successfully in India, the English no longer required our tea. The trade trickled down to nothing.'

'I know,' Gold moaned. 'I am reduced to selling on the local market. It's very hard, I had to dismiss half my workers. I may lose part of the plantation.' He brightened. 'But that means less opium.'

'True,' Xuan Wu said. 'So the streets of the southern provinces were full of addicts with no supply. The tea merchants were forced to dismiss many of their staff. Suddenly the streets of Guangdong were full of addicts in withdrawal, and workers with no livelihood.'

Gold was silent. He hadn't seen it that way.

'When there is poverty, there is unrest. The obvious ones to blame were the foreigners. Many of the homeless men joined secret societies of martial arts practitioners. They worshipped *me*.'

Gold began to feel that things were once again not going his way.

'They believed that I protected them against the Westerner's weapons,' Xuan Wu said. 'They attacked the foreigners in their enclaves.'

He leaned back and glared at Gold. 'The Dowager Empress supported them. They killed every foreigner they met. Women and children as well.'

'They were freeing our nation,' Gold said. 'I have heard that the foreigners were carving up our country.'

'The Empress fled.' Xuan Wu thumped his fist on the table. 'The foreigners put down the rebellion and the Empress *ran*.' He leaned back and sighed with exasperation. 'The Westerners have taken over. Heavenly Mandate has been removed. The Empress will last no more than a couple of years. Very soon she will poison *her own son* to stop him from taking control when she dies, because she fears that he will bring China the reforms that it so desperately needs. She will set up a three-year-old as Emperor, to keep this country stunted and backwards.'

THE EMPIRE HAS ALREADY FALLEN, GOLD.

Xuan Wu continued. 'You are a very small Shen. You do not know the extent of the suffering that our country is about to encounter. Millions of people will starve to death.'

'I have no vision of the future, my Lord,' Gold said. 'I am too small.'

'Be glad of that. If the tea trade had continued, it is possible that we may have maintained enough control of our economy to lessen this disaster. It is impossible to tell how much the theft of the tea contributed to these catastrophes.'

Gold moaned. 'I helped do this.'

'The Jade Emperor would like to speak with you.' Xuan Wu rose and pulled out a vermilion scroll bound with gold ribbon — an edict from the Jade Emperor.

Gold shot to his feet, then fell to his knees. '*Wen sui, wen sui, wen wen sui.*'

'Present yourself at the Imperial Cell Complex in the Celestial Palace,' Xuan Wu said. 'You are to be held at the mercy of the Jade Emperor.'

'This small Shen is honoured.' Gold rested his forehead on the floor. 'No.'

'I will give you a day to organise your affairs,' Xuan Wu said. 'Do you have any children?'

'No, my Lord,' Gold said without rising. 'But I have three wives.'

'Human?'

'Yes.'

'They will never see you again,' Xuan Wu said without emotion. 'Say your goodbyes. Settle your affairs. I will be acting as Celestial General when next you see me.' His voice softened. 'Rise, Gold.'

'I can understand why you have done this, but the Jade Emperor is furious,' Xuan Wu said. 'You have openly disobeyed an Imperial Edict. You have meddled in human affairs. Be ready, stone, this will be very bad for you.'

꧁꧁꧁꧁꧁꧁꧁꧁꧁꧁꧁꧁꧁꧁꧁

The next day, Gold presented himself to the Imperial Cell Complex. He was placed in a cell usually reserved for the worst Celestial offenders. As he sat down in his cell, he looked around, and spotted a familiar face.

It was Jade, hair and clothes dishevelled. She was sitting in the cell next to his, with her head buried in her knees to hide her tears.

JADE!

!

OH, GOLD!

I AM SO SORRY, GOLD ...

NO ...

IT WASN'T YOUR FAULT. YOU DIDN'T FORCE ME.

WE BOTH THOUGHT WE WERE DOING THE RIGHT THING.

ENOUGH. THE JADE EMPEROR IS WAITING.

Xuan Wu walked through the open doors of the dungeon, with Jade and Gold trailing him. His pace was quick, and he led them through a number of dark twisting passages, lit by small torches on both sides.

Midway through the long walk to the Jade Emperor's audience chamber, Xuan Wu changed his form. He was now in full Celestial Form, with black lacquer armour and the Seven Stars sword on his back.

Jade and Gold followed quietly, Jade visibly quivering with fear. Xuan Wu escorted them into the small audience chamber; obviously they weren't important enough for anything grander. The Jade Emperor appeared small and elderly on his golden throne, and Xuan Wu took position as First Heavenly General at the Jade Emperor's right hand, emotionless and intimidating.

YOUR MAJESTY, THE JADE EMPEROR.

Jade and Gold fell to their knees and touched their foreheads to the floor. '*Wen sui, wen sui, wen wen sui.*'

The Jade Emperor had taken human form for the audience. He watched the two Shen prostrate themselves with amusement.

RISE.

Jade and Gold rose and carefully didn't look into the Emperor's eyes.

'Read the charges,' the Emperor said. He raised a tea cup from a small table next to the throne and sipped the tea.

The guard behind Jade and Gold moved forward to stand next to them. He opened a scroll. 'Princess Jade of the Dragons.'

'This small Shen is present and honoured, Celestial Majesty,' Jade said.

'Golden Boy, child of the Jade Building Block.'

'This small Shen is present and honoured, Celestial Majesty,' Gold said.

'These Shen are charged with interfering in Earthly matters. They aided a Westerner in the theft of one of the Middle Kingdom's greatest treasures. This interference was in direct contravention of an order issued to all Shen by your own Celestial Majesty that Shen were not to interfere in Earthly affairs during this time of unrest.'

'How do you plead?' the Emperor said, returning the teacup to the table.

'Guilty as charged, Celestial Majesty,' Jade whispered.

'Golden Boy?' The Jade Emperor's amused expression didn't shift.

'Guilty as charged, Majesty.'

'No argument, stone?'

'It was a foolish thing to do, Majesty.'

'What shall I do with them, Ah Wu?' the Emperor said without looking at Xuan Wu.

'I'll take them, Majesty,' Xuan Wu said. 'I may have need of their abilities.'

'Oh, come on, Ah Wu,' the Emperor said. He raised his tea cup and swept his long sleeve out of the way. 'You have an army on the Mountain at Wudang, you have the entire Northern Celestial Heavens, and you claim need of these two? I think not.'

'Celestial Majesty,' Xuan Wu said.

'You always were too soft, Ah Wu.'

'My nature is yin, Majesty.'

'That it is. Summon the Azure Dragon of the East,' the Emperor said.

Jade stiffened and Gold squeaked.

Qing Long appeared next to Jade and Gold. He fell to his knees and touched his head to the floor. '*Wen sui, wen sui, wen wen sui.*'

'Rise,' the Emperor said.

Qing Long rose beside Jade and Gold. He glanced at them, his long serene face emotionless.

'These two have offended Heaven,' the Jade Emperor said. 'You want them?'

Qing Long folded his hands into his long sleeves and studied the dragon and stone next to him.

'Are they good for anything?'

'Jade Dragon, list your accomplishments,' the guard said.

'Embroidery, ink painting, pipa, erhu ...' Jade began.

'No!' Qing Long snapped. '*Useful* stuff. Any Earthly qualifications?'

'I can read and write, add and subtract, I know all of the laws and the precepts,' Jade said stiffly.

'Stone of Gold,' the guard said.

'I am a stone. We are renowned for our mathematical abilities. I also know all of the laws and precepts,' Gold said.

Qing Long turned back to the Jade Emperor. 'I'll take them, Majesty.'

'Write out an edict, Ah Wu, and give this worthless pair to Lord Qing Long,' the Jade Emperor said.

'As you wish, Celestial Majesty,' Xuan Wu said.

The Emperor put his teacup carefully on the side table. 'The Jade Girl and the Golden Boy are to serve the Azure Dragon of the East until I decree otherwise. They are both to retain human form,' he glanced at them, '*constantly*, day and night, while they are serving him, unless he permits otherwise.'

Jade and Gold didn't look at each other but they were both clearly completely mortified. Human form, twenty-four hours a day? Eating, sleeping, washing, all of the human inconveniences ... It was worse than being bound in True Form.

The Jade Emperor watched their reactions carefully. 'Concluded. Dismissed.'

Qing Long bowed deeply, his hands still in his sleeves. 'Celestial Majesty.' He beckoned towards the two Shen quivering next to him. 'Come with me. I have a lot of work for you to do.'

Jade and Gold both touched their foreheads to the floor. 'Thank you for your merciful correction of our erroneous ways.'

'Next time I will not be so lenient,' the Jade Emperor said. 'Take this as your final warning, both of you. Next time it will be a very long visit to Hell.'

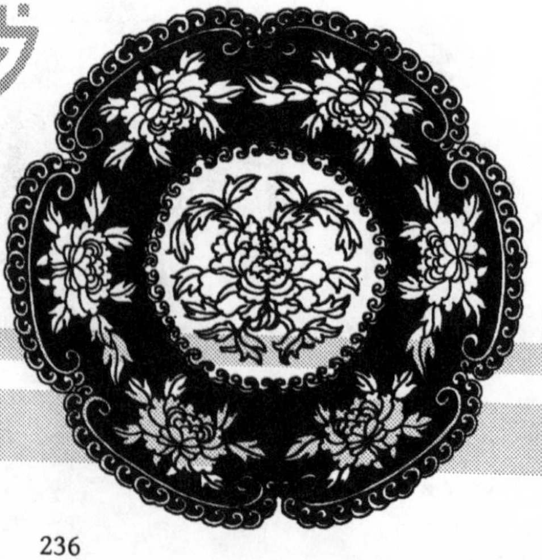

THE YEAR
1999

THE
CELESTIAL
PLANE

꧁꧁꧁꧁꧁꧁꧁꧁꧁꧁꧁꧁꧁꧁꧁꧁

Gold hesitated at the entrance to Thunderbolt's pavilion. The building was a small house on the edge of the Celestial complex, traditionally designed with minimal windows on the outside. Thunderbolt was a highly revered Shen, having fought bravely in the Shang--Zhou Wars even though his True Form had been horribly changed so that he could participate. Gold had never met this powerful spirit, but the Celestial bureaucracy had assured him that Thunderbolt was a great sorcerer and the person to talk to for anything computer-related. Charged with the task of syncing the Dark Lord's Heaven and Earthly databases, Gold could only hope that Thunderbolt would be of help.

Gold tapped nervously on the double wooden doors. He heard footsteps and steeled himself, then the door opened a crack.

'Who is it?' the man on the other side of the door said.

'The Golden Boy, on an errand from the Dark Emperor of the Northern Heavens to request help from Honoured Lord Thunderbolt. I have authority from the Jade Emperor to be here.'

The door opened wider. The man behind it was a young Chinese, appearing thirty years old and only five and a half feet tall, with large metal-rimmed glasses. He wore a black T-shirt and a pair of scruffy jeans. 'Oh yeah, they told me you were coming. Come on in.'

Gold followed the man through a tastefully decorated living room with comfortable Western-style furniture to a workshop. The large room had workbenches along three of the walls, with the fourth wall of double doors opening out to the house's interior courtyard. The courtyard was a simple square area paved on one side, with a ceramic outdoor table and chairs next to a small tidy lawn.

The man who'd let Gold in went to one of the benches. The table was strewn with a variety of circuit boards, a well-worn soldiering iron, and a couple of voltage testers. A wooden board sat in the middle with a stone about the size of someone's fist attached to it by four large nails, and wires from the stone connecting to a number of circuits on the board.

'You might be able to help me with this,' the man said. 'This stone isn't sentient, but it has been on the Celestial for a very long time. It should have some sort of attunement to Celestial Harmony, but I'm getting nothing.'

Gold approached the bench and studied the stone. 'May I touch it?'

'Go right ahead.'

Gold looked from the stone to the man who'd let him in. 'Are you Lord Thunderbolt?'

'Oh, yes, of course, sorry for not introducing myself.' Thunderbolt quickly saluted Gold. 'Thunderbolt.'

'I was expecting someone ...' Gold's voice trailed off.

'I stay in human form most of the time, my True Form tends to scare people,' Thunderbolt said. He gestured towards the stone. 'You're a stone, aren't you? Have a look at this, tell me how much Celestial attunement this thing has? It's supposed to have much more than I'm reading here.'

Gold touched the stone and studied it. 'How long has this stone been on the Celestial?'

'Four hundred years. One of the Tiger's sons sold it to me, cost me a fortune.'

'That's nonsense. If a stone had been on the Celestial that long, I'd expect something from it. This is just an ordinary rock.'

'Thought so.' Thunderbolt took the stone out of the board and threw it into the courtyard. 'I'll have to find myself another.'

'What are you trying to do?' Gold said, studying the circuit board.

'From what I've heard, I'm trying to do the same thing you are. Sentient stone Shen aren't all that eager to act as communication devices, it's too boring. But stones that have been on the Celestial for a long time become attuned to Celestial Harmony, and we may be able to use that attunement to transmit data.'

'Fascinating,' Gold said. He took True Form, made himself the size of the stone that had been on the board, and slotted himself into position. 'Put the wires on, let me see.' He sent his awareness through the wires as Thunderbolt attached them. 'These circuits are extremely elegant! Did you do this?'

'Yup.' Thunderbolt carefully attached the last wire. 'There. Do you see anything?'

'I see what you're trying to do,' Gold said. 'But I can't connect with the stone on the other side of the room.'

Thunderbolt looked back. 'Yes, I have one set up in a similar rig on the other side. At least you can tell it's there, that's a start.'

'I saw it when I walked past, nothing to do with the rig,' Gold said. He pushed more energy through the circuits, seeing them snap shut. 'Something just isn't happening here.'

Thunderbolt grinned ruefully. 'You don't need to tell me that.' His face cleared. 'You wouldn't possibly have some spare time you could help me with this, would you? You can tap into the stone network and get them to help as well, I'm sure they wouldn't mind.'

'Let me see what I can come up with. I've had some experience fiddling with Celestial Harmony myself, I'll go back to the Earthly and do some research. Mind if I take the plans for this with me?'

'Go right ahead,' Thunderbolt said.

Gold disconnected himself from the apparatus and drifted off, taking human form again.

'I thought you weren't allowed to take True Form,' Thunderbolt said.

'I'm permitted to take True Form at my own discretion when I feel that it's necessary,' Gold said. 'They keep an eye on me, believe me. If I do it too much, the Celestial enforcement people are in touch very quickly.'

'Let me find another Celestial stone, and we can get together and see if we can get this working,' Thunderbolt said.

'I'll keep in touch,' Gold said.

※※※※※※※※※※※※※※※※

Gold returned to the Dark Lord's apartments in the centre of the Jade Emperor's Celestial Palace to screams from Simone and shouts from Michelle. He hesitated outside the door, then steeled himself and went in.

Michelle was clutching the screaming Simone, with what appeared to be vomit down the back of her shirt. She was yelling at Xuan Wu, who did not seem to be making too much of an attempt to defend himself.

'What sort of monster are you to terrify your own child!' Michelle yelled at Xuan Wu. She saw Gold. 'Gold! Find a servant. Simone has soiled herself and me.'

Xuan Wu spread his hands. 'I honestly didn't think she would be so upset, love.'

'Upset!' Michelle screeched. 'You changed into a monster, and took her into a hall full of monsters! Why did you not tell me they would all be in True Form!'

Gold quickly contacted the palace staff, searching for a tame demon servant to help out. Michelle was right; in her terror, Simone had clearly soiled herself and was crying with fear.

'Michelle, she has to get used to it some day,' Xuan Wu said, keeping his tone reasonable. 'She will need to conquer her fear and learn to live with everybody here.'

'Not if I have anything to say about it!' Michelle said. 'Gold! Where are those servants?'

'I have some tame demons coming to help us, ma'am,' Gold said, wishing that he could take True Form and shrink to a tiny pebble.

'You're overreacting, love,' Xuan Wu said, his tone still reasonable. 'She's resilient. She'll get over it. Stop making a fuss.'

'I'll show you a fuss!' Michelle said, casting around. She lowered Simone gently to the floor and led her into the bedroom. She returned alone with a small revolver, closed the door behind her, and without hesitation shot Xuan Wu right between the eyes. He fell without flinching and his body disappeared before it hit the floor.

Michelle dropped the gun and returned to the bedroom, collecting Simone in her arms. 'Nobody will scare you any more, Simone. I will keep those horrible things away from you.'

'Daddy was scary, make him stay away,' Simone said into her mother's shoulder, still tearful.

'Daddy will be gone for a couple of days, ma petite, and when he returns he will not be scary, or I will send him away again.' Michelle glanced up at Gold. 'This means that we are stuck here until he returns, doesn't it?'

Gold wanted to shrink even smaller. 'I'm afraid so, ma'am. You'll be much safer here than down on the Earthly without his protection.'

'Well, then I hope I taught him a lesson. What's that expression you people use? "Meditate on his faults."'

'I'm sure you did, ma'am.' There was a tap on the door. 'Here are the servants to help you.'

Michelle opened the door. Two tame demons, appearing as elderly women in black and white servants' uniforms, stood smiling in the doorway.

'Thank you, Gold. I suppose I must manage as best I can now that I am prisoner here by his stupidity. Find me a full-time nanny for Simone, I must practise. And Gold?'

'Ma'am?'

'Pop back down to the Peak and bring me my Playstation?'

Gold bowed. 'Ma'am.'

꒰꒱꒰꒱꒰꒱꒰꒱꒰꒱꒰꒱꒰꒱꒰꒱

Six weeks later, Gold and Thunderbolt had found another

stone that a Celestial was willing to part with — this time it had cost them a great deal of jade and they were assured it would work. Gold sat in True Form on the workbench next to the board as Thunderbolt connected the wires.

Thunderbolt connected the final wire, and attempted to send a signal across the room to the other stone. Nothing happened.

'I hate to think you've spent all this time working on this only to have it not work,' Gold said, watching the circuits as the energy of the Celestial Harmony flowed through them perfectly but with no result.

'I just don't know what's going on,' Thunderbolt said. 'Everybody says this should work. The stones are intensely attuned to Celestial Harmony. They should be able to connect.'

'I can't see anything wrong with it,' Gold said. 'This is so frustrating!'

'Have you found another stone Shen who'd be willing to help us out by sitting in the other board?' Thunderbolt said, pressing the wires harder into the stone.

'I have a couple of people,' Gold said.

'We might have to do that then. I just feel bad about making people act as stones.'

'It's what we are,' Gold said. 'The only thing they're not sure about is being parts in a glorified radio. We stones are very particular about the way we're used by Celestials, and really prefer, if anything, to be put in jewellery and kept as something very precious.'

'Precious is the word,' Thunderbolt growled under his breath. 'Okay, one last try. Stay put, I'm going to take True Form and see if I can't shock this thing into life. Be ready, though, the True Form is quite intense.'

'Go right ahead, I work for the Xuan Wu, and nothing is as ugly as that, and that's his own words.'

Thunderbolt concentrated and took off his glasses, placing them carefully on the bench next to Gold. He grew and spread, and sprouted feathers all over his body. The clothes disappeared, and his face changed to something very much like a bird's, with a large, fearsomely sharp eagle-like beak. He hunched over, then stretched back and huge bird wings shot out of his shoulders, sending a couple of feathers flying. He stood nearly eight feet tall, with greyish brown feathers and a bird-like face, and hands that now appeared to be more like eagle claws.

'Impressive,' Gold said. 'But I don't think you're that scary.'

'Humph,' Thunderbolt said, and clacked his beak. He rested

one clawed hand on the stone set into the board. 'Move back a bit, I'm going to send a shock through it.'

Gold shifted away. Thunderbolt concentrated and the air filled with the smell of ozone. There was a loud crack, and a spark shot from the stone on the bench to the stone on the other side of the room. Both circuit boards blinked into life, the circuits shut, and the connection was established.

'Needed kickstarting,' Thunderbolt said with amusement.

'We still have a long way to go,' Gold said.

Thunderbolt shrank back to his human form. 'I need to replicate this design, and package it into something that's both a little more durable and way more pleasing to the eye. We need to find one attuned stone for each node on the network. We'll also need something that's analogous to bridges and routers on a standard LAN to route the traffic from stone to stone.'

'And most of all, we need to test how it works from Earthly to Celestial,' Gold said.

'Well, let's do that now,' Thunderbolt said. 'Take this board — carefully — down to the Earthly, with the circuit still working, and let's see if the connection survives.'

Gold lifted the circuit board and drifted towards the Earthly plane. He took his time, making sure that the circuits were not rattled. It took him nearly an hour to reach the nearest interface between the Celestial and the Earthly. 'Okay, I'm here.'

'Don't hesitate, take it through,' Thunderbolt said. 'Not too slow, not too fast.'

Gold couldn't take a deep breath but he wished he could. He steeled himself and drifted carefully at a constant speed through the curtain between Earth and Heaven.

When he reached the other side, he floated holding the board. 'Is it still ...?'

Thunderbolt's whoop of triumph in his head answered his question. 'It works!'

Gold nearly dropped the board in excitement.

'Okay, bring it back, carefully, now,' Thunderbolt said. 'Damn, this is exciting! Thanks for your help.'

'My pleasure,' Gold said. 'I just hope the Dark Lord doesn't call for me in the next hour, because I'm taking my time coming back again.'

'I don't think he'll mind when he discovers that he'll finally have data that's up to date.'

Later that evening, Gold went to the Peak apartment to share his excitement with Leo. With the research and building he'd been doing with Thunderbolt, combined with the constant treks carrying data backwards and forwards between Earth and the Mountain, he hadn't spent an evening alone with Leo in a good seven or eight weeks. This was nothing on a geological scale, but he knew that by human terms it was close to neglect, and he felt guilty about it. He hoped that Leo would forgive him.

When he arrived at the Peak apartment, Monica grimaced. 'Master Leo has gone out again, Gold.'

'He's gone out? Where?'

Michelle was sitting on the couch in the living room talking on the phone, she put her hand over the mouthpiece to speak to Gold. 'I became sick of him moping around the house waiting for you,' she said with disdain. 'He's out having fun at that new bar in Lan Kwai Fong — the "Last Hurrah". Do him a favour, and leave him there.'

Gold ducked his head with shame, and Michelle returned to the telephone.

There you are, Gold, come into my office.

'So you are finally getting somewhere,' Xuan Wu said when Gold had explained the breakthrough. 'And we might have you back where you belong, working as my legal advisor, and helping to guard my wife and daughter.'

'Believe me, my Lord, there is nothing more I would rather do. We have made a connection between stones on the Earthly and the Celestial. The prototype is working. Now we need more stones that are attuned to Celestial Harmony, and to make more chassis units to hold them. After that, the rest is a simple matter of installation.'

Michelle burst into the office without knocking. 'Lo Wu! It is incredible!'

'What is, love?'

Michelle's smile was huge. 'The Academy for Performing Arts has finally decided to put on a full-length opera, and I am to star! I am to play Tosca!'

Xuan Wu rose, went around the desk, and held her hands. 'I am very much looking forward to seeing you.'

'Gold, this is wonderful news. It will be the first full-length that I have performed in, since ... I don't remember how long! It will be a triumph.' She returned her attention to Xuan Wu. 'I will be helping to produce it, and it will be staged in only six months! We will have to work so hard!' She jiggled with excitement. 'And! My father has completed his chemotherapy, and the tumours in his ear have become smaller. Now they will do a six-month course of radiotherapy, and at the end of that, he may be free of the cancer.' She released Xuan Wu and jumped in a circle, clapping her hands. 'It is so wonderful! All of it!'

Xuan Wu glanced at Gold. 'Make this connection work, Stone, because very soon all of us are going to be spending a lot of our time minding Simone and guarding Michelle.'

'As soon as I find some more stones, it will be done, my Lord.'

Three weeks later, Gold arrived at the Peak apartment at one pm to interchange the data between the Mountain and Peak databases. The database system was relatively new, only a year old, and the staff of the Mountain had quickly come to appreciate its benefits and had asked for a variety of supplementary information to be stored in its matrix. The database kept growing, and the interchanges took an increasing amount of time to complete. It would soon reach the stage where he wouldn't be able to keep up. He just needed to find those damn stones.

He entered the living room; Monica was in the kitchen, and Leo and Michelle were out — he winced, he hadn't seen Leo since Michelle had told him about the Hurrah. Xuan Wu was with little Simone in the martial arts training room.

Curious, Gold went to the door of the training room and watched the father and daughter together. Xuan Wu was teaching Simone, who was only about a year and a half old, a Chen tai chi set; her hazel eyes were wide and her mouth fixed in concentration as she performed a graceful 'Part the Horse's Mane'.

'Very good, now step back, like Daddy ...' Xuan Wu performed the move for her, and Simone mimicked him. 'Perfect. Do you think that's enough for the day?'

'Can we go through it one more time, Daddy?' Simone said, her little face still fierce with concentration.

'You sure you're not too tired?'

Simone shook her head. 'I'm having fun.' She grinned up at Xuan Wu. ''Cause I'm with you.'

Xuan Wu crouched to speak to Simone. 'And I'm having fun 'cause I'm with you. Now, one more time, and then you should go do something else.'

'Okay, Daddy,' Simone said, and moved into the start position.

Gold turned to go into the office but stopped when the front door opened and Leo and Michelle came in. Michelle poked her head through the kitchen door. 'Where is he, Monica?'

'Training room, ma'am,' Monica said from inside the kitchen.

Gold ducked into the office, leaving the door open, and changed to True Form — a tiny stone — ready to begin the data transfer. He had to do the transfer in True Form, but incidentally he could also see the rest of the household with his inner eye.

Michelle went into the training room, Leo trailing behind.

'Lo Wu! We were attacked, and Leo was magnificent! He destroyed them completely!' Michelle said with triumph.

'I wasn't that great, ma'am,' Leo said, sounding deeply embarrassed.

'And how is my little Simone?' Michelle said, scooping Simone up into her arms.

'Hello Mummy!' Simone said, and kissed Michelle loudly on the cheek. 'Me and Daddy have been doing koo foo!' She looked at Leo. 'Did you get some bad people?'

Michelle spun Simone. 'Yes! We had some bad people, but Leo made them all disappear, because Leo is fantastic!'

Simone nodded, her little face serious. 'I know. Leo is really good.'

'My turn to spend time with Simone,' Michelle said.

'Yes, I need to review some figures,' Xuan Wu said ruefully. 'Then we will have dinner together.'

'Would you like to play with me?' Michelle asked Simone.

'Only if Leo plays too,' Simone said, cheeky.

'I think that can be arranged,' Leo said.

They went into the television room together, and Xuan Wu entered the office.

'What happened, my Lord? Was it another demon attack?'

'Yes. Michelle had a meeting at the Academy for Performing Arts. Leo was magnificent; he fended off three level thirty humanoid demons without injury.'

'That's very impressive, sir.'

'He is coming along, I am most pleased with his progress. Now. Your progress leaves very much to be desired. What is the hold up? I really cannot afford to have you spending all your time acting as a courier between the Mountain and the Earthly! Leo may need your assistance guarding.'

'We have the circuitry all ready, my Lord. Everything is in

place. What we are lacking, though, is enough stones with Celestial attunement. Those who own them want extremely high prices for them — sometimes the equivalent weight in fine Celestial jade —'

'That's ridiculous,' Xuan Wu said. 'A non-precious Celestial stone in trade for jade? Tell me who these people are, and I will deal with them.'

'If you become involved, people might refuse to provide them at all,' Gold said. 'Please, give me a little more time to work something out.'

Xuan Wu's eyes unfocused for a moment, then he snapped back. 'Go to the Undersea Palace of the Azure Dragon of the East. He says he may be able to help you.'

Gold hesitated, then he said in a small voice, 'Qing Long?'

'He says you have thirty minutes to get there, otherwise the offer — whatever it is — is off. Move yourself, stone.'

'My Lord,' Gold squeaked.

Gold took human form and drifted to the sea bottom outside the crystal palace of the Azure Dragon of the East. A few dragons grinned menacingly at him as he made his way — with some difficulty in human form — to the main gate. The gates opened for him and he moved from water to air and entered the Grand Audience Hall.

The Azure Dragon was in True Form, stretched out on the cobalt-blue floor tiles in front of his throne. He opened one eye when Gold approached, then lazily pulled himself to his feet. He looked around. 'Where is the Jade Girl?'

'She is busy attending to the Dark Lord's accounting procedures,' Gold said. 'This task, of communicating the data between Celestial and Earthly, has been passed to me.'

Qing Long lowered his massive head to gaze into Gold's eyes. 'Next time you come, you bring the Jade Girl. Understood?'

Gold shrank back slightly. 'Yes, my Lord.'

'Very well.' The Azure Dragon took human form, a tall slim man with long turquoise hair and a grey silk robe embossed with a turquoise scale pattern. He raised one hand and the double doors of the throne room swung open silently. 'I hear from Ah Wu that you need stones.'

'Yes, my Lord. We need stones that have been on the Celestial Plane for at least four hundred years, and that have become attuned to Celestial Harmony.'

The Azure Dragon led Gold down one of the underwater breezeways, and stopped when he heard this. 'Jade? Celestial Jade?'

'No, my Lord, jade short-circuits the mechanism we have built.

Our preferred choice is quartz, but any sort of ordinary rock will do, as long as it's reasonably attuned to Celestial Harmony.'

The Dragon turned back and continued to lead Gold down the hall. 'Interesting. I think I may be able to help you.' He led Gold through a maze of corridors, gradually heading down until they were below the sea floor. A heavily barred gate creaked open before them, and they descended into what had to be the palace basement. Gold peered at the glinting precious metals through some of the barred doors to either side, but the Dragon moved too quickly for him to stop and study them. The Dragon led him to the end of the corridor and opened the bolted door of what was obviously a strongroom.

There were shelves all around the room, and on all of the shelves a variety of stones sat in small bamboo baskets, cushioned with red silk. Gold gasped; many of the stones were large pieces of exceptionally fine Celestial Jade; the room was a fortune house.

The Dragon gestured to one of the lower shelves further in. 'Those are the ordinary stones. Take whatever you need.'

Gold crouched to see; the stones were about the size of a human fist, and most were comprised of a similar mix as Gold himself; clear quartz with shining bands of gold.

'My Lord, these are absolutely perfect,' Gold said with awe. 'How much do you want, for about six of them?'

'You can have them on two conditions,' the Dragon said.

Gold rose and turned to see Qing Long. 'What conditions are those, my Lord? It is my employer, the Dark Lord, who is the one to make the actual purchase.'

'One: you put nodes for the network in both the Eastern and the Undersea Palaces; and hook them up to my own LAN and my email servers in Japan so that I may have communication between the Earthly and the Celestial as well. No way is Ah Wu having this excellent technology without me getting a part of it. Two: You must absolutely vow to never tell anyone — except those higher in precedence than me, of course — that I have given these stones to you for free. I have a reputation to maintain.'

Gold saluted the Dragon. 'I'm sure those terms are most acceptable, my Lord. When may I collect the stones?'

The Dragon waved one hand airily at the stones and turned away. 'Just take whatever you need. Since you don't need any jade, leave the jade here. You can have as many of these stones as you like. Just don't tell anyone that I did this for you.'

Gold fell to one knee and saluted the Dragon again. 'I thank you, my Lord.'

The Dragon turned back. 'Oh, cut it out, take the stones, and get lost. I thought I got rid of you a while ago.' His turquoise eyes focused heavily on Gold. 'Just make sure to bring the Jade Girl with you if you are ever ordered to visit me again.'

'Certainly, my Lord.'

THE YEAR
1969

QING LONG
WORKS
PEOPLE HARD

1969
SOMEWHERE IN THE PALACE OF QING LONG, THE DRAGON, LORD OF THE EAST.

HEAVENS, I'M SO TIRED...

I'M STUCK IN THIS FORM, AND I REALLY NEED TO TAKE A BATH.

FLOP

YOU ALL RIGHT?

I'LL LIVE, I HAVEN'T SLEPT IN DAYS.

IF WE'RE LUCKY, LORD QING LONG WILL WORK US TO DEATH.

HELL WOULD BE TEN TIMES BETTER THAN THIS.

FLOP

GOLD...

YOU EVER CONSIDERED SUICIDE?

YOU TOO, EH?

WE'D JUST SPEND A FEW YEARS IN HELL AND THEN END UP BACK HERE WITH OUR SENTENCES EXTENDED. COMPLETE WASTE OF TIME.

HELL WOULD BE A *HOLIDAY* COMPARED TO THIS.

'I had to go through every single contract in his records room. Every single one. Looking for loopholes. Some of them are more than five hundred years old.' Gold stretched and his joints cracked. 'It took me three weeks. I had to sleep on the floor in there. I ache all over. I *hate* being human.'

Jade threw the covers off and staggered to Gold's bunk. Before he could protest she sat next to him on the bed, lifted his plain white cotton shirt, and rubbed his back.

Gold relaxed. 'Thanks, Jade.'

'Nothing more,' she said. 'Friends.'

'Frankly, I'm too exhausted to be interested, anyway.'

'Me too. It's been ages.'

'How long have we been working for Lord Qing Long?'

'Must be close on seventy years,' Jade said with a sigh. 'We've served him well. We perform our duties diligently and without complaint. When will we be freed?'

'When the Celestial Majesty wills it, and not before,' Gold said. 'I'm really past caring anyway. My human form is aging. I didn't know that I could die of old age in this form. It will be an interesting experience.'

'How long do humans live here on the Celestial Plane? That never occurred to me. I thought the wrinkles were from overwork. I'm getting *old*?'

'I think humans live about twice as long on the Celestial Plane,' Gold said. 'Some of them have a name for it. "Shangri-La". I don't know about stones or dragons, but we both seem to be growing old.'

Jade stopped rubbing Gold's back and returned to her own bunk. Gold hoisted himself with effort, fell to sit next to her, and massaged her shoulders. She stretched her neck beneath his hands. 'Thanks.'

'I've seen some of the other poor workers here, the tame demons particularly, and compared to them our working conditions are luxurious. At least Qing Long allows us to sleep.'

'I know,' Jade said. 'I suppose we'll stay here serving Lord Qing Long until we die as humans.'

Gold returned to flop on his bed again. 'It's all the same to me.'

Jade fell back onto her pillow. 'Me too.'

'At least I have your friendship,' Gold said into his pillow. 'I don't know what I'd do without you to talk to, Jade. I really appreciate it.'

'I feel the same way, my friend,' Jade said, but Gold was already asleep.

'Why do you drag those two little Shen around with you everywhere you go?' the Red Phoenix of the South said. She banged her tile on the table, and the colours in the scarlet fabric of her robe rippled. 'Pung.'

'Shit,' the White Tiger said. 'Yeah, Ah Qing, there's no shortage of servants here. There's nothing for them to do while you're visiting. Why the hell don't you just leave them in the East?'

Qing Long glanced at Jade and Gold who knelt to one side watching the game without interest. 'Aren't they decorative, though? So pretty. And I love the way people react when they discover who they are.'

Xuan Wu lifted a tile from the wall and checked it. He slammed it into the discard at the centre of the table, making the other tiles rattle.

'They look awful,' the Phoenix said. 'What have you been doing to them?'

'They're just soft,' Qing Long said. 'A proper day's work is a new experience for both of them.'

'You'd better be sure her father isn't too upset,' the White Tiger said.

Qing Long raised a tile from the wall and waved it airily. 'Frankly I don't think the Dragon King is even aware of her existence. She's number eighty something, a long way down the list.' He slammed the tile onto the table. 'Damn.'

Jade sagged slightly over her knees.

'Pung,' the Phoenix said, and snatched the tile Qing Long had just discarded.

The Tiger groaned.

The Phoenix shuffled her tiles, her face alight with grim satisfaction. She pulled one tile out of the group and put it into the discard.

'Sik,' Xuan Wu said, and flipped his tiles so that the others could see them.

All three of the other Shen groaned and tipped their tiles over.

'Another round,' Xuan Wu said.

'I'd rather hear about the West,' the Phoenix said. She opened the drawer in the table and counted her cash, then handed Xuan Wu a gold coin. 'You've reported to the Celestial. Tell us about it.'

'Yeah, I'd like to know what happened as well,' the Tiger said. He handed Xuan Wu three gold coins. 'You've been gone an awful long time, Ah Wu, was it really worth it?'

'It was worth it,' Xuan Wu said. 'Let's sit beside the pool, I'll tell you about it in True Form while I have a swim. I wasn't able to take True Form nearly as much as I would have liked in England, and I'm using every opportunity.'

'My Lord,' the Phoenix said.

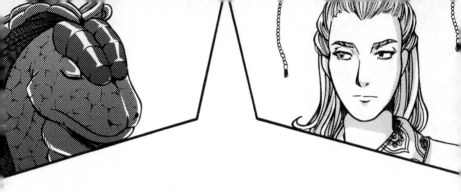

They rose and sat at a table near the pool bar. The demon from the bar quickly brought drinks for them.

Xuan Wu changed to True Form; the black serpent and turtle. The two reptiles separated and the turtle slid into the pool.

'You'd live in that pool if you had the chance,' the Tiger growled. He took tiger form and flopped to lie sideways. He stretched, sheathing and unsheathing his claws.

The Phoenix and Dragon both remained in human form and sat at the table.

The Serpent stretched out on the warm pavers. 'I'd been watching England for a while. I went there to learn two things: one, how long I could stay so far from my Centre without suffering unduly. None of us had tried this, and it was an interesting experiment.'

'But you're the only one really big enough to do it for two years straight,' the Tiger said. 'You spent five years there, and only came back twice.'

'I proved that it can be done. The second thing I wanted to learn was the impact of the changes in society that have been happening the last few years. It was most enlightening.'

'Tell us,' the Phoenix said. 'What did you learn? Did you have much difficulty living as one of them?'

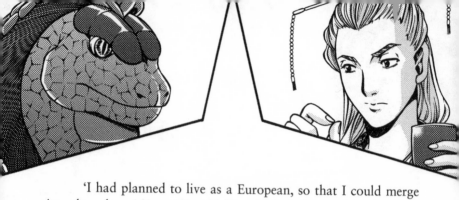

'I had planned to live as a European, so that I could merge into the culture,' Xuan Wu said. 'I couldn't do it. I couldn't hold the shape for long stretches. Eventually I had to take my usual human form.' The Serpent raised its head slightly. 'I experienced racism for the first time in my history. It was most unpleasant. That was the worst part about being there.'

The Tiger chuckled. 'Well, you're home now, you collected your doctor or degree or whatever that thing was, gathered plenty of information, and the Jade Emperor is mightily glad to see you back.'

'All of us are,' the Phoenix said. 'It was extremely worrying to have you so far away. The demons could have attacked us, and it would have taken you days to return.'

'Hell has been quiet, I've been watching,' Xuan Wu said. 'The Jade Emperor wouldn't have sent me if we thought there was any danger. With modern transport the travelling time is only hours, now, in human form. The world is shrinking. We may even begin to see powerful demons and Shen from other Centres come and visit us in China. The Jade Emperor and I wanted to see what was happening in Europe. I may visit America next. And it was a PhD, a Doctorate in Philosophy, and you can call me *Doctor* John Chen, now.'

'Doctor Serpent,' Qing Long said under his breath. The Serpent fixed its small black eyes onto him and he looked away.

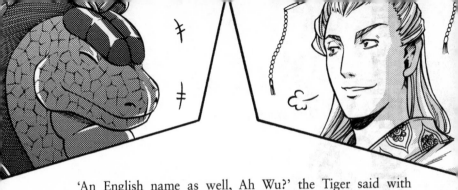

'An English name as well, Ah Wu?' the Tiger said with disbelief. 'Turncoat. Did you meet any Western Shen? What did they have to say when they saw you?'

'Now there's a strange thing.' The Serpent coiled its body and raised its head. 'I did not encounter a single Western Shen the entire time I was there. Demons, yes. Western demons are extremely interesting. In many ways similar to ours; in many ways different. But Shen; no.'

'Did you see any of those new people in London? The ones we've heard about?' the Phoenix said.

'Hippies,' Xuan Wu said. 'I joined a commune for a while during semester break. They are searching for the Tao. They are following the Hindu and Buddhist scriptures, they have gurus. They are regarded as highly fanatical and dangerous. Because they search for the Tao.'

The Tiger chuckled.

'One of the gurus tried to show me the error of my ways, and put me onto the correct path towards Enlightenment,' Xuan Wu said with amusement. 'Apparently knowing some Chinese Taoism is a great help in my search for the True Way.'

The Tiger laughed, his feline vocal chords making his voice a throaty growl. 'I'm sure you were suitably humble and attempted to learn from the sage. And the verdict was?'

'He said with exasperation that I would never get there.'

THE YEAR
1999

HONG KONG

꿹꿹꿹꿹꿹꿹꿹꿹꿹꿹꿹꿹꿹꿹꿹꿹꿹꿹

How far away from the Peak are you, Gold?
About half an hour, my Lord.
Good. I've decided to post you as an extra guard when Leo collects Michelle's parents from the airport. Take the form of a tiny stone and accompany them.
My Lord.

꿹꿹꿹꿹꿹꿹꿹꿹꿹꿹꿹꿹꿹꿹꿹꿹꿹꿹

Leo parked the Mercedes in the airport car park and he and Michelle worked their way along the walkway towards the terminal. Gold was a tiny pebble in Leo's pocket. The new airport was a very long way from the city, on a huge area of reclaimed land that had once been the island of Chek Lap Kok.

The airport's structure was a series of interconnected arches, all side by side, gleaming white. The walkway leading to the arrivals hall was two storeys high with a loft level containing restaurants and other walkways to the departure levels.

The arrivals hall itself was twenty times the size of the old arrivals hall in Kai Tak; it must have been nearly four hundred metres across. There were two exit gates, one at each end of the long wall, with 'one' and 'two' in large letters next to them. An airplane of the Wright Brothers era hung from the ceiling with a dummy jauntily sitting in it, complete with an aviator's cap and scarf.

'Gate two,' Michelle said, and they took the transparent elevator down to wait. While they were in the elevator alone, Gold floated out of Leo's pocket and took human form again. Leo ignored him.

The hall was the full height of the airport, the curved roof flowing overhead. Michelle looked around. 'It was so pleasant to greet the other performers when they arrived in this airport. It's new, it's clean, it's so bright compared to the old one. It gives them a very good first impression — before we move over to the island and the filthy high-rises.'

Leo didn't reply, he just watched the gate.

A steady flow of people came through the frosted glass double doors; many of them stopping the minute the doors opened and standing stunned in the doorway, obviously confused. A few tourists caused a major traffic jam as they milled around, trying to decide where to go and oblivious to the chaos they were causing behind them.

The way cleared, and Michelle jumped and waved. 'Maman! Papa! Daniel! Here!'

Michelle's parents and brother waved when they saw her. Michelle's mother and father were both significantly shorter than Daniel. Michelle's mother had a youthful face and immaculate hair, and wore a dark blue tailored suit. Michelle's father had a kind, wrinkled face, thin grey hair, and wore a sport jacket and tailored slacks.

Michelle threw herself at her parents and hugged both of them at the same time, jiggling with delight. 'It is so wonderful to have you here!'

Michelle's mother pulled back to touch her cheek. 'It is wonderful to be here.' She looked around. 'Where is the little one?' She saw Gold, and moved closer to whisper to Michelle. 'Is that your husband? He looks so young.'

Michelle's father shook Leo's hand. 'Leo, my friend, good to see you.' He turned to Gold and held his hand out. 'And you are John?'

Gold shook Michelle's father's hand. 'No, Mr Chen is back at the Peak, he stayed behind with Simone so that there would be room in the car for all of you. I'm Gold, Mr and Mrs Chen's lawyer. I'll see you to the car, then take a taxi back to the Peak.'

Michelle approached with one arm around Daniel and one around her mother. 'I am so glad you are well again, Papa! Yes, this is Gold, my husband keeps him around to do computer things and carry messages. Leo.' She gestured towards the luggage trolleys. 'Can you help us with the bags, dear Leo? My father is still weak.'

'I am not weak!' Michelle's father said, moving purposefully to take command of one of the trolleys. 'I am perfectly fine!'

Daniel shrugged and rolled his eyes. 'He hasn't changed, Mimi.'

Michelle hugged her father with one arm. 'And I am very glad he hasn't.'

※※※※※※※※※※※※※※※※

When they returned to the apartment, Simone was in the living room with Xuan Wu, clutching his hand, her little face stiff with nervousness. She cringed slightly as her grandparents and uncle entered, then released her father's hand and ran to her mother, raising her arms to be held.

Michelle picked Simone up with difficulty and sat on the couch, putting Simone into her lap. She spoke into Simone's ear. 'This is your grand-père and your grand-maman, and you remember Uncle Daniel?'

Simone stared at her relatives, wide-eyed.

Michelle's mother gently approached Simone and took her hand. 'Hello, little Simone. You have the same name as my mother, your great-grandmother, you know that? And she was as beautiful as you are.'

Simone hesitated a moment, studying her grandmother, then said, 'You smell nice.'

Everybody laughed at that, and Simone buried her face in her mother's shoulder.

'I agree with you,' Michelle's father said. 'You can call me Victor, don't call me Grandpapa, I'm not old enough for that yet.'

Simone nodded, serious. 'I don't think you're old enough yet, either.' She turned to study Michelle's mother. 'Are you my Lo Poh?'

'Wai Poh,' Xuan Wu said.

Simone wriggled free of her mother's lap and stood. She bowed to her grandmother and said, 'Wai Poh.' Then she bowed to her grandfather and said, 'Grandfather Victor.' She turned to Daniel. 'Uncle.'

'Did you teach her that?' Michelle demanded of Xuan Wu.

'No, I didn't,' he said with awe. 'And I have no idea where she picked that up.'

'Aunty Jade has been teaching me the right way to talk to elders,' Simone said. 'So I'm not scared next time I talk to the Jade Emperor.'

'I'm not your Chinese grandmother, so you don't need to call me a Chinese name,' Michelle's mother said. 'You can call me Grandma Violetta, if you like.'

'Violetta is a flower, right?' Simone said.

Violetta nodded.

'You smell like flowers. Your name suits you,' Simone said. She approached Violetta and raised her arms for a hug. 'Hello, Grandma Violetta.'

Violetta hugged Simone, her face warm with pleasure. 'Your daughter is as delightful as you are, Michelle.'

'And as delightful as you are, Maman.'

Victor went to Xuan Wu and held out his hand. 'Pleasure to meet you, John. Michelle has told me a lot about you.'

Xuan Wu shot a nervous look at Michelle as he shook his father-in-law's hand. He turned back to Victor and bowed his head slightly. 'Likewise. I am honoured to meet you.'

Violetta released Simone and strode to Xuan Wu and enveloped him in a huge hug. 'And you are my new son. I am so lucky, to have two such strong tall sons.'

Xuan Wu went stiff with shock at the embrace, then patted Violetta's back lightly. 'Thank you.'

'Well!' Michelle said. 'Let me show you all where you are staying. Then, if you are hungry at all, we have dinner ready for you.'

'Whatever's cooking in there smells as good as something that Reid would make,' Victor said jovially.

'Monica, my housekeeper is a treasure, Reid taught her everything,' Michelle said. She gestured. 'Come this way, I will show you your rooms.'

🀫🀫🀫🀫🀫🀫🀫🀫🀫🀫🀫🀫🀫🀫

Gold followed Leo to his room. 'Can we talk?'

Leo studied Gold for a moment, then held his door open. Gold sat on the couch and, after a moment's hesitation, Leo sat next to him.

'I'm not seeing someone else, if that's what you're thinking,' Gold said.

Leo carefully looked at Gold again, then relaxed.

'I've been spending all of my time transporting the database backwards and forwards between here and the Mountain. We have to keep the data up to date. I've been doing it every day. When I'm not doing that, I'm working on getting some sort of connection established so that we can synchronise the data and free me up.'

'And this is taking all your time?'

'Pretty much.'

'What about your days off? We haven't spent a weekend together in forever, man.'

'I don't get them any more.'

'That's not right. Mr Chen wouldn't do that to anybody.'

'I'm doing it to myself. The data needs to be kept synchronised.' Gold sighed. 'It's exhausting.'

'Isn't there someone else who could help you?'

'No.'

'So when do you think you'll have this link thing done?'

'We'll be installing it in about two weeks.'

265

'And then you'll be free?'

'Leo ...' Gold's voice trailed off, and he rallied. 'Leo, I think we should cool it for a while. I can't have a proper relationship with anybody, I can't give you the attention you deserve, because I'm not free. I'm Xuan Wu's slave, his bonded servant, and if he decided to move, I would have to move with him, with or without you. I cannot give myself one hundred percent to anybody. It's not fair on you.'

Leo relaxed. 'I was thinking the same thing. Maybe we should cool it off for a while.'

'Go meet some humans, Leo, you deserve better than a Shen who isn't even free to commit to you.'

'And you shouldn't be spending your time with someone who's completely smitten with someone else. It's not fair to you.'

Gold pulled Leo into a quick hug. 'But best friends still, I hope.'

Leo clutched Gold. 'Absolutely. And you make sure to take some time off, and spend it with me, man, especially when you're finished with this computer thing. I miss you.'

'I miss you too,' Gold said into his shoulder. 'I have to go, I'm exhausted.'

'I understand.' Leo pulled back and smiled at Gold. 'But this weekend, you're taking a couple of hours off and beating me at Star Destiny Fortune.'

'It's a date,' Gold said. He rose. 'Take it easy, Leo, I'll see you on the weekend.'

'Take care, Gold.'

Gold presented himself to Xuan Wu in the office before departing. 'By your leave, my Lord.'

Michelle came in. 'Simone loves them, and they love you. This is working out so well!' She saw Gold. 'Gold, please ask Jade to call me and tell me how the preparations for Simone's birthday party are proceeding? I would like to know.'

Jade, please call Lady Michelle about the birthday party preparations.

Oh, look who's here, Mister I'm-Not-Around Stone.

Jade, Xuan Wu broke in, *Gold is working twelve hours a day, seven days a week keeping the data synchronised. Would you like to assist him?*

266

Sorry, my Lord, Jade said, sounding chagrined. *I will call in a moment.*

'We have a busy couple of weeks,' Michelle said. 'My parents here, Simone's birthday party tomorrow, the opening of Tosca in three days. It is wonderful!'

'How is Daniel liking Paris?' Xuan Wu said.

'That is the best news of all. He is engaged to a wonderful young woman he has met there. They have been living together for half a year now, and he says he has eyes for no one else. He is looking forward to starting a family with her. The wedding is in three months, and we are invited.'

'In Paris?' Xuan Wu said, grim.

'Yes of course in Paris!'

'I may not be able to travel that far.'

'Well, you will need to find a way, because there is nothing I would like to see more than my brother in a happy relationship with a good woman.'

'I will see what I can do.'

Monica poked her head in the door. 'Dinner is ready, ma'am.'

'Thank you, Monica,' Michelle said. 'Will you stay for dinner, Gold?'

'It would not be right for me to encroach on your family time, ma'am,' Gold said with a small bow. 'But I will certainly be here for Simone's party tomorrow.'

Michelle's smile widened. 'It will be so much fun.'

'Dismissed, Gold,' Xuan Wu said, pulling himself out of his office chair.

'And do not disappear in front of my family,' Michelle warned. 'Go out the front door like a normal person.'

'Yes, ma'am.'

The phone rang, and Michelle answered it. 'Quickly, Jade, dinner is served. Is everything prepared?'

Gold bowed to Michelle and Xuan Wu and went out.

卍卍卍卍卍卍卍卍卍卍卍卍卍卍卍卍

The birthday party was held at lunchtime the next day in the function room on top of one of the five-star hotels in Admiralty. The tables, each for six, were decorated with pink tablecloths, white ribbons, and white and pink balloons. Simone sat in a high chair at the head table, attended by Monica, Xuan Wu, and Michelle's family. Another table behind was piled high with birthday gifts. Simone sat

267

in her chair, wide-eyed and intimidated, while Monica talked softly in her ear.

Michelle drifted through the crowd, laughing and joking with her friends from the Academy for Performing Arts and the visiting performers for the upcoming *Tosca*. Xuan Wu stood behind her and slightly to one side, silent and wary.

'Fabulous job again, Jade,' Gold said quietly as they stood in the corner of the room together.

'I agree with Xuan Wu that there is insufficient security,' Jade said.

'They are all human. There aren't any Shen here.'

'That's the point. With no Shen here, there is nobody to defend them if the Demon King decides to show.'

'He won't come for this.'

Michelle spread her arms. 'Everybody, please be seated. Lunch will be served in a moment.'

Waiters appeared, bearing Western-style dishes, placing them in front of each guest. Gold studied his plate suspiciously. 'What is this?'

'Leo's is seafood terrine with French bread and lemon mustard mayonnaise,' Jade said smugly.

'You know about Western food?' Gold said. He looked at his own plate; it was a more familiar large mushroom, but stuffed with something orange and unrecognisable.

'Lady Michelle did most of the choosing,' Jade admitted. 'Yours is stuffed mushroom with sweet potato and leek puree. Slice a piece off, and place it on a piece of bread the same way that Leo has with his.'

'It's very good,' Leo said through a mouthful of bread. 'Shame you're vegetarian, Gold.'

Gold sliced his mushroom and put it onto the bread. He took a bite, still suspicious, then was surprised at the burst of combined flavours of sweet yam and tangy mushroom. He grinned through the food. 'It's very good!'

'Of course it is, this is costing about a thousand a head,' Jade said, still smug.

Xuan Wu suddenly shot to his feet, touched Michelle's arm, and strode out the door. *Jade, Gold, Leo with me.*

The three of them quickly rose and hurried around the edge of the room to follow him.

He'd cut off a demon that was attempting to enter the room. It appeared as an ordinary young human dressed in a business suit.

It stopped when it saw Xuan Wu, then grimaced, turned, and walked away. Xuan Wu stood at the door of the room, watching it go, then relaxed. 'It's gone.'

'That was the same one that attempted to enter the Mountain in disguise,' Gold said.

'A demon prince?' Jade said.

'Yes, I recognise it now,' Gold said. He nodded to Xuan Wu. 'It inherited Twelve's holdings when Twelve was destroyed.'

'I know the one you mean,' Xuan Wu said. 'It has been quiet these last hundred years, consolidating its hold over Twelve's empire. Looks like it has decided to take a higher profile. It has chosen the wrong Shen to deal with.'

'It is unbelievably stupid if it thinks it can pick a fight with you,' Jade said with disbelief. 'You are the greatest demon destroyer on any plane, my Lord.'

Xuan Wu turned back to re-enter the room and dropped his head. 'Right now I am not, Jade. I need to return to the Mountain again soon, to rebuild.'

'When, my Lord?' Jade said.

'As soon as Michelle's family depart, and the opera's run is completed. Week after next. I will take Michelle and Simone with me. The demons will learn of Simone's existence soon, they must, and then I will need all my strength. It was just a stroke of luck I sensed this one in time to stop it entering the room and seeing her.'

They went back in. Xuan Wu went to Michelle, whispered in her ear, and sat next to her. He studied his plate suspiciously.

'I think the Dark Lord is having as much trouble with the food as I am,' Gold said as they seated themselves at the table.

'He lived in Europe for a while in the sixties, though,' Jade said. 'Remember him talking about it at the Western Palace, when we were bound to the Dragon?'

'According to Michelle, while he lived in London he taught all his staff to cook Chinese food,' Leo said with amusement. 'His housekeeper in London makes a mean congee.'

'You've been?' Gold said.

'A couple of times, before he became too weak from staying in human form all the time. He has a couple of really nice people looking after his house in London. It's a sweet setup, just a shame he can't go any more.'

Jade sighed and rested her chin on her hand. 'He has sacrificed so much for their love.'

'So has she,' Leo said to his food. 'She had a sweet setup in

Florida too, before she met him.'

After the entrees had been cleared, Michelle rose. She glowed with happiness and smiled broadly at all present. 'Dearest people. Thank you all for coming. Thank you to the cast and crew of *Tosca*, who are here visiting from so many foreign lands. And the local members of the Academy for Performing Arts, who are doing so much to bring Western gifts to the Chinese community — and who have been touring Chinese performances throughout the West. These interchanges can only raise the cultural awareness of both sides!'

There was a smattering of applause from the guests, and she nodded. '*Tosca* opens in two days — Hong Kong's first locally produced full-length Western opera. You have all worked so hard, it will be a triumph. This lunch, in a way, celebrates that.' She turned to her family. 'But for me, it celebrates something much more important. My father has recently fought cancer, and the doctors have informed us that he has won. He is clear of the disease. Bravo, Papa.' There was another smattering of applause. 'My brother, Daniel, has announced his engagement and will be married next year. I cannot wait!' She smiled down at Xuan Wu. 'And in a couple of weeks, I will have been married to John Chen, a man who is full of so much contradiction — so much strength, and so much frustration and joy — for four years. I will celebrate four years with him, and look forward to many more, because he has given me my greatest gift.' She stood behind the high chair, and put her arms gently around Simone's neck, smiling down at her. 'He has given me little Simone, who is the most precious gift that anyone has given me. Five years ago, a journalist asked me what my greatest gift was, and I said it was my voice. Now, I have a much greater gift; that of my family. Mama, Papa, Daniel, Dear Lo Wu, and,' she smiled down at Simone, 'my darling Simone, who is two fabulous years old today. You are all the greatest gifts that life has given me.' She released Simone and returned to stand behind her chair. 'So please, all, celebrate, the greatest gift that life can give us — our families.'

The guests raised their glasses and toasted Michelle amid more applause, and she sat. Xuan Wu took her hand and kissed her, then spoke quietly to her. They shared a small private toast.

Jade wiped her eyes with her napkin, and sighed. 'I am so privileged to have been a part of this. This story will go down in the annals.'

'The stones wanted someone here to transmit the proceedings to everybody on the network,' Gold said with amusement. 'I refused. I said it was invading a private family party.'

'So they don't have someone to eavesdrop?' Jade said.

'No. This is for us. Family only.'

'Hear, hear,' Leo said.

Leo parked on top of the Star Ferry car park, next to City Hall. The car park was only two storeys high, even though it was close to the middle of Central District, a mass of high-rise office towers.

Leo pointed out the landmarks. 'The building with all the large round windows is Jardine House. Across from that on this side is Exchange Square. The new building next to the harbour over there is the International Finance Centre.' He turned and gestured inland. 'The weird looking coat-hanger building in front of us there, is the Hong Kong Bank Building, I should take you inside, all the lifts are glass. Left of that, the tall building with all the X shapes on it, is the China Bank building.'

'You do not need to tell Victor any of this,' Violetta said. 'He knows them all.'

'Did you know, that the Hong Kong Bank Building actually hangs off the eight pillars, two on each corner?' Victor said. 'There are no internal supports, and all the services, including the air conditioning, are in the floors. When you call it a coat hanger, you don't know how correct you are. It's a feat of engineering, to have the glass curtain walls —'

'Enough!' Violetta cut him off. 'Now you've done it, Leo, you've started him talking about architecture.' She linked her arm in Victor's. 'You are retired, now, my love, no more big buildings for you.'

'I've been wanting to come here for a long time, the buildings here —'

'Are spectacular,' Violetta finished for him. 'And we are going to enjoy them as tourists, without making a single scale drawing. All right?'

Victor turned around, pulled out his camera, and took a photo of the HSBC building. 'That was me being a tourist.'

'An architecture tourist,' Violetta said. She turned to Leo. 'If we linger here, we may miss this ferry you talk about!'

'No chance of that, they run continuously,' Leo said.

'That is not what I wanted you to say!' Violetta said.

They walked down the stairs of the car park and across to the Star Ferry terminal. The building was old and low ceilinged, with a concrete plaza in front, covered in rusty green metal roofing. A taxi rank had a long queue of red taxis and a similar long queue of people lining up to wait for them. An elderly woman begged from person to person in the queue, prodding them with her outstretched hand and beseeching them in a high-pitched voice in Cantonese for money.

'They have beggars here?' Violetta said, horrified. 'This place seems so modern and wealthy.'

'They have a pension system, I've heard tales about these beggars being driven home in Mercedes,' Leo said. 'Let's go in.'

Leo handed each of them a few Hong Kong coins to pay the fare and they went through the turnstiles into first class, and up some stairs into the terminal. A light indicated which side the ferry would be coming in; the ferries docked on both sides of the terminal. The walls were painted green on the bottom half and white on the top half. The end of the terminal was a semi-circular wall with windows overlooking the harbour. Plastic chairs were placed around the walls, but most people stood impatiently at the large metal gate blocking the gangway down to the ferry.

A Star Ferry pulled into the wharf, oval-shaped with its lower deck painted green and its upper deck painted white. The people piled out of the ferry the minute the deckhand lowered the gangway. When all the people had left the ferry, the deckhand opened the gate, allowing people to board.

Leo guided everybody onto the ferry, taking the back of one of the wooden bench seats and pushing it so that the seat now faced in the other direction.

Violetta looked around at the open deck with the wooden bench seats. 'This is first class?'

'Second class is the lower deck,' Leo said. 'Next to the engine, so it's very loud, and if it's a bit rough, you'll get wet.'

'Sounds like fun!' Daniel said, leaning his arm over the back of the chair. 'You said it's a short ride?'

Leo indicated towards the front of the ferry, where a separate air-conditioned compartment had windows all along its semi-circular wall. 'You can see the Cultural Centre there. It looks like a big brown ski jump.'

Victor laughed. 'That it does. But it's an elegant design, and I've heard that the acoustics are excellent as a result.'

'Michelle has said similar.'

Violetta shoved Victor. 'Stop working!'

He turned to her, mouth open to protest, then saw that she was laughing and subsided.

The deckhand raised the gangplank and the ferry pulled away from the wharf into the choppy harbour.

'What are those boats, with the funny booms on them?' Victor said, pointing at a barge that was twenty-five metres long and ten wide, with a long steel pipe stuck at an angle from the wheelhouse.

'They're lighters,' Leo said. 'They're everywhere. They carry containers and bundles of cargo from the container ships moored in the harbour to the docks at the shore. A lot of the container boats go to the container terminals, where there's huge modern cranes to move the containers around — but some of the cargo is moved around on these old-fashioned barges.'

'So much seaborne traffic,' Violetta said.

'This is a major port,' Victor said. 'One of the world's largest. I think just about everything that's made in China to go to the West passes through here.'

Daniel turned to Gold. 'John is in import-export, he must have a lot to do with the way goods are transferred. Do you think he can help me do a photo study, comparing the modern container management with the old-fashioned lighters? I'm sure there are some real characters that I could include portraits of, to spice up the story — the human face of traditional cargo management.'

Gold looked to Leo for help. Leo shrugged.

'Um ...' Gold said. 'I don't know how much of Mr Chen's products are shipped by sea, I think they may be carried by truck from the Mainland ...'

'Oh, that would be even better,' Daniel said, becoming excited. 'I could track a container from China where it is loaded, onto the truck, then onto the container ship and to its destination.'

'I'll see what I can do,' Gold said weakly.

'Thank you!'

'Oh, we are docking already,' Violetta said. 'I wish the boat would take us around the harbour rather than directly across.'

'I can organise that for you, if you like,' Leo said. 'There's a Star Ferry that does an evening cruise around the harbour, it's a fun ride.'

'Oh, yes please,' Violetta said, glowing with pleasure.

The deckhand lowered the gangway and they walked across and up the ramp to exit. Behind them a group of people waited impatiently behind the gate blocking them from boarding.

They walked out onto the concourse outside the ferry terminal. Directly in front of them was a bus terminal, full of double-decker buses and smaller sixteen-seater 'public light busses'. To the left, Ocean Terminal jutted into the harbour, a couple of massive cruise ships moored along its length. Star House, an office tower, was across the road from them.

'Star House joins up with Ocean Terminal, and then there's a row of buildings along that street that stretches for a long way, and you can walk inside the full length of them,' Leo said. 'When we come for the *Tosca* performance, we'll park on the roof, the view is great. There's a whole row of expensive apartment blocks and hotels, all joined together with the mall underneath. It's huge.'

'Sounds like fun,' Violetta said. 'And we're going there after we visit Michelle?'

'Absolutely,' Leo said.

The Cultural Centre was on their right, a massive sloping brown building with no external windows. A wide, paved concourse skirted it, edging the harbour, with a few tourist groups and locals wandering around and taking photos of Hong Kong Island on the other side of the water. Leo led them to the edge of the harbour, and let them enjoy the view for a while.

Gold stood next to Leo. 'You're a great tour guide, Leo.'

'I like sharing Hong Kong. It's an amazing place.'

'I'd like to visit the West one day. I've never tried. I wonder if I can go.'

'I can't see any reason why not. When you get this data link thing sorted, go take a vacation somewhere.'

Gold dropped his voice. 'We Shen can't travel far from China, our Centre. I'm a very small Shen, so I don't know how far from China I can travel.'

'Wouldn't Mr Chen be able to help you with that? He's one of the biggest Shen. He was in Florida for a long time.'

'I honestly don't know. I would like to try, though.'

'What if you were to hop on a plane, and it went too far? You wouldn't die or anything, would you?'

'Probably,' Gold said. 'But remember, when we die, we just come back a while later, so it would only be an inconvenience.'

'Death, an inconvenience,' Leo said, and shook his head.

'Come on, you two,' Daniel said, wrapping one arm around each of Leo's and Gold's shoulders. 'We want to see Michelle!'

'This way,' Leo said, leading them towards the Cultural Centre, then he stopped. 'Gold.'

Gold saw them at the same time as Leo. Demons; two of them, looking like Chinese men in their mid-twenties, wearing slacks and polo shirts, fitting in with the other people on the promenade. Gold and Leo shifted so they were between Michelle's family and the demons.

'They won't try anything here, it's too public,' Gold said.

'I know,' Leo said. 'I wonder if they're waiting for us to be somewhere less open.'

'I could contact the Dark ... I could contact Mr Chen and have him come down from the rehearsal,' Gold said.

'What's going on?' Victor said.

'You know we told you that Mr Chen has some enemies among the Triads? Well a couple of them just turned up,' Leo said.

'Oh, how exciting!' Violetta said. 'It's like a crime novel. Which ones are they?'

'It might be better if we just ignore them, and go inside,' Gold said. He turned to guide them into the Cultural Centre. 'This way.'

'Michelle told us that John does martial arts,' Violetta said. 'It's just like a movie! I hope we can see him fight some of these gangsters!'

'I'd prefer you didn't,' Leo said. 'When we're home, though, ask Mr Chen to show you some moves, he has a training room in the apartment where he teaches and practises.'

'Did he know Bruce Lee?' Victor said as they entered the Cultural Centre and crossed the lobby to the lifts.

'Actually, yes, he did,' Gold said.

'Did he *learn* from him?'

Gold hesitated. Lee had been one of the most talented students on the Mountain until he had a huge argument with one of the Masters about the nature of chi energy, and had stormed out.

'I think they were just acquaintances,' Gold said.

'I wonder if he has any photos of them together,' Victor said.

'Michelle's husband just becomes more and more interesting all the time,' Daniel said. 'I might do a photo essay on *him*.'

Gold and Leo shared a horrified look as they entered the lift, then grinned together. Daniel's curiosity had changed direction, but it was still as problematic as ever.

Xuan Wu and Simone were sitting at the back of the room, listening, while Michelle and the chorus practised one of the songs for the opera. When Michelle saw them, she waved, but continued to sing.

'That was absolutely terrible,' the director said, when the cast finished. 'All of you, go away, have some lunch, those of you who have been eating or drinking dairy products *get the hell off them*, and come back in two hours ready to sing instead of sounding like a herd of cattle in heat.' He snapped his folder closed, and headed for the door, stopping in front of Gold's group on the way out. 'I don't know what you think you are doing here, but this is a rehearsal. If you want to see the show, pay for tickets like everybody else.'

'Maurice,' Michelle said behind him, and he rounded on her. 'Maurice,' she said again, and indicated the group. 'This is my husband, John Chen, who as you know is sponsoring most of the opera and has paid for all the costumes and most of the sets. This is my father, Victor LeBlanc, the famous architect; my mother, Violetta, the artist; and my brother Daniel, the award-winning photographer who is considering doing a photo essay on the first full-length Western opera to be shown in Hong Kong — for *Time* magazine.'

The director's menacing expression didn't shift. 'I don't care if they are the royal family of the Sultanate of Brunei. They do not attend rehearsals.' He waved one hand at Michelle. 'Get them out of here.'

'Humph,' Michelle said, and tossed her head. 'You are a despicable little man, and I hate you for the rest of my life.' She took his hands and kissed him on the cheek. 'See you in two hours.'

He kissed her affectionately back. 'See you in two hours, darling.'

'Come with me,' Michelle said to the others. 'We will go next door to the Regent Hotel, they have a delightful lunch buffet in the café there, overlooking the harbour. The view is wonderful, and the food is excellent.'

'Not yum cha?' Daniel said.

'Daniel, you have had yum cha every morning since you arrived, aren't you ready for a change?' Michelle said.

Daniel grinned with mischief. 'Jade and Gold have me addicted to it.' He smiled down at Gold. 'And I've found an excellent Chinese restaurant on the Left Bank that serves fabulous yum cha — you must all come to Paris to visit, and try it.'

'We will be coming for your wedding, silly Daniel,' Michelle said as they walked along the promenade towards the imposing Regent hotel.

They're still there, Leo, Gold said.

Leo nodded. He'd noticed the demons tailing them as well.

They have been hanging around here every day, Xuan Wu said. *This is why I have not left Michelle's side. Is all well at home, Jade?*

Very quiet, my Lord. They are obviously still unaware of Simone's existence, there is no demon presence anywhere nearby. I have taken True Form and scouted the area, it is clear. All the demons are on you.

Michelle jabbed Xuan Wu with her elbow. 'Talk out loud,' she whispered.

He bent and kissed the top of her head. 'Sorry my love. Silly god business.'

Michelle tossed her head and rolled her eyes. 'Silly god business, indeed. Well, I sure hope you'll keep your silly god business out of my Tosca opening night.'

Xuan Wu smiled. 'I promise you it will be the best opening night of your life.'

At that, Gold could not suppress a frown. With all these demons around, he could only hope it would be true.

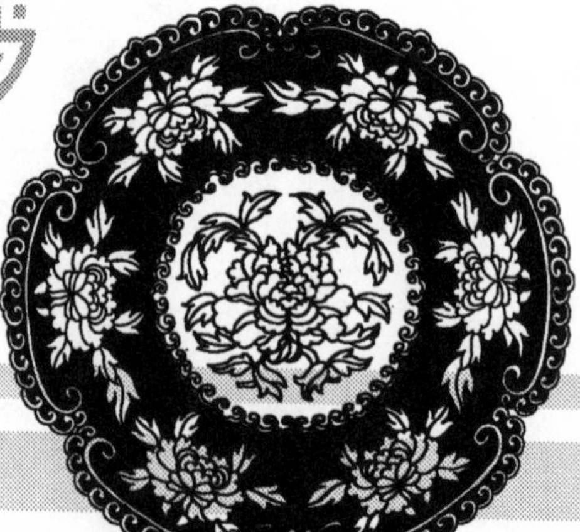

THE YEAR
1992

TO LOVE
A HUMAN

1992

THE UNDERWATER PALACE OF QING LONG, DRAGON LORD OF THE EAST.

BUT WHY ME?

THE WORKINGS OF THE FEMALE HUMAN MIND ARE AS MYSTERIOUS TO ME AS THEY ARE TO YOU. ASK THE TIGER.

IF I WERE TO USE THE TIGER'S ADVICE SHE WOULD LEAVE ME IMMEDIATELY.

THE PHOENIX HAS HAD HUMAN WIVES.

SHE HASN'T TAKEN MALE HUMAN FORM IN MORE THAN FOUR HUNDRED YEARS, AND YOU KNOW IT.

AND DON'T SUGGEST THE JADE EMPEROR, HIS FAMILY IS ABOUT THE MOST DYSFUNCTIONAL ON THE ENTIRE CELESTIAL PLANE.

ONLY YOU COULD SAY THAT AND GET AWAY WITH IT, AH WU.

WHAT ARE YOU DOING HERE?

I FINISHED THESE CONTRACTS AND I WAS RETURNING THEM TO THE RECORDS ROOM, SIR.

!

The Dragon turned to Xuan Wu, his turquoise eyes flashing in the reflected ripples of the water. 'This is the one you should be asking, Ah Wu. It holds the record for seducing the greatest number of Shen on the Celestial. There are very few small Shen anywhere that have not seen the underside of its sheets.'

Xuan Wu studied Gold expressionlessly, his dark eyes piercing. He thought for a while, then appeared to come to a conclusion. 'Lend it to me for a week or so. Let me talk to it.'

The Dragon turned back to Gold. 'Return those scrolls to the Records Room, then present yourself at the Hall of Undersea Delights. If you mention the purpose of this trip to anybody, I will eat you myself.'

Gold bobbed over his knees. 'I understand, My Lord.'

'Go.'

Gold rose, picked up the scrolls, stole a quick glance at Xuan Wu's fierce face, and hurried away.

CELESTIAL MOUNTAIN OF WUDANG-SHAN.

HER NAME IS MICHELLE.

'I met her in Florida. She was singing. I had never heard anything like it.'

'You'd never heard Western opera before?' Gold said.

'Of course I had. But this was different.' Xuan Wu studied his teacup, his face rigid with control. He glanced up and looked into Gold's eyes. 'Her voice went straight through me, like an arrow. Pleasure and pain.'

'That can happen, my Lord.'

'And then I met her at the backstage party, and it was ...' He was obviously lost for words, then gathered himself. 'She is French Canadian. She has courage, and spirit, a spark you don't often see in humans. She lives for her art, and she sings like the Heavens. She has a temper that even I find intimidating.' He sighed. 'She is wonderful.'

Gold poured the tea. 'I think I understand. When you encountered this with other human women, what did you do? What mistakes did you make? Human women are different to Shen, particularly animal Shen like dragons. They must be approached more cautiously.'

'I have never loved a human woman.'

'You are one of the oldest of us all, my Lord. You have been around since the Dawn of Creation; you are North Wind. I have heard that you were already old when humans began to walk the Earth.'

'And I have never loved a human woman.'

Gold poured the tea. 'This one must be exceptional.'

Xuan Wu sighed. 'She is.'

'Well then, let's win her for you.'

'No deception. No use of the fact that I am a Shen. I want to win her as a human man. I want you to help me win her, not by doing what you would do, but help me to avoid the mistakes I could make because she is human and therefore different.' Xuan Wu sagged slightly. 'I do not want to lose her.'

'When she finds out what you really are, you may lose her forever, my Lord. Your True Form is ...' Gold hesitated.

'I am well aware of the fact that my True Form is one of the ugliest in creation,' Xuan Wu said evenly. 'Even without the Serpent, I am truly horrifying.'

'Without the Serpent?'

'I have no idea where it has gone, Gold. I have searched the planet, from pole to pole, and it does not answer the Turtle's calls. Right now I am only Yin Turtle. The Yang Serpent is out there somewhere, hiding.'

'I had not heard about this happening, my Lord.'

'And you will not share it. The residents of Hell must not know about this.'

'I understand. You have my word, I will tell no one. When did this happen?'

'About twenty years ago. Nineteen seventy three.'

'Has this happened before, my Lord?'

Xuan Wu turned his teacup in his long fingers. 'No.'

'That may explain some of the strange weather patterns in the last ten years. The Serpent affects the weather.'

'I am well aware of my own abilities.'

'Apologies, my Lord, you are the only Shen who is two creatures. It must be very difficult for you, being in two pieces with one half gone.'

'You have no idea.'

Gold straightened and changed the subject. 'So. This woman. Tell me what you have done so far, and I will help you to take this further. Is she still in Florida? I don't know if I can travel that far from the Centre, I am very small.'

'She is in Hong Kong doing a concert series. This is the perfect time.'

Gold raised his teacup and smiled up at Xuan Wu. 'Let's win you this exceptional woman.'

Xuan Wu leaned back. 'Good.'

285

HERE. IDENTITY DOCUMENTS, ENOUGH CASH AND A COUPLE OF CREDIT CARDS TO COVER EXPENSES.

GO OVERBOARD WITH THE SPENDING AND I'LL REMOVE AN EQUIVALENT AMOUNT IN GOLD FROM YOUR OWN STONE SELF.

SIR...

'I understand, my Lord, but there is no need,' Gold said. 'Lord Qing Long sent me down here to study Law about ten years ago. I'm a registered barrister both here and on the Mainland, and I already have a small bank account and full identity papers.'

'Really? Useful,' Xuan Wu said. 'Why not accounting? That would be more in line with your talents as a stone.'

'Jade is the accountant. My skills as a stone allow me to connect with devices that are also made of stone. Silicone. Computers.'

'You can hack into networks?'

'No computer system is closed to me. I have been through every major system in the world.'

'It is not honourable to be prying like that.'

'Lord Qing Long doesn't seem to be very bothered about those details, my Lord.'

'Stop calling me that in public. Here I am Mr John Chen. Just "sir" is enough.'

'Sir.'

'As I said, back here at seven. You can come with me to the Cultural Centre, and we'll begin.'

'Sir,' Gold said.

The bag was already in Gold's room when he went in. He went straight into the bathroom and had the longest, hottest bath he'd had in years.

QING LONG'S AUDIENCE HALL.

I AM FINISHED WITH IT, AH QING. IT HAS BEEN EXTREMELY USEFUL.

GOOD. RETURN TO THE HALL OF RECORDS, GOLD.

YES, MY LORD.

STONE.

DO NOT THINK FOR ONE SECOND THAT YOU WILL RECEIVE ANY SPECIAL TREATMENT BECAUSE OF THIS.

AND DO NOT MENTION THIS EPISODE TO ANYBODY, OR IT WILL GO VERY BADLY FOR YOU.

... I UNDERSTAND, MY LORD.

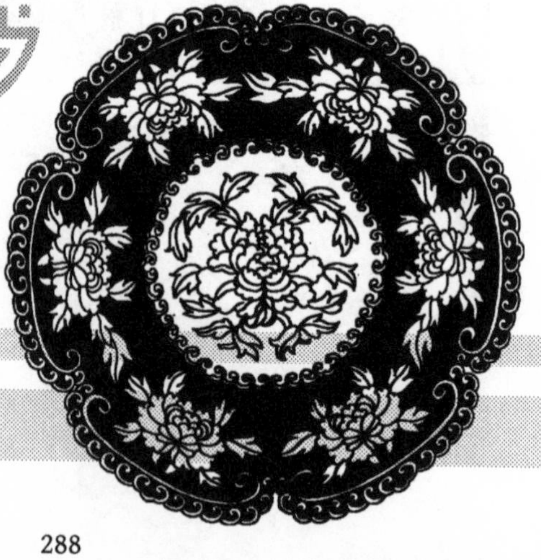

THE YEAR
1999

HONG KONG

The next day they attended the opening night of *Tosca*. They met Michelle in her dressing room, which was overflowing with flowers and costume pieces. She sat at her dressing table with the make-up charts in front of her, putting the finishing touches to her face. Her hair was a high, elaborately designed wig, and her dress was heavy golden velvet with complex silken trim in an Empire style, the skirt gathered beneath her bust and full to the floor.

She turned and smiled when Xuan Wu guided Simone into the dressing room. Simone stopped and stared for a moment, then approached Michelle.

'You are so beautiful, Mummy!' Simone exclaimed.

Michelle's brows furrowed and she glanced up at Xuan Wu. 'What did she say?'

'She said you're beautiful,' Xuan Wu said. 'And I agree with her. That dress is spectacular.'

'We had to have it made to measure,' Michelle said. She saw Gold. 'Is that you, Gold?'

Gold bowed slightly. 'Yes, ma'am, I have taken female human form and I'm pretending to be Simone's mother out in the audience, so they don't suspect that she is yours.'

Michelle turned back to the mirror. 'That is completely unnecessary, we are well protected by Lo Wu and Leo.' She spun back and glared at him. 'Have you been teaching my little Simone Chinese, Gold? Because Lo Wu never speaks Chinese to her.'

Gold and Xuan Wu shared a confused glance, then turned back to Michelle.

'You heard that as Chinese?' Xuan Wu said.

'Yes, Simone said something in Chinese,' Michelle said. She bent to speak closely to Simone. 'You are very clever, my darling.'

'Nobody's been teaching her anything, ma'am,' Gold said. 'Shen just speak our language, Chinese, and we are understood by all.'

'Is she a Shen?' Michelle demanded of Xuan Wu. 'Is she one of you?'

'No, no, no,' Xuan Wu said, moving closer to Michelle, then hesitating at her expression. 'She is a perfectly normal child, love. She has probably just picked up some Chinese from being with Gold and Jade.'

'But they don't speak Chinese,' Michelle said, gesturing towards Gold. 'They speak English.'

'Actually, we speak Chinese, and because we are Shen, you can understand us,' Gold said. 'Being with the Dark Lord also allows you to understand any Chinese spoken to you.'

'Well, then why isn't it working now? And will my daughter be able to speak English at all?'

'I can understand you, Mummy, don't worry,' Simone said.

Michelle relaxed. 'So you have just been picking up some Chinese after all. I am glad.'

'She has probably been speaking some Chinese and some English all along,' Xuan Wu said. He grimaced. 'I am very low on energy, Michelle, I wanted to talk to you about it later this evening ...'

'Oh no,' Michelle said. 'Not again.'

'As soon as the season finishes, we will go up to the Mountain for about a week, and all will be well.'

'A week!' Michelle raised her hands with horror. 'I will miss all of the press reviews, all of the after-production parties, I will miss *everything*!' She turned back to the mirror. 'I will stay here with Leo and your pet small Shen. I will be fine. You go.'

'It's too dangerous,' Xuan Wu said. 'They will find out about Simone eventually. As soon as they do, I'm not sure Leo will be able to hold them off by himself.'

'Pfft.' Michelle waved him away without looking at him. 'Three weeks ago he destroyed three big demons without difficulty. He has always been more than enough of a guard for me. I will be fine.'

'I'd prefer you went to the Mountain with me.'

'We will discuss this later,' Michelle said. 'I will be on stage soon. Go out to the audience, and enjoy.' She turned back and held Simone's little hands. 'There will be people pretending to get hurt and die on the stage, Simone, but it is all just acting. Even me. All right?'

Simone nodded, her little face serious.

'Now go, everybody, and enjoy the show,' Michelle said.

Someone tapped on the door. 'Ten minutes, Miss LeBlanc.'

'Shoo!' Michelle said, her smile wide.

※※※※※※※※※※※※※※※※※

At first Gold was fascinated by the elaborate sets of the opera, but he soon found the singing a tedious repetition of the same words, even though the story was a high drama full of love, sacrifice, and betrayal. He hooked into the stone network to find someone to talk to while he waited for the opera to finish.

The shared stone consciousness was curious, many Chinese stones had never even heard of Western opera and wanted to share his experience.

He connected the input to the network so that all could share.

'So she loves him ... but she's jealous, and thinks that he's fooling around with her ...' one stone said.

'Isn't there any *fighting*?' another stone said.

'Apparently not,' Gold said. 'No martial arts involved. Just singing and acting out the story.'

'Well, that's boring,' a couple of stones said, and dropped the connection.

'Which one is Xuan Wu's wife?' one of the stones asked, curious.

Gold indicated Michelle.

'Damn, she's loud.'

'She has a microphone. It's not visible from here.'

'The singing is so strange. Her voice is so *low*!'

'They think Chinese opera is sung very high.'

'And do they depict Western gods in these stories? It would be interesting to see which gods they have over there.'

'No, just people. They only really have one god, but he's divided up into some family thing. Quite complicated really. They say they have one god, but really it's three.'

'Only three? Visiting the temple must be really boring,' one stone said. 'Imagine if there were no small shrines for the little village gods.'

'With the Western gods being followed in China, and the recent ban on religion, those shrines for the little village gods are becoming obsolete anyway,' Gold said.

'Hey, I'm a little village god. Am I going to be obsolete?'

'We're all obsolete,' one stone said sadly. 'Nobody puts incense in our roadside shrines any more. Nobody thinks that mystic stones like us have spirits any more. One day we'll all be ordinary rocks.'

'As long as the other Shen treat us right, we'll be okay.'

'Yeah, and as long as the Golden Boy doesn't do anything else to ruin our status and give us a reputation as troublemakers.'

Gold disconnected from the network, settled himself into his seat more comfortably, and prepared himself to be bored for the next two hours.

Two weeks later, Jade, Gold and Xuan Wu met to arrange the trip to the Mountain.

'The timing is perfect, my Lord,' Gold said. 'Lord Thunderbolt will be on the Mountain as well to kickstart the network. Without his electrical power, the connection doesn't work. We will do the Mountain machines first, power up the router, then come down here and complete the connection. With your family all on the Mountain, and Michelle's family going home tomorrow, it will be easy.'

'I've delayed the trip a couple of days so that Michelle can attend the post-production party,' Xuan Wu said. 'But I really am fading and must go up there as soon as possible. I've received notes of concern from the staff of the Mountain, they can sense the energy drain from there.'

'You won't lose it, my Lord, will you?' Jade said, worried. 'It would be awful if Lady Michelle had to go to the Celestial full-time to wait for you to return.'

Xuan Wu rubbed one hand over his face. 'I doubt she would agree to it. We just have to ensure that I do not fade away.'

'Do you think you could take True Form and retain your intelligence for a while?' Gold said. 'It would be an ideal solution to the problem, just ask Lady Michelle to release you from your oath.'

Xuan Wu looked down at his hands. 'That is no longer an option. The animal is strong. If I were to take True Form now — I would be gone.'

Michelle burst into the room, full of excitement. 'Lo Wu! It is unbelievable! Unheard of! A triumph!'

'What is, my love?'

'They are extending the season! There are to be five more performances. We knew the show was sold out, but there are still people lining up to buy tickets, it has been so popular that they have had to double the run. This is one of the longest-running operas I have ever been involved in. Some of the majors cannot stay, but talented youngsters from the academy will take their places.' She jumped in a circle with excitement. 'A triumph!'

'Five more performances?' Xuan Wu said with horror.

'Two weeks more!'

'Two *weeks*?' Gold said. He turned to Xuan Wu. 'Will you last another two weeks, my Lord?'

Xuan Wu ran his hands over his face. 'I suppose I must.'

'Go up to your silly Mountain,' Michelle said. 'I will be fine, I have Leo here, Gold and Jade are here, and my family are going to stay until the end of the opera. Daniel has pulled out his camera to do the photo essay, and my parents say they want to take a small trip into China and visit ...' She grinned with mischief. 'Lo Wu.'

Xuan Wu glanced at Jade and Gold, thoughtful.

'I won't be here for a couple of days during that period,' Gold said. 'I will be on the Mountain setting up the network.'

'Postpone it,' Xuan Wu said.

'I can't,' Gold said. 'Lord Thunderbolt has agreed to set up a similar network for the Jade Emperor right after he's done with the Mountain. It has to be done now, so that the Celestial One may be connected at the arranged time.' He grimaced. 'You yourself agreed to share the data on the Mountain cohort.'

'And you do not make the Jade Emperor wait,' Xuan Wu said. He looked up at Michelle, beseeching. 'Are you sure you must do this? I do not want to leave you alone!'

'I will not be alone! I will have Leo, and Gold, and Jade. They are more than enough to guard all of us.'

'I will be gone ...' Gold began.

'For two days. I know. Two days out of two weeks.' Michelle waved one hand airily. 'That is no time at all.'

'What do we tell your parents?'

'We tell them that you have to go across the border into China on a business trip. They are probably more surprised that you haven't been to China in the time they've been here. You are supposed to have a large company there, remember.'

'I suppose.' Xuan Wu rubbed his hands over his face. 'I really don't like this.'

'You don't have a choice.' Michelle turned to go out. 'This opera has made history, Lo Wu. Be proud.' She grinned broadly. 'Because I am!'

⸻⸻⸻⸻⸻⸻⸻⸻⸻⸻⸻⸻⸻⸻⸻

'Can't this business trip wait?' Daniel said as they said their farewells at the base of the apartment building. 'I want to come with you, and see your operations in China!'

'I'm sorry, Daniel, it takes at least twenty-four hours to get a visa for China,' Michelle said. 'But in a couple of days we will all take a quick trip to the border, and have a look across the "bamboo curtain".'

Simone ran to her father and threw herself at him. He lifted her and held her on his hip, and she buried her face in his shoulder. 'I want to come too, Daddy.' She wiped her eyes. 'I like the Mountain. I like the dragons.'

'You can't go to the Mountain without Mummy, and Mummy still has the singing thing,' Xuan Wu explained sadly. 'But next time I go to the Mountain, you can come too, okay?'

Simone nodded, serious, and wriggled to be released. Xuan Wu let her down and she returned to her mother and held her hand. 'Don't worry, Daddy, I'll look after Mummy and make sure the bad people don't get her.'

'We have Leo and Jade and Gold,' Michelle said. 'We'll be just fine.'

'Simone, come with Grandmama Violetta and Grandpapa Victor, and let your mummy and daddy say goodbye,' Violetta said.

'Okay, Grandmama,' Simone said. She took her grandmother's hand. 'Want to play "Go Fish" while we wait for them to do their icky stuff?'

Violetta laughed. 'That sounds like a good idea.' She looked around. 'Come on everybody, let's go up.'

As Gold went up with the rest of the family, Leo started the car, ready to take Xuan Wu to a private place where he could summon his cloud. Michelle and Xuan Wu moved closer to each other, their faces full of longing.

'Gold!' Violetta called, and Gold jumped, then hurried to enter the lift.

꧁ ꧁ ꧁ ꧁ ꧁ ꧁ ꧁ ꧁ ꧁ ꧁ ꧁ ꧁ ꧁ ꧁ ꧁

Gold was working on the new node to be installed in Xuan Wu's office when Leo entered a couple of days later. 'Got that stuff working yet, Gold?'

Gold changed back into human form and stood up. 'Just need Lord Thunderbolt to send a spark through it, and we should be good.' He grinned at Leo. 'Then I'll have a lot more time to spend beating you at Fantasy Battle.'

Leo grimaced. 'I sort of met someone.'

Gold didn't hesitate. 'That's great, Leo, good to hear.'

'It's real casual at this stage ...'

'Even better. Exactly what you're looking for. Human?'

Leo checked behind him, then lowered his voice. 'Yeah, a real nice human guy. American, like me.' He shrugged and smiled slightly. 'You should meet him.'

'I'd love to.' Gold ducked under the desk, checked the cable between the stone node in its sleek black box, and then stood back up again. 'I need to head to the Mountain, Lord Thunderbolt is already there waiting for me to connect this up, and then it will all be active.'

'I'm going to take Michelle and her family to Sheung Shui, to the border, to have a look across to the Mainland,' Leo said. 'We'll probably have lunch at the country club out there. Jade's gonna fly overhead and keep watch.' He gestured towards Gold. 'Why don't you come and meet us later?'

'I will.' Gold bent so that he could see down the hallway. 'Nobody there?'

'Nah, they're all asleep. They had another party last night, they may not even wake up until lunchtime. If so, they'll have lunch at the country club first before we go sightseeing.'

'I should be back in a couple of hours, call me on your mobile phone when you head out,' Gold said. He returned to True Form to travel to the Mountain. 'I'll be back soon.'

'Okay,' Leo said, and went out.

'All ready?' Thunderbolt said.

Gold changed to True Form and settled on top of the PC. 'Go for it.'

'Uh ...' Thunderbolt grinned at Gold through his glasses. 'Are you sure? This is going to be about six hundred volts.'

Gold wished he could grin back. 'It's fine, I'm a rock.'

'Okay, here goes.'

GOLD! Jade shrieked in Gold's lattice. *We've been attacked! HELP! Leo is down, I think they're dead. Help me!*

'Stop, Thunderbolt,' Gold said.

Thunderbolt hesitated, his hand over the node box. 'Changed your mind?'

'No, my family's been attacked.' *Where are you? Send me a signal!*

Leo, Daniel, Victor — here. Jade indicated a location near the border in Sheung Shui. *I'm chasing the demon prince — that same one — it has Michelle and Violetta. Go to the men! The Dark Lord is pursuing the demon with me.*

Simone? Gold said.

Jade didn't reply.

Jade? Where is Simone?

I don't know, Jade said, her voice small. *Go help Leo, please don't let them die! The Dark Lord thinks that Simone is with Michelle and Violetta.*

'I have to go,' Gold said. 'It's bad — Jade thinks they're dead.'

'I'll come with you. You can move faster than me, I'll follow.'

Gold landed in a grassy hilled area near the Sheung Shui prison, a compound of high steel fencing with barbed wire on top. A few farmhouses, barely more than shacks, dotted each side of the road, and a cow was tethered to a stake nearby. The Mercedes was parked at the side of the road, a good vantage point to see across the Closed Area towards Shenzhen, its tall buildings shrouded in a haze of pollution.

He found them in a ditch near the Mercedes. Victor lay on his back, his neck obviously broken, his eyes wide and unseeing. Daniel was a few steps away, the grass around him crushed by the struggle and stained from the blood where his chest had been smashed.

Leo was on his belly nearby, a sword in his hand. As Gold approached, Leo moved slightly. Gold ran to him, turned Leo onto his back, and cradled his head. Leo's head lolled, his mouth open. Gold quickly checked him over; he'd lost a lot of blood, he had multiple fractures, one leg was almost torn off, and he had massive internal injuries. His liver was macerated. He didn't have long. Gold hunched over Leo and made a soft sound of misery.

'Find ...' Leo gasped. 'Find! Michelle!'

'We're following Michelle,' Gold said. 'Where's Simone?'

'Simone ...' Leo said, and then lost consciousness.

Do you need me, Jade?

No! Stay with them! We cannot find Simone, where is she?

I don't know ... I think Leo knows ...

Find Simone! I think she may be all he has left, Gold ...

No!

Find Simone!

Leo was barely breathing, his breath rasping through his throat. 'Leo, Leo, where's Simone? Where is she?'

Leo didn't come around. Gold dropped his head, took a deep breath, and fed Leo all of the chi energy from his human body. He threaded the energy through Leo's broken bones and destroyed blood vessels, knitting up his liver, cleansing and restoring his internal organs. He turned Leo on his side with what remained of his strength, and slapped Leo hard on the back to make him spit out the contamination from being assaulted by the demons. Leo vomited up a large amount of foul goo, then collapsed back again. He opened his eyes, and pulled himself up with difficulty.

Gold shrunk back into True Form and fell onto the grass, completely drained.

Leo saw Daniel and Victor. 'Oh, God, no,' he moaned. He looked around. 'Gold?'

'Where's Simone, Leo?' Gold said.

Leo staggered to the Mercedes and leaned on the front bonnet. He gestured with one hand. 'She's in the car, she fell asleep, and we left her.' He leaned heavily on the car and peered inside. 'Looks like she's still asleep.' He went to the back of the car, opened the door, and checked inside. He pulled his head back out again. 'She's alive. Looks like she hasn't been touched. Where are Michelle and Violetta?'

'Demon ...' Gold gathered the last of his breath. 'Demon got them, Leo. Jade and the Dark Lord are pursuing.'

Leo staggered back to Gold and sat on the grass next to him. 'Whatever you did, I think you saved my life.'

'I did,' Gold said, fading fast. 'But unfortunately, it killed me.'

Thunderbolt landed in a flurry of feathers. 'Ouch, this is a mess. Humans murdered by demons? That hasn't happened in a long time.' He saw Gold. 'Where are the demons that did this?'

Gold tried to tell them about Jade and Xuan Wu.

'Gold?' Leo said. 'I can barely hear you ...'

꿔꿔꿔꿔꿔꿔꿔꿔꿔꿔꿔꿔꿔꿔꿔꿔꿔

Gold was in a courtroom, dressed in the white cotton pants and shirt of a criminal on trial. Guards in Tang livery stood on either side of the room, and the judge sat at the end behind his desk on a dais.

'The prisoner will present,' one of the guards said.

Gold moved forward and prostrated himself in front of the desk. '*Wen sui, wen sui, wen wen sui.*'

'Golden boy. It has been a while since you were here,' the judge said.

Gold didn't look up from the floor. 'I have worked hard to cleanse my record, my Lord.'

Gold heard papers shuffling, and the judge grunting to himself as he read the record of Gold's most recent incarnation. 'Get up.'

Gold rose and stood, head bowed, in front of the desk.

The judge wore a robe that crossed over at the front with toggles and loops, elaborately embroidered with four-toed dragons in black and red. His black hat stood high and square, with long extensions on either side. He wore steel-rimmed, old-fashioned glasses as he perused Gold's file with his lips pursed. Finally he dropped the paperwork and glared at Gold over his glasses. 'Well?'

Gold tried to control the urgency in his voice. 'Permission to return to the Earthly immediately, my Lord, the Dark Lord's family has been kidnapped by demons and his father-in-law and brother-in-law have been murdered by them. It is most urgent that I return! Lady Michelle is in the gravest of danger —'

The judge cut him off with a dismissive wave of his hand. 'Too late. They're all dead.' He tossed the file onto the desk. 'A most regrettable situation. First time humans have been killed by demons in nearly two hundred years. Ah Wu disobeyed the Celestial, and now he must reap the consequences. It's only a shame that his child — a half-Shen child with enormous potential — has to suffer because of his stupidity. He should be thrown from Heaven.' He threw his glasses onto the file on his desk. 'You, on the other hand, show improvement. You have served him loyally and well, and you gave your life for a human Retainer.' The judge picked up his glasses again and opened the folder. He took a brush hanging from a rosewood rack in front of him and dipped it into a pool of ink on an ink stone. He held the brush vertically and with economical sweeps of the brush, wrote out Gold's sentence and his reasoning.

He didn't look up from the folder. 'Return to the Dark Lord's household and continue to serve in the manner already arranged.' He snapped it shut, then glared down at Gold. 'Continue your efforts to improve your erroneous ways, and you may be eventually freed. The Xuan Wu, however, deserves nothing but condemnation for its part in this disaster, and I hope you do not learn from its irresponsible ways.'

Gold hesitated, wanting to set the judge straight about the Dark Lord, then changed his mind. The most important thing was getting back to the family — the tragedy. He fell to his knees and touched his forehead to the floor. 'This small Shen thanks you for your correction of its erroneous ways.'

'Back to the Earthly with you,' the judge said.

回回回回回回回回回回回回回回回回回

Gold arrived at the Peak to find the front door hanging open. Leo and Monica sat on the couch with Simone between them, both of them holding her. Jade sat on the other couch, distraught. Gold checked the household; the Dark Lord was nowhere to be found.

Gold entered and sat on one of the chairs opposite them. He smiled gently at Simone, but she didn't appear to notice him. Leo wiped his eyes; he, Monica, and Jade had been weeping.

Gold ran his hands over his face.

They are all dead. Michelle, Violetta, Victor, Daniel — they are all dead, Gold, Jade said. *The demon ...* Jade dissolved into tears and Gold went to her and held her. She turned on the couch and clutched him. 0Jade couldn't control her sobs, and Simone buried her face harder into Leo's chest. *It did terrible things to them, Gold, horrible things! Their faces ... I will never forget their faces ...* She took a deep breath, conjured a box of tissues, and wiped her eyes, then blew her nose. *I am so glad Simone did not see it, and that the demon did not find her ... it is so cruel ... it played with them, like toys, it used them, the Dark Lord took one look at them and said ...* She blew her nose again.

'Is Jade telling you?' Leo said softly.

Gold nodded a reply.

Leo shook with restrained grief. 'Okay.'

What did the Dark Lord say? What is he doing now?

He said, 'It is so stupid. It killed them by mistake. That demon had all of Hell and all of the Celestial in its grasp, and it killed my loved ones by mistake.' Then he went out, and has not returned.

I see, Gold said. *I knew that demon a long time ago. It enjoyed making humans suffer. Particularly women. It would not have been able to resist.*

Stupid! Jade said, threw herself up, and went down the hall towards the bathroom. *It had the Dark Lord in its power and it threw its power away — to have some fun hurting humans!*

Leo smiled wanly at Gold. Gold dropped his head to see Simone's face. 'You okay, Simone?'

'I want Daddy. I want Mummy. I want them to come back.'

'Mummy, and Grandmama Violetta, and Grandpapa Victor, are never coming back, sweetheart,' Leo said, his voice breaking. 'They're dead.'

Monica threw herself up off the couch and raced into the kitchen. The door to her quarters closed.

'No, when you die, you go away for a few days, and then come back again.' Simone moved one hand slightly in Gold's direction. 'That's what you just did, Gold.'

'There's a difference,' Gold said, touching Simone's shoulder. 'I'm special. Your Daddy is special. Leo, and Mummy, and your grandparents — they're not special, they're just ordinary. And when they die, they're gone forever.'

'Is Daddy coming back?' Simone said. She looked up at Leo, beseeching. 'Where's Daddy?'

'I'm going to go out there right now, and look for your daddy,' Gold said. 'He can't die, so he has to be out there somewhere, and I'll find him. And I'll get some people to help me.' *Jade?*

Of course. Let's go. I can show you where the demon took them, and we can try to work back from there.

'What if he changed?' Leo said.

'Changed?' Simone said.

'He can change, like I can, and Jade can,' Gold said. 'But he promised your mummy he wouldn't do it, cause it scared her.'

Simone buried her face in Leo's chest. 'He scared me too. He was big and scary.'

'Huh?' Leo said.

He took Celestial Form and carried her through the palace to see the Jade Emperor when she was about a year and a half old, Gold explained for Leo. *It scared the life out of her. That's why he never took Celestial Form again around her.*

Leo nodded, understanding. 'He may have changed into something even scarier, and forgotten all about you. It doesn't matter, Simone, Jade and Gold will find him.'

Jade came in, her face composed but her eyes still red. 'Come on, Gold, let's find this turtle.'

'I'm here,' Xuan Wu said. He stood in the doorway, leaning heavily on it, his hair completely grey. 'I searched for the demon. Everywhere. I never found it.' He looked haggard and old.

Gold rushed to help him, but he waved him away. 'Don't touch me. I don't think I could control myself. I'd drain you dry.'

Simone threw herself up from Leo's lap, raced to her father, and hit him hard. He hoisted her and held her close, his eyes tight shut.

'Are they not coming back, Daddy?'

'They're not coming back, sweetheart.'

Simone dissolved and sobbed into Xuan Wu's shoulder. He staggered to the armchair and sat, rocking her in his lap.

'Go to the Mountain, my Lord. You need to rebuild, and do it quickly.'

'I cannot. I am too drained to make the journey.' He switched to silent speech. *I am finished. I have ordered a couple of Celestial Masters to come down here and assist you in guarding her. I only have a couple of days at the most. You have all the documents prepared. I thank you for your assistance, Jade, Gold; when I am gone you are free, but I hope you will remain to help Leo guard my daughter.*

'No!' Jade choked, and left the room again.

'What?' Leo said.

Gold explained silently for Leo. Leo dropped his head into his hand and sat unmoving.

'You'll stay with me, won't you, Daddy?' Simone said into Xuan Wu's shoulder. 'You won't leave me too? Gold said you're special.' She nuzzled his shoulder, her tears soaking the fabric of his shirt. 'And you won't go away.'

Xuan Wu rose, still holding Simone. 'Let's go to your room, Simone, we need to talk.'

'There you are.'

Gold turned to see who had spoken, and quickly fell to his knees. Kwan Yin, the Holy Bodhisattva of Mercy, stood in the doorway in human form, appearing as a slim, elegant middle-aged Chinese woman in a white silk pants suit. 'I heard you have put yourself into very deep trouble, again, Ah Wu, and many are suffering.' She entered the room, and stopped at Gold. 'Up you get, little stone, I have been watching you. Your heart is becoming more pure every day.' She leaned to touch Leo on the hand, and his expression changed from grief to beatific. 'Leo Alexander, heart of a lion.' She swept to Xuan Wu and took Simone in her arms. 'Hello, Simone, I'm your Aunty Kwan. I'm here to help out, because your mummy and your grandparents are dead, and your daddy thinks he's going to die too.'

'I don't want him to die,' Simone said.

'And I won't let him,' Kwan Yin said. She turned. 'Come sit on the couches, and I will tell you what I will do for you.'

'Can you bring Mummy and Grandmama and Grandpapa and Uncle Daniel back?' Simone said, her little face full of fierce hope.

'No, I cannot do that,' Kwan Yin said. 'That would be wrong, it would be against the order of things. But I can help you, and I can help your daddy.'

'I think I am past help, Lady,' Xuan Wu said.

Jade entered, her face full of wonder. She fell to her knees, bowed three times to Kwan Yin, then rose again. 'My Lady.'

Kwan Yin nodded gracefully to Jade. 'Princess. Very well; here is what we will do.'

She switched to silent speech. *We must first stage something to make their deaths acceptable to the authorities. I know this is hard, but if we do not, the police will pursue Ah Wu and accuse him of killing them. Particularly since he is well known as a practitioner of the Arts of War.*

Xuan Wu's face went grim.

Jade and Gold; this is a task for you. I will handle Xuan Wu and Simone. Gold, take Leo's form, put the bodies in the Mercedes, and drive out on the Tolo Highway. Jade, take male human form, steal a truck, and run headlong into them. Jade, die. Gold, suffer injuries. Leo will come with me and Ah Wu and Simone for a while; Gold, take Leo's place in the hospital and recuperate as him.

Gold nodded. 'Yes, my Lady.'

Jade looked horrified. 'I don't want to touch ...' She changed to silent speech. *I don't want to touch them, I love them too dearly, I cannot do this to them ...*

You must. Gold will handle the bodies. All you need to do is steal the truck, take human form, and die.

Jade dropped her head. 'Yes, ma'am. I only hope I can fulfil this duty.'

'You will be fine. Now, you two, go.'

What about the Dark Lord? He is dying, Gold said.

I will feed him energy. Enough to keep him here with Simone, until she is old enough to fend for herself.

'The minute you do that, the demons will attack us,' Xuan Wu said, grim. 'If they find out the state I'm in, they'll want to take advantage of it immediately.'

'I will give you enough to keep you going for a couple of days, here and now,' Kwan Yin said. 'Then, I want you to fly to Paris. I have a house there; it is not real, but it will suffice. It is an extension of Potala Island, a small part of Purity in the city of Paris. Go there; I will give Leo directions. There will be a car waiting for you at Charles de Gaulle Airport. I will be at that house, and I will feed you energy for a few days. It should be enough to last you six or eight months, provided you do not overexert yourself. You must live, as much as possible, as an ordinary human, and conserve your energy.'

'And Daddy can stay with us, if we do that?' Simone said.

Kwan Yin nodded.

Simone threw her tiny arms around the Bodhisattva's neck. 'Thank you!'

Kwan Yin returned the embrace. 'You are most welcome. Now, your father and I must go into the training room together, and I will provide him with some energy to keep him going until he gets to Paris. Gold and Jade have some errands to do.' She looked around. 'Does everybody understand?'

'I feel okay now,' Simone said with wonder. 'Like, everything's going to be all right, even though they're all dead. Because I still have Daddy, and Leo, and Jade and Gold, and Monica — everything's going to be all right. You make everything better.'

Kwan Yin jiggled Simone in her lap. 'That's what I do.'

Simone threw her arms around Kwan Yin's neck again. 'Thank you!'

꿈꿈꿈꿈꿈꿈꿈꿈꿈꿈꿈꿈꿈꿈꿈

Michelle's extended family in Quebec asked for the bodies to be returned to them for burial there, then refused all further contact with Xuan Wu except to ask for a contribution to the costs. He paid it all, and they stopped talking to him altogether. He seemed happy with that situation and didn't pursue it.

After the memorial service held at the Hong Kong Funeral Home in North Point two days later, they returned to the Peak exhausted and subdued. They still had to pack to travel to Paris the next day. Xuan Wu went straight to the training room and proceeded to repeat a low-level sword kata over and over. Monica took Simone into the kitchen, and Gold followed. Monica sat Simone at the table, no longer in a high chair, and started preparing some noodles for her.

Gold went to Leo's room and tapped on the door. He heard Leo moving inside, but there was no answer. He tapped again. 'Let me in, Leo. Just to talk.'

'Gold ...' Leo said, almost too soft to hear. Gold opened the door and went in.

Leo wasn't in his little living room, he was stretched out on the bed, fully clothed, his forearm over his face. Gold sat on the bed next to him. 'You okay, Leo?'

Leo didn't reply, and then Gold saw the open bottle of pills on the side table. He picked them up; a powerful sleeping drug, bought over the counter at one of Hong Kong's many pharmacies, where any type of drug could be bought without a prescription. He looked at the date on the bottle; it had been given to Leo the day before, but it was empty. Gold dropped the bottle and quickly checked Leo; he'd taken all of them.

My Lord, Leo's attempted to kill himself.

Gold heard the weapon hit the floor with a thump in the training room and then Xuan Wu raced into Leo's room. He took Leo's hand and studied him. 'Damn!'

'I can heal him, my Lord.'

'No,' Leo whispered. 'Let me die.'

'Do it,' Xuan Wu said.

'No!' Leo gasped, and attempted to move away.

Xuan Wu spoke to Leo as Gold moved the cleansing energy through Leo's body. 'You are such a coward! Running from failure, and not even clearing your shame honourably — to die by the sword.' He dropped Leo's hand. 'I should dismiss you from my service for this. Hasn't Simone suffered enough, to have lost nearly all those dear to her? But you would take another? She loves you like a father, Leo, and this is how you repay her love.'

Gold was horrified at Xuan Wu's cruelty. 'My Lord!'

'Heal him. Then I will punish him,' Xuan Wu said, his voice icy. He turned his attention back to Leo. 'Coward. Running away when things become difficult.'

'It was my fault,' Leo gasped. 'All my fault!'

'That's right it was!' Xuan Wu snapped. 'And it was my fault too, I let them stay when I should have told them about myself, and taken them all to the Mountain with me! You think you are the only one who feels responsible? I have killed them all!' he dropped his head with misery. 'I should have known that becoming involved with a human woman would only end in tragedy.'

Leo was silent.

'But Simone needs us,' Xuan Wu said. 'She needs all of us, to gather around her, and help her to recover. We need to be strong — for her. We may blame ourselves and punish ourselves as much as we like — but not in front of her. Because whatever happens, she must not suffer any more.' He rose. 'Now as soon as Gold has finished saving your worthless life again, you will rest, and then you will come out, and you will help me to look after this wonderful little girl that both of us have betrayed so completely. She trusts us, Leo, even though we have killed her mother.' His voice broke, and he took a deep breath. 'And I do not want to betray her trust again, by leaving her. And neither should you. For her sake, Leo, live.' He spun and stalked out.

Gold didn't say anything, he just continued to cleanse the drugs out of Leo's system. Leo remained motionless on the bed.

When Gold was finished, he dropped Leo's hand. Leo still didn't move. 'Are you okay, Leo?'

'He's right. I need to live for both of them.' Leo turned his head to see Gold. 'And you've saved my life again. I don't deserve it.'

'Of course you do.'

'No, Gold, I don't! I started seeing Rob long before you and I broke up.' Leo looked away. 'I cheated on you.'

Gold took Leo's hand again. 'Leo, I knew for a long time that you'd been seeing Rob. I was glad for you. You didn't betray me, I left. I wasn't able to give you what you needed.' He squeezed Leo's hand. 'Rob makes you happy, so stay with him.' He rose. 'Now rest, and do as the Dark Lord ordered. You're a Retainer, you're sworn to obey him, so I suppose you have to.' He went to the door to go out.

'Gold,' Leo said.

'Hmm?'

'Thank you.'

'Just get better, okay? And be strong. All of us need to be strong. For Simone.'

With that, he closed the door, before any of his tears fell.

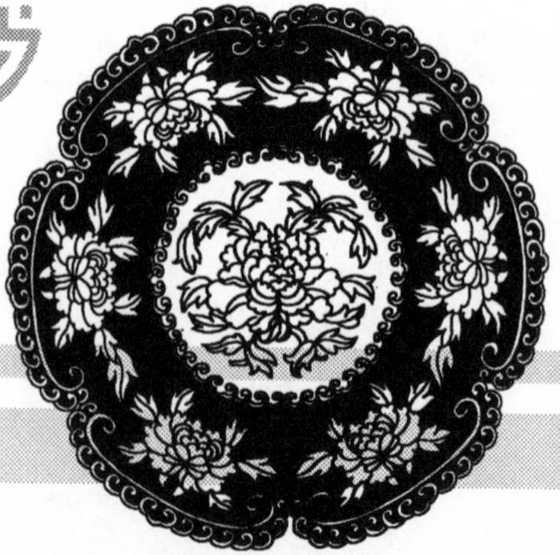

THE YEAR
1995

FAREWELL
TO HEAVEN

1995

THE GREAT HALL OF CELESTIAL AUDIENCE

REMEMBER, GOLD. RECORD EVERYTHING YOU SEE.

IF WHAT I'VE HEARD IS CORRECT, THIS SHOULD BE VERY, VERY GOOD.

WHAT BUSINESS HAVE YOU HERE?

CLUNK

309

CLANK

CLANK

CELESTIAL MAJESTY.

EMPEROR ZHENWU OF THE DARK NORTHERN HEAVENS. ARISE.

311

'This humble servant petitions your Celestial Majesty with a request,' Xuan Wu said, his deep voice echoing through the hall.

'Name it,' the Emperor said.

'This humble servant has married a human woman and requests permission to join her and live on the Earthly plane as a human.'

'What of your duties as First Heavenly General?'

'I would that they were delegated to Er Lang, Second Heavenly General.'

'Your dominion, the Dark Northern Heavens?'

'My Generals will manage the Heavens in my absence.'

'Your Mountain?'

A soft rustle echoed through the hall, the hissing sound of moving silk. None of the gathered Celestials said a word, but everybody present knew how much the Celestial Mountain of Wudangshan meant to the Dark Lord.

Xuan Wu waited until the noise died to silence. Then he raised his head and looked the Jade Emperor in the eye. 'I have lieutenants capable of running the Mountain in my absence. I request permission to remain on the Earthly.'

'Permission denied,' the Emperor said. 'You are needed on the Celestial Plane, Dark Lord of the Arts of War. We cannot spare you. Bring her to the Celestial, she will be welcomed and given full honours as your Empress.'

The rustle of moving robes hissed through the hall, then once again there was silence.

'She refuses to leave the Earthly,' Xuan Wu said. 'If it needs be, I will forsake my dominion for her.'

'Permission is still denied, you are not given Celestial consent.' The Jade Emperor spoke with an edge of exasperation. 'This has been discussed and negotiated. The position of the Celestial is clear.' His voice became vehement. 'You are needed here.'

Xuan Wu raised his head with defiance. 'I will do it anyway, Celestial Majesty. With your permission or without it, I will be with my wife.'

The rustle of robes was accompanied by a gentle hush of voices which trickled to silence.

The Jade Emperor spoke loudly and clearly. 'You will not do this.'

'Arrange someone else to fulfil my duties for the next hundred or so years, Majesty, I will be living on the Earthly.'

The Jade Emperor banged the arm of the throne. 'You will not do this, Ah Wu, I forbid it!'

Xuan Wu took two steps towards the dais.

I WILL DO IT ANYWAY.

The Jade Emperor rose, stepped forward, and glared with menace. 'You are walking a very fine line, Ah Wu, *do not disobey me*!'

'Go to hell.'

And with that, Xuan Wu stalked out of the hall, surrounded by a dull roar of astonishment.

Oh my, that was better than I expected, the Dragon said silently to Gold. *Did you get it all?*

Yes, my Lord, Gold said. He hesitated, then, *If I had known it would lead to this much trouble I would not have aided him.*

He may be thrown from Heaven, the Dragon said, still amused. *There are many who question his place here, and this is exactly the excuse they have been looking for.*

The Celestials filed out of the hall, quietly discussing the events once they were through the door. Gold and the Dragon followed the crowd. It took some time for them to reach the door, and they were the last people in the hall to leave.

GOLDEN BOY!!

GOLDEN BOY, CHILD OF THE JADE BUILDING BLOCK.

APPROACH!

Gold slumped and wiped his hand over his face. Not *again*.

'Azure Dragon, you are dismissed,' the Jade Emperor said. 'I wish to see the Golden Boy alone.'

You're on your own, the Dragon said, and disappeared.

Gold sighed and walked to the dais. The empty hall echoed with his footsteps. He fell to his knees in front of the dais and spoke the obeisance with resignation. '*Wen sui, wen sui, wen wen sui.*'

'Rise,' the Emperor said.

Gold rose and waited.

'Find the Jade Girl. Bring her here to my private apartments in one hour. I wish to speak to both of you.'

Gold took a deep breath, hesitated, and then threw his life away. 'Celestial Majesty.'

The Jade Emperor had turned to sit on the throne. He paused for a moment, then sat and leaned his elbow on his knee. 'Speak.'

'Celestial Majesty.' Gold fell to his knees again. 'If it pleases your majesty, the Jade Girl was not involved in this. It had nothing to do with her; it was all my doing. I take full responsibility. Please do not punish her for something she did not do. It was me and me only who assisted the Dark Lord in this matter.'

'Did you hear my order, stone?'

'I did, Celestial Majesty, and still I beg for my friend's life. She was not involved.'

'Your *friend*, eh?' The Jade Emperor didn't move. 'I repeat my order, stone. Return with Jade Girl to my private apartments in one hour. Do not even begin to think of running. You will obey me.'

'I will obey you, Lord, you know I have no choice.' Gold dropped his forehead to the floor. 'This humble Shen is honoured.' He shook his head, still with his forehead on the floor, and whispered, 'No.'

'Go.'

Gold pulled himself to his feet and went.

Gold sat in the office chair next to her at the desk. 'You remember when the Dark Lord asked for my help to win the human? How we laughed about that?'

Jade smiled down at the printouts then back up at him. 'That was delightful, the most I'd laughed in twenty years.'

Gold's voice was hoarse. 'He married her, and now he's forsaken his duties and wants to live on the Earthly with her as a human.'

'He just had a major altercation with the Jade Emperor. Let me show you.' Gold concentrated and presented the recording so that Jade could view it.

When the recording had finished Jade shook her head, confident. 'Without the Dark Lord to defend it, Heaven is at the mercy of the demons. They won't throw him from Heaven, it's simply not possible. Besides, he's the North Wind.'

'With him full-time on the Earthly, Heaven is at the mercy of the demons anyway,' Gold said. 'This is just the excuse his enemies have been looking for.'

'He has no enemies.'

'He is Yin itself, he refuses to play the political games and is straightforward in all his dealings. Of course he has enemies.'

Jade sighed. 'I hope it doesn't happen, I have a great deal of respect for him. And he tried to help us when we were in trouble, by taking us into his service.'

'Jade.' Gold fingered the printouts. He sighed. 'This is very hard.'

Jade touched Gold's hand. 'Go on, I trust you, my friend.'

Gold didn't look up from the paper. 'The Jade Emperor wishes to see me in his private apartments in forty minutes. Apparently my interference, once again, has returned to bite me on the ass.'

'He wants to see you too.'

Jade shot to her feet. 'No!'

Gold put his head in his hands. 'I am so sorry.'

Jade grabbed Gold's forearm and hauled him to his feet. He watched with confusion but didn't attempt to defend himself.

She threw her arms around him and held him close, pulling his face into her shoulder. 'Don't worry, whatever happens, it will work out.'

'I hate to think what our sentence will be, Jade, and it's all my fault.' He nuzzled her shoulder. 'And you had nothing to do with it at all.' He gripped her tighter. 'This shouldn't happen to you!'

WELL, WHEREVER WE'RE GOING,

WE'RE GOING TOGETHER.

I JUST KEEP MAKING PEOPLE SUFFER.

GOLD... DON'T WORRY.

WHEREVER WE ARE, WE'LL ALWAYS HAVE OUR FRIENDSHIP.

WE'LL DO THIS TOGETHER,

I KNOW WE CAN...

JADE EMPEROR'S APARTMENT

WEN SUI, WEN SUI, WEN WEN SUI.

RISE.

YOU SURE THEY WON'T BE MORE TROUBLE THAN THEY'RE WORTH?

I THINK THEY'LL BE USEFUL.

Xuan Wu turned to the Jade Emperor. 'The Dragon released them, Celestial Majesty?'

'He had trouble finding them more work. He said they were just redoing tasks because he'd run out of things for them to do.'

'Well, I'll have plenty for them to do.'

Jade inhaled sharply but didn't look up.

'Jade Girl. Golden Boy,' the Jade Emperor said sternly.

'Celestial Majesty.'

'The Xuan Wu is so obviously insanely in love with this human woman that the Celestial has seen fit to give him permission to remain on the Earthly with her for a human lifetime.'

'The Xuan Wu will obviously require assistance whilst living on the Earthly, and he has suggested that you worthless pair may be of some use.'

'Where should they present themselves, Ah Wu?'

Xuan Wu shifted slightly. 'Hong Kong, Peak. One Black Road. Top floor.'

'You heard him,' the Jade Emperor said. 'You have three hours to collect your belongings and present yourselves there. You are to remain in human form while in the Dark Lord's service, you have not atoned completely for assisting the foreigners to steal China's greatest treasure.'

'Don't bring too much, Hong Kong is very small, there won't be room,' Xuan Wu said. 'One bag apiece. If you need more you can purchase it later.'

'Celestial Highness,' Jade said.

The Jade Emperor waved them away. 'Go.'

JADE AND GOLD'S ROOM

HEY,

DO YOU KNOW ANYONE WHO'S WORKED FOR HIM?

NO.

HE'S SO SENIOR THAT EVEN HIS RETAINERS ARE TOO BIG FOR ME TO KNOW.

I'VE HEARD THAT HE IS A HARD MASTER.

HARDER THAN THE DRAGON?

I DON'T THINK ANYBODY IS HARDER THAN THE DRAGON.

HA HA... YES, YOU'RE RIGHT.

323

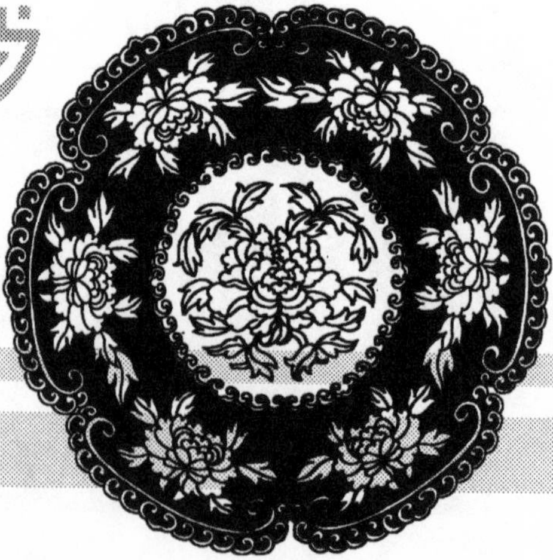

THE YEAR
2002

HONG KONG

Gold entered the living room and stopped. Simone was playing with Lego on the living room floor, the pieces strewn all over the carpet. A young European woman was talking to her in English, and Simone was replying, telling a story.

Simone saw Gold, jumped up, and ran to him. 'Hello Gold!'

The young European woman rose as well, and stood with her hands clasped in front of her. She was in her mid-twenties; about five six tall with mid-brown hair tied back into an untidy ponytail. She wore a plain blue T-shirt and a pair of jeans, both of which had seen better days. Her eyes were a clear shade of blue, standing out in her face which was pale without make-up. Compared to the immaculately turned-out and made-up Hong Kong women, she was a refreshing blast of naturalness, and Gold found himself immediately intrigued.

'And who is this?' Gold asked Simone.

'This is Emma, she teaches me English,' Simone said. She dropped her voice and her eyes went wide. 'Well, she's supposed to teach me English, but most of the time we just play together. Don't tell Daddy.'

The young woman bowed slightly with her hands in front of her in the traditional Chinese way; she'd been learning or had been in Hong Kong for a while. 'Good afternoon, I'm Emma Donahoe.'

'I'm Gold, Mr Chen's lawyer, I'm here for a meeting,' Gold said.

The door opened and Jade entered. She stopped when she saw Emma. 'Miss Donahue,' she said coldly.

'Actually, it's Donahoe, I believe it's a more ancient form of the traditional Irish name,' Emma said without rancour.

'Donahue, Donahoe, whatever,' Jade said, and shoved Gold. 'He's waiting for us, let's move.'

Gold bent to speak to Simone. 'I have a meeting with your dad, okay?'

Simone nodded. 'That's fine, me and Emma are wan wan Lego.'

'English, Simone,' Xuan Wu said from the doorway of the dining room. He gestured with his head. 'In here, Jade, Gold, I've been waiting for you.'

This one might last a little longer than the others, Gold said to

Jade as they walked to the dining room for the meeting.

I hope she doesn't, I don't like her, Jade said. *She doesn't know her place.*

They entered the dining room. Xuan Wu stood at the doorway, watching Emma and Simone play with the Lego, and then came in and closed the door. 'That Emma is remarkable. She has taught Simone so much — and has demanded that I buy Simone books and videos that will entertain and educate her.' He sat at the table. 'There really is much more to her than meets the eye. Kitty Kwok did me a huge favour recommending her.'

'She comes in three days a week, my Lord?' Gold said.

'Yes, three afternoons, when she's finished at Kitty's kindergarten.' His expression became wistful. 'Leo says I should put her on full-time as a nanny for Simone, to free Monica up from caring for her. It might be a good idea.'

'She is after you,' Jade said grimly.

Xuan Wu stared at her. 'Don't be ridiculous.' He swept one hand across the table. 'I am done with human women forever. Never again. I may offer her a position as a human nanny for Simone, that is all.'

'Get a tame demon or a Shen,' Jade said. 'Not a human.'

'Simone needs to learn how to interact with humans, and this one is perfect,' Xuan Wu said. He rested his elbow on the table. 'She has a strong personality and is not afraid of anything. She's very impressive. Simone adores her. And she has the most astonishing blue eyes ...'

'You've certainly had problems keeping domestic staff, my Lord,' Gold said with grim humour. 'They all run when they see the weapons in the training room.'

'I don't think this one will. Anyway.' Xuan Wu picked up the folder in front of him. 'Regardless, that is a decision to be made in the future. Right now, I need to make another trip to Paris, and I need you to buy me an airplane.'

Gold and Jade stared at Xuan Wu, aghast. 'An airplane?'

'Just a small one, to take to Paris for my energy visits with Kwan Yin.'

There was a tap on the door, and it opened. 'Sorry to disturb you, guys,' Emma said. 'But Simone's spilled her drink on the carpet. Can someone show me where I can get stuff to clean it up?'

'I will,' Xuan Wu said, and rose from his seat. 'She does that all the time.'

'She'll grow out of it,' Emma said, smiling up at Xuan Wu. They went out of the room together, talking about Simone's clumsiness.

Simone came into the room holding a collection of Lego blocks smashed together in a multicoloured tangle. 'Look what I made.'

Gold took the Lego. 'That's very clever, Simone.'

Xuan Wu came back in, followed by Emma.

'Let them have their meeting, Simone, let's go make something else,' Emma said.

'Okay, Emma,' Simone said with delight, and went out.

Emma smiled at Xuan Wu. 'Thanks for the help, Mr Chen.'

'My pleasure, Miss Donahoe,' Xuan Wu said, and she went out.

'You should keep her, my Lord, she makes Simone very happy,' Gold said.

'That's what Leo says,' Xuan Wu said. 'And I'm beginning to think that it might be a good idea. Oh, she left her Lego here.'

Jade made some small sounds of derision and they pulled out the brochures on private jets to compare them. Xuan Wu picked up the Lego and took it out to Emma and Simone. Gold watched him as Jade remained oblivious, looking at the brochures.

It was Gold who spoke.

Butterflies
~ By Yunyu ~

Scan this QR tag with your smartphone to receive
your **FREE** copy of the song '*Butterflies*'

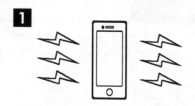

Download the **FREE** QR Scanner app to your
smartphone, from your app store.

Scan the QR tag on the top of this page with
your QR Scanner.

Scanning the tag will take you to a secret
webpage. Follow the instructions there.

You now have your own copy of '*Butterflies*',
the book soundtrack for *Small Shen*!

What is a QR tag: A type of barcode, when scanned by a QR scanner on a smartphone,
will send you to a particular internet page, *without* needing to type in the internet address.